roughstuff

rough stuff

tales of gay men, sex, and power

edited by simon sheppard and m. christian
with an introduction by pat califia

alyson books
los angeles | new york

MANUFACTURED IN THE UNITED STATES OF AMERICA.

THIS TRADE PAPERBACK ORIGINAL IS PUBLISHED BY ALYSON PUBLICATIONS, P.O. BOX 4371, LOS ANGELES, CALIFORNIA 90078-4371.
DISTRIBUTION IN THE UNITED KINGDOM BY
TURNAROUND PUBLISHER SERVICES LTD.,
UNIT 3 OLYMPIA TRADING ESTATE, COBURG ROAD, WOOD GREEN,
LONDON N22 6TZ ENGLAND.

FIRST EDITION: MARCH 2000

00 01 02 03 04 a 10 9 8 7 6 5 4 3 2 1

ISBN 1-55583-520-1

LIBRARY OF CONGRESS CATALOGING-IN-PUBLICATION DATA
  APPLICATION IN PROCESS.

CREDITS
"DIRTY PICTURES" © 1997 BY TOM CAFFREY, FIRST APPEARED IN *BUTCHBOYS*, REPRINTED WITH PERMISSION OF THE AUTHOR.
"BUT FOR INSOUCIANCE THERE GO I" © 1996 BY MIODRAG KOJADINOVIC', FIRST APPEARED IN *POWERPLAY* MAGAZINE, REPRINTED WITH PERMISSION OF THE AUTHOR.
"WHOSE LITTLE BOY ARE YOU?" © 1994 BY WENDELL RICKETTS, FIRST APPEARED IN *DOING IT FOR DADDY*, REPRINTED WITH PERMISSION OF THE AUTHOR.
"AEGIS" © 1996 BY D. TRAVERS SCOTT, FIRST APPEARED IN *BEST GAY EROTICA 1996*, REPRINTED WITH PERMISSION OF THE AUTHOR.
"IDOL" © 1994 BY LUCY TAYLOR, FIRST APPEARED IN *UNNATURAL ACTS AND OTHER STORIES*, REPRINTED WITH PERMISSION OF THE AUTHOR.
COVER PHOTOGRAPH AND COVER DESIGN BY PHILIP PIROLO.

Dedicated to the memory
of Scott O'Hara

Acknowledgments

First and foremost, thanks go to Scott Brassart at Alyson for suggesting this project; he's been a total pleasure to work with. And a big hug to M. Christian—coeditors don't come any better.

And thanks to my pals in the smut-writing community, a great bunch of perverts. Special recognition goes to a few: Years ago, Bill Brent suggested I might try writing my first story; Scott O'Hara bought it; Pat Califia has always been an inspiration, and it's an honor to have her associated with this book. A long list of other writers and editors have provided aid and comfort. You know who you are; sincere gratitude to you all.

Thanks also to all the bottom boys, top men, and switches who've passed through my life. I've learned so much from you guys and, for at least a split second, I've loved you all.

Above all, thanks to William for putting up with me all these years. I'll always love you.

—Simon Sheppard

Big hugs to the two wonderful men without whom this book would not been possible: the fantastic Scott Brassart at Alyson and Simon Sheppard—whom I respect, admire, and still love...even after finishing this book.

Thanks to the friends who've always been there, in print as well as in the flesh: Pat Califia, Thomas S. Roche, Carol Queen, Pamela Briggs, Lynn, Martha, and all the rest of the divinely crazy writers and special lovers in my life. Special praise goes to everyone in these pages—we've made one terrific book!

Finally, to you out there: all the men, boys, and everyone betwixt and between. May you live long—and break all the rules!

—M. Christian

Contents

Foreword

This book is dangerous.

Dangerous because sex is dangerous, desire is dangerous, life is dangerous. The tales this book has to tell are stories of some of our deepest secrets, the needs we're not supposed to speak aloud. Inconvenient facts: the realization that the use and misuse of power are part of our desire; that there are links between pleasure and pain; that we long to explore dark, hidden places the world tells us we must not go. For some of us, such stories are texts for jacking off, the fuel for fantasies better left unfulfilled. For others, they're the guideposts by which we lead our lives.

This is, in some sense, the era of S/M. The discourse about kink and leather sex has never been more public, more insistent. Images of bondage are appropriated to sell shoes and cigarettes. Kink-themed dance parties are the rage. Men in harnesses cavort in trendy productions of operas; queer theorists write theses on fisting; music videos broadcast stuff that would have been unspeakable a few short years ago. Clearly, the concept of "taboo" has lost its tang.

Once just the playground of a select few, power-based sex has become an open secret. So this might be an ideal moment to go beyond the conventions of leather porn, to explore what the extremities of sex and desire really feel like, what they really mean. And queer men are in a perfect position to lead the way.

Our straight allies might be willing to grant us a place at the table, but most of them would strongly prefer we keep our flies buttoned while we're seated there. For the world at large, male-male sex remains a topic of both fascination and repulsion. The moment a guy sucks dick, he places himself beyond the pale.

And since we are each and every one of us still—still!—a sexual outlaw, since we've already stepped over that line, we have the freedom of outlaws. For gay men, sex is not utilitarian. We do not use sex as a means of reproduction, as a way to establish a socioeconomic dynasty, as a means of gaining status in the world at large. Our desire is our own, what sets us apart, plain and never simple. We're already fags; if we want to be kinky fags, so be it.

Which is not to say that every gay man thinks it's a great idea to explore the more baroque perversions. Vanilla can taste good too. But queer sex, delinked from the imperatives of "family," "long-term commitment," and "respectability," can be quite a fertile field in which to muck around.

It helps that the people involved are both (or more than both) male. Heterosexuality suffers from millennia of enforced, standardized power dynamics. A male-female domination scene either plays to tradition (male top) or against it (female domme). When it's just guys everything is up for grabs. Without a one-size-fits-all model against which to measure things, power relationships become a lot more fluid, more complex. This is not to say there aren't still stereotypes: older=top; stronger=top; more butch=top. But these "rules" are more likely to be broken in a variety of amusing, challenging, scary ways.

Also, the male of the species is just plain expected to engage in power plays, both in the sack and in the world at large. Putting on leather just makes it all more visible. The growth of a worldwide leather community that engages in "safe, sane, consensual" kink has helped many men discover important things about themselves. But not every guy in leather is into S/M, and not everyone into kink wears the uniform. Even the very notion of "sane and consensual" is a lot trickier than it may appear. One might argue that the playroom door is a kind of magical gateway, and when we enter a dungeon space, we leave our civilian selves behind. But can we easily say that being tied up and groveling for hours at the feet of a jackbooted gentleman is "sane"? And if we do think of it as just another diversion, doesn't that take some of the fun out of it? Some of the heat? Some of the meaning? When one "consents" to be a "slave," doesn't that transform the meanings of both words? Can we truly say our sexual desires, the very core of our being, can be dissociated from our out-of-leather selves? The deeper we go into the dynamics of consensual power sex, the more we dance along the knife-edge of ambiguity. And the more S/M play helps us discover who we really are, the scarier and more comforting things get. Strange indeed.

There is, to be sure, more to the subject of sex and power than pricey whips and safe words. No matter how consensual and careful many of us are in real life, there's that sticky subject of fantasy. We're each and every one of us entitled to our libidos. But it's one thing to play out a carefully orchestrated, well-negotiated flogging scene and another to fantasize about nonconsensually kidnapping, whipping, and fucking some attractive guy, safe words be damned. So just how OK are these fantasies, really? Don't they express who we really are? Anybody who's ever been in a really good S/M scene has been to that place where the pretending ends, where what's happening ceases to be just a game. Leather rituals can help keep things structured, but every time we step into a playroom, so much is at stake: self-image, self-respect, even sanity. What we're playing with is not just power over another person but power over ourselves, our needs, even our mortality. Our bodies, our vehicles of pleasure, are always only partly under our control. Ultimately, no matter what the scene, desire is our master, and we're all slaves to limitation. We can try to step over the boundaries, but, damn it, those boundaries are still there. Limits are made to be tested, even broken, but limits there always will be, even the final limit of death. When we enter the realm where opposites are reconciled, where pleasure and pain, love and annihilation are one, things can get pretty weird. Pretty dangerous.

And that's what this book is about.

M. Christian and I have set out to collect maps of that dark terrain where forbidden lusts take their pants off and get down to fucking. Some of these stories will turn you on, and some may challenge you. Some may surprise you; I know that a few astonished me. We hope a few will take you to places you've never been, be you a blushing virgin or a boy who just got pissed on and pierced at last night's play party. A story or two may even help you grow, explore, discover something about who you really are. And even if they don't, you can always jack off to 'em.

A word of advice: Don't try this at home, kids. While many of the stories are about consensual, well-regulated scenes, even they may describe activities that are dangerous in the wrong hands. These stories are fiction, remember? We don't advise the unprepared among you to blunder off and act them out any more than the readers of *Peter Pan* should think happy thoughts and try flying out the window.

Neither, though, must you keep everything in the realm of fantasy. If you're something of a novice, there are plenty of good S/M handbooks with plenty of good advice and lots of experienced players who've been there already and will be happy to lend a gloved hand. And if you decide you never want to play rough, that's OK with us too.

But we do hope some of these stories touch your head, your heart, and your dick. For me, power-based play is a great way to find out who I am, who other people are, and to have a damn good time while I'm doing it. And, yes, it's scary to be vulnerable. Vulnerable to restraints, signal whips, the pleas of a bottom, the demands of a top. Vulnerable to desire, to love, to life. But without vulnerability you might as well be dead. One way or another, we're all gonna get hurt. Because life is dangerous.

And I hope this book is dangerous too.

—Simon Sheppard

Introduction
Snips and Snails and Puppy Dog Tails
by Pat Califia

Who, or what, then, is serious?

Discounting that which everyone does, and which is nothing, there are these three routes: Leather and Rough, which are open to all, or nearly all, and the remaining one which is The Real Thing.

A person may, of course, go more than one route. Purists, for instance, are frequently Rough. Indeed, I have seldom encountered one that did not like to make it that way. But they are all like puppies, like bear cubs, like youths at play: they are merely rough. Their principal advantage to us is that we can relax around them, and they are excellent at arranging things.

—William Carney, *The Real Thing*,
New York: G.P. Putnam's Sons, 1968

"Never confuse sensitivity with kindness."

—Herself

William Carney's novel *The Real Thing*, published in 1968, is a pre-Stonewall peek at a scene for sexual outlaws who would have guffawed at the term *leather community*. This one-sided instructional correspondence between a self-schooled, accomplished sadist and his novice nephew is the *Urban Aboriginals* of its decade. When I happened upon it in the late '70s, thanks to the bibliographic fetish of a slightly older masochist, I was relieved to encounter a literate voice of experience that mirrored my own. Carney's narrator has little use for women, though he does offer grudging praise of female stamina and tolerance for pain. But he spoke with a passion and dedication about the antisocial art of erotic domination and torture that I found riveting. In the anonymous narrator's obsession with etiquette, rules, grades, ranks, divisions, and classifications of "the Way," I saw a reflection of my own need to bring a little order, or at least some formality, into a troubled and chaotic world. I also recognized our shared need to feel important, despite our real-world status as objects of ridicule, horror, and pathology. It's a classic defense mechanism—turning stigma into superiority, marginalization into elitism.

The nature of sadomasochism has changed a great deal since 1968, thank Medusa. I've tried to turn a couple of younger twisted literati on to Carney's masterpiece, but most of them find it boring or too upsetting to be instructional. The world-view of the book's hero is that of a genuine outcast who is more than a bit sociopathic. (The eponymous "real thing" gives new meaning to the phrase *like lambs to the slaughter*.) Although this voice is rich with irony and sharp observations about human nature, it's a point of view that is too bleak for most modern "leather people," who cherish a vision of safe, sane, and consensual S/M—a mutually pleasurable power exchange between equals.

Since I am one of the activists who brought sadomasochism a little closer to the light of day and tried to make it more understandable by emphasizing consent, safety, and fantasy role-playing between equals, it's ironic, I think, that today I find so much truth about my sexuality in *The Real Thing*. This is a world where tops and bottoms are not on the same side, where degradation is genuine, the infliction of pain is not prettied up by talk about intense sensation, and the top man pays a heavy emotional price for his royal status. Carney's leathermen don't care about education or activism. Their realm is hidden, to preclude the need for public relations.

Perverts, even radical perverts, have a hard time hanging on to their own history. But I think it's important to remember that there was a time when a penchant for restraint, pain, or submission could only be gratified by locating an underground whose gates were remote and making it past the Cerberus of cops, newspaper exposés, and Freudian psychoanalysts. There was another option as well, primarily open to men who sought the not-so-loving attentions of other men—cruising for rough sex with straight trade. Even in the 21st century you know exactly what I'm talking about, because it's still a staple of pornography—blue-collar workers, soldiers and sailors, cops, bikers, bodybuilders, cowboys. Any straight guy with a mean attitude, a leather belt, and a burning desire to both get his dick sucked and punish the fag who did it will fit the bill. Being rough is a perfect excuse for a straight man to act like a fag for just 15 minutes. From Phil Andros to Jack Fritscher and beyond, it's a tried and true scenario that makes even smooth-shaved circuit party gym bunnies who don't like S/M clutch their cocks and give it up.

The nearly universal appeal that fantasies about rough trade have held for gay men also speaks of their determination to survive in a homophobic milieu. The pre-Kinsey powers-that-be said homosexuality was as rare as it was pernicious, but gay men knew in their hearts and loins just how many ostensibly straight men took their pleasure in subway bathrooms and freeway rest stops. Getting off on straight trade is one way to thumb your nose at gay haters, by fetishizing them and getting illicit pleasure from them. This makes it difficult to ferret out the meaning of such encounters. From the outside it may look as if the straight boy is using or abusing his subservient and maybe even self-hating gay victim. But if the cocksucker is savoring every moment of the encounter and suffused with a delight the putative "top" would find repulsive and upsetting, who exactly is being exploited?

Sex with rough trade and, by extension, a great deal of casual, anonymous vanilla sex, is also a way to insulate oneself from the rejection gay men routinely mete out to one another, as if any hint of a desire for intimacy has to be ruthlessly stamped out. By eroticizing "the Man," or masculinity in general, one becomes less hurt by the rudeness or unavailability of one particular man. Perversely, a straight-appearing sex object may offer more ego insulation than a butch queer because the script is predetermined. There will be no romantic sequel. Of course, the straight man rejects you. He can't hurt you because you expect nothing else. Besides, he is a fool about the real nature of what has happened, a pawn, a hick who has just been gulled out of his zipper and conned out of his spunk.

Historically, rough sex was part of a cultural matrix that created the possibility of masculinity for gay men. The stereotype of masculine behavior, especially in the sexual realm, is that of aggression, selfishness, and brutality. If you put two "real men" together, what else can you have but rough sex squared, even if one of the men is an avowed homosexual? It's no accident that many physical attributes linked to male secondary sexual characteristics are part of the rhapsodic semiotics of rough sex: beards that rub skin raw, like sandpaper, so that the ephebe experiencing that abrasive contact is remade and shaped into a new being; calluses, especially on the hands, a mark of harsh treatment of the self that foreshadows an expectation that one's victim will be worked even harder; a penchant for quick penetration, devoid of the irksome foreplay that is mandated by the presence of romance or a woman; hard, fast fucking, a pace made necessary by the supposed distaste of a "straight" top man for the fag; the physical strength to back up a threat, particularly a threat of rape or ravishment.

But here's what takes this paradigm beyond the aping of the polarized male-female dyad. Rough sex is an affirmation of butch identity for *both* male partners. You have to be tough

enough to dish it out and tough enough to take it. Thus we have
the Tom of Finland icons whose huge nipples and bubble butts
denote them as queers and bottoms but nonetheless manly men.
And early S/M fiction is full of jibes about "sweater queens,"
whose femininity fucked with the butch-on-butch dynamic.
Eventually even orifices, which would seem to be inextricably
linked to girliness, could aspire to butch status. This hardihood
was manifested by an ability to tolerate extreme penetration.
The guy whose asshole, in porn at least, swallowed ten-inch
poles without lubrication, or stretched enough to accommodate
a quart of Crisco and a fist, was "taking it like a man." *Like a
real man, baby. Yeah!* (Said in an utterly unselfconscious basso
profundo while incongruously lighthearted Malibu Adult Video
music clutters up the background.) As Ian Philips has pointed
out in his deliciously lewd lampoon "Man Oh Man," the
hybrid of masculinity and an open hole is an uneasy one. It
seems it must be constantly reinforced with the modifier of
man/male/boy. So the personals abound with boy pussy, man
holes, male cunt, etc. Even boots, mustaches, and furry chests
must have their precarious homomasculinity reinforced with
odd xy specifiers. Mating such paradoxical concepts seems a
great deal more difficult than humping booty.

It's not surprising that these harsh and convoluted coping
mechanisms have been transformed by activism into something
more humane and direct. As we teeter on the edge of the mil-
lennium, a gay boy who wants to come out into leather will
probably take the careful, well-considered route of reading the
literature, joining a club, and cruising at leather bars. He will
most likely receive his initiation from a Master who is literate,
considerate, and a long-term subscriber to *Dungeonmaster*. Let
me be clear: I would not turn the clock back. I would not willingly return to a time when that boy would be more likely to
figure out his sexual needs by falling to his knees in dark alleys,
dangerous bars, or dirty strip joints, knowing he had a 50-50

chance of receiving a real beating or even losing his life because he wanted to pleasure and serve another man. I don't want to give up the leather shops full of a thousand expensive and well-made gadgets for seasoning scenes or turn my back on bookshelves full of a dozen "how-to" manuals on safety and technique for newcomers.

But for me S/M has always been an inherently risky business. Even if a scene has been tamed and dumbed down to the point where no actual physical risk exists, there is an emotional and psychological risk. The most dangerous thing that can happen to someone who follows this Way is the acquisition of self-knowledge. A broken nose will heal, but you can't gainsay an erection that points straight at something unspeakable. That sort of insight is hard to erase—especially for a sadist. One of the ways the modern S/M community tries to expiate its collective guilt is by focusing on the well-being and gratification of the bottom. We have not put nearly as much emphasis on making sure tops get what they are looking for in a scene, much less an S/M relationship. I think that as a group we are still afraid to ask what it is that sadists are looking for, what makes them tick.

I'm fond of the concept of choice as the basis for sexual orientation. This point of view is unpopular in an era in which every claim for gay rights is based on pseudoscientific sulking about how we can't help being queer; we're just born that way. Thanks, but I don't want to receive my civil rights as a charity fuck bequeathed on me by my genetic superiors. When it comes to sadism I believe I have chosen to deploy my talents between the boundaries set by the bottom's consent and my hunger. If I am kind, considerate, or obliging, it is because that is how my whimsy takes me. There's also a certain amount of self-preservation involved. I have no interest in being incarcerated. Genuine violence doesn't interest me much because it's a simple matter of employing the laws of physics. The use of force does not require much intelligence. Although it can have a certain raw beauty, there is not much sensuality to it. I am a sort of ring-master of sexualized travail, and I want my circus to have a few more clowns and trapezes and flaming hoops than the Punch-and-Judy dumb show of simple brutality. Human suffering is so much more tasty when it is dressed up in the victim's need, expi-ation, and transcendence. It acquires a complex aesthetic, a fine-tuned stomach-shivering delight, the illusion that I am a con-noisseur rather than a thug. Or, I should say, *merely* a thug.

But not every bottom wants to be hooded and shackled by someone like me. Many, if not most, prefer a top who has been trained like a captive hawk to the fist. Indeed, some bottoms can barely tolerate the knowledge that there is another person in the room with them and their precious fantasies. The pleas-ure they seek is a narcissistic one—assisted masturbation, ego-centric ecstasy without the lonely bits. I used to say I would only do this kind of scene for money, and now there's not enough money in the world to pay me to waste my time. As sadists age, I think we become less afraid of saying no. We have given up on the hope of being loved or admired. What we want is authenticity, a chance to reveal even a portion of ourselves to someone who will not flinch or rat on us. Since every bottom's primal fear is that no one will ever really want to do such sweet and terrible things to them, I wonder why so few of them are ready to look up from their own tumescence for a split second and catch a glimpse of me relishing their predicament. Do bot-toms not desire to be out of control? Then why spurn my authority? Despite all their prating about trust, I've learned that this does not equal "allowing" me to use my own judgment about what's best for them. I'm too old for paint-by-numbers scenes. Be my willing canvas, adore the vulnerability of waiting to be spattered by my tools, or get the hell out. Here's your cab fare, honey.

Perhaps Carney, and Gilles Deleuze in the brilliant essay "Coldness and Cruelty," which accompanies the 1989 Zone

Books edition of *Venus in Furs,* are correct when they say that sadists and masochists do not share a common agenda and are doomed to be at perpetual odds with one another. In that case, one could abandon the search for one's counterpart and simply play the game out as one more dangerous liaison. Carney's isolated, superior, and misanthropic top man would never stoop to explaining himself or justifying himself to a bottom man. He believes that an element of mystery, the air of being a different order of being, was essential to the proper conduct of the Work. Like it or not, modern pervs behave as if that were still true. I think we are still enslaved by certain basic dynamics that make the fantasy of rough sex so reliable: The top will have genuine power in the real world, and this is the source of his sexual power. He will be a different sort of person than his victim. His desire to use, hurt, overpower, or destroy will be authentic and dangerous. There will be a real possibility that things could get out of hand.

No matter how much education is done about S/M safety and technique, I believe that there will always be a broad, less organized category of experience called "rough sex" that is a sort of precursor to or underpinning of S/M, a first cousin of leather sex. There are a lot more people having rough sex than there are individuals taking on the stigmatized identities that comprise the leather family's taxonomy. (And not all of them are fags and straight boys.) These experiences are not carefully thought out or planned. The only negotiation may be a slap or a fierce thrust and a hand over the throat, accompanied by the whispered sneer, "You like it this way, don't you?" Consent is expressed by the failure of the bottom to escape. The victim's refusal to scream his head off is the equivalent of a safe word. Rough sex is clandestine, rushed, made more thrilling by the fear of detection. This is in sharp contrast to the days of planning and cleanup that even a moderately complex S/M scene requires. Any pain is provided by the simple expedient of a blow or a bite. Specialized S/M equipment would be counter-erotic. If restraint is enforced by mechanical means, the equipment has to be stuff that you would expect to be near at hand—an MP's handcuffs, a rancher's lariat. Because it has no pretensions of being healthy or politically correct, rough sex can proceed in a more fluid fashion, without the yawnsome interruptions for polemics that pepper the Marquis de Sade's and John Norman's works.

Carney's protagonist dismisses Rough as a sort of leather day-care center for learning-disabled pervs or a primeval swamp out of which something really interesting might evolve. It is the first pen to contain the herd and serves to divide the completely clueless from those who might have some spark of potential. But those who have aspirations to more serious Work proceed rapidly into a smaller holding area. In his disdain the narrator overlooks or willfully ignores a split in leather aesthetics that has existed pretty much from the '50s on. This division was most neatly articulated by the late Louie Weingarden of Stompers Gallery, a habitué of the Mineshaft who explained this as "military spit-and-polish leather" versus "dirty biker" leather. The sadist-pedant Carney so vividly brings to life is definitely in the former camp. So, I think, is most of the modern leather community. We imagine that the existence of bureaucracy, codes, rules, procedures, precedents, and ranks will tame the wild heart of the experience we seek and make it possible for us to have our cake and eat it too. We invite Dionysus into the temple of Apollo as if we could tame and contain him there without diminishing our enjoyment of the intoxication he offers.

Thus we have bizarre occurrences like people being thrown out of leather bars or play parties for being too exuberant and noisy—having, in effect, too much fun. I have frequently been found guilty of the strange crime of doing S/M at an S/M event. But it's not really funny—the consternation evoked more than once by a bullwhip being wielded in the leather section of a gay pride march makes it clear that there is a deep schism in the leather community about such things, a conflict we may never resolve. Despite all the public education I have done on behalf of my community, I sometimes wonder if there is not something about S/M that can never be made palatable to the lockstep tyrants of hegemonic vanillaism. I also wonder if, when we put on our best shiny leather apologetics and polish the buckles of our public relations finery, we are not changing our community into a place where I, for one, do not belong.

Modern tops and bottoms expect to be able to juggle with the fire of sadomasochism without ever being burned. More than once I've listened to traumatized players who could not digest the fact that they went further than they thought they could or wanted something they thought they should not desire. A little more experience with the unpredictability and intensity of rough sex might do these folks some good. S/M is not a sitcom. If the script gets followed to the letter, you are not really playing. You're holding a funeral for Eros, squeezing a modicum of clammy pleasure from his corpse.

The entire realm of extreme sex attracts us because we know we are sickly and overcivilized. We've been poisoned by images, drowned in brand names, racked by 9-to-5 jobs. It's safe as houses—boring, predictable, and false. But inspiration is a fanged and feral state.

If you go knocking on the door of tough love, you ought not to piss and whine if its claws are sharp and its breath a little fetid. Predators are like that. They can't help it and won't. As your elder and better, I sincerely advise you to stay at home and watch televised pictures of tigers hunting and copulating. Do not willingly go among them and offer your own flesh for their consumption or instruction. To do such a thing would be quite mad—as mad as emulating any of the acts that you are about to read about in the pages that follow...

Just Like You
By Samuel Cross

*Some of the stories that came our way took our breath away.
This is one of them: relentless, edgy, hot, and sick as fuck.
Samuel Cross takes us on a swift, rough ride, one where power
is the ultimate aphrodisiac. Strap yourself in and get ready.*

"Unh!"

I'd been with Evan for eight months. I had the scars to prove it.

My grandmother, who raised me, taught me that all sex is
sin. I don't know that I believed her. Then again, the dark fires
she described frightened me to death. I'm not even a religious
person. Not really. But she started on me young, burned it right
in my head. Why take chances? With Evan my needs were ful-
filled. I had no choice, no control. So my soul was safe.

"Unh!"

Don't let the name fool you. Evan was a big guy, a dark guy.
Burnt skin and curly brown hair. Blue eyes, though. Blue like
the devil's and every bit as convincing. I just couldn't see them
at the moment. He had a paper bag over my head, cartoon
smile and daisy eyes drawn on the front. Inventive fucker, at
least when it came to humiliating me. Evan was a poet. Taught
depressed girls at the community college how to hate men.

So he had me kneeling naked in his desk chair. I typed blindly
while he dictated one of his foul poems. It was my duty to get every
word right, every letter in place. If I didn't, he'd make it hurt. Maybe
I'd screw up or maybe I wouldn't. I mean, that was the point, right?

I didn't have to decide. I had a guilt-free hard-on as I hit the keys, and if the cigar burn on my back distracted me, then so be it.

Hair singed, skin melted: "Unh!"

The typewriter said ding! and I groped to reset the carriage. I could smell the sweat under my arms, rising up into the paper tent over my head. Fear sweat. It smelled like puberty, but I guess we're all afraid then. Evan was on his last words, and my fingertips brushed the final keys. Silence. My cock throbbed, leaking a cold little stream down my shaft to my balls. I sensed my Master looking over the typed page. Checking it like Teacher. I sort of missed the days when a simple whipping or some candle wax would do as foreplay before he put his cock in my most available hole. Not that I minded the games. He was the foreman, the Master. But I wondered if maybe he was getting bored. Artists are like that, you know. In love one moment, jaded the next.

He leaned. Hand on my back, cigar between his fingers—my weak shoulders rose at the momentary sizzle of flesh. He smacked the bag off my head and it sounded like a gunshot.

No paper. No fucking paper. The typewriter was empty.

My eyes squinted up. My cock strained like I was going to come. Evan grabbed me by the neck and pushed my face into the keyboard, kicked the chair out from under me. My ass was on fire as he squeezed my face into that oily-smelling monster. Leather and denim pressed from behind. He dropped his cigar onto the keys, just in front of my eyes.

"Fucking games!" he said. His fingers tightened around my neck. My heart raced, breath held. I waited for the sound that never happened, the delicious noise of his brass zipper tearing open, the sound of flesh slipping over denim as Master pulled out his enormous cock. My anus throbbed, waiting for it. I didn't have to *want* him to dry-fuck me into oblivion. He always spared me the sin of choice. He just gave it to me. Gave it to me hard and fast—heart-pounding, clenched-jawed, blood-and-sweat *good*.

He let go of my neck. I heard him breathing. Then he turned away and left the stuffy little room with the windows closed and sunlight pouring in. I didn't move. Just left my head there on the typewriter as I listened to him go downstairs and tear his apartment apart.

"Fucking games!" he bellowed again and again. "Small-town fuck, stupid goddamn games!

I take responsibility for nothing, so nothing is my fault. Least of all Evan's frustration. Blame this town, a fleck of fly shit on the map of the Midwest. Evan came up in July from Atlanta. He was in his teens when Atlanta really came into its own, just buzzing with any kind of scene a fiery young cock-sucker might like. I won't judge his choices in life. Hell, I don't even like talking about him like this. But what could he expect, pursuing a degree in the arts? A job in Hollywood? Berlin? Paris, maybe? He would've liked that. Especially Berlin. But he came here, where someone would hire him. Not much of a scene here. Just me. Just this flesh and bone. I was all for his pleasure.

But I was safe. The meek shall… Well, you know the routine. It might've been perfect except that Evan was just so fucking bored here. I could've gone on like that forever. Taking it. It wasn't my fault that my dick grew when he hit me, that I came when he did. Everything was perfect, but then he got tired. He had to fuck it all up.

What happened next—it's not my fault.

Not my fault that I *liked* it.

"I got something you're going to do for me."

I didn't look up. Not when Evan spoke to me. That was one of the rules.

I told him I'd do anything. My mouth bled when his black boot heel struck the very next moment. Head snapped back. I didn't lick the blood from my lips. He liked the way it looked running down, so I left it there.

"Don't interrupt me. *Ever.*" He continued eating. I listened to him chew, heard his fork scrape the plate. Chicken and dumplings, pie, and tea. A Southern meal. My stomach rumbled as I waited on all fours beside the kitchen table, and I prayed he didn't hear. My mouth watered. I tried to swallow, but the yellow-orange twine around my neck was too tight and it hurt. My head hurt. I sometimes wondered if he'd kill me. Just a fantasy.

"How dare you speak out of turn?" he growled after a while. "I'll fill your mouth up. Suck my cock."

I hesitated.

"Suck it!"

I crawled and started to unfasten his buckle. Again, a strike from his boot. It ached—lovely. I fell away, and he snapped off his belt and twisted it around his fist. My cock was growing. I'd taste that leather yet. Still in his chair, he unfastened his pants and pulled his meat out. Shy as a kitten, I crawled over and nuzzled between his legs. I licked around his crown and tasted his slit, the way he likes, to make him hard. I slobbered all over him. Like I said, the twine was too tight to swallow.

"Kid in my class," Evan explained, seeming satisfied for the moment, talking between bites. "Skinny geek in a sea of fat whores. Even a skinnier piece of inbred shit than you are. Blond. No style. Adam's apple bigger than his elbow. Looks just like you. Just like all of you boys here. Probably has a crush on his sister, too."

"Yes," I said with my tongue out. I waited for him to kick me, wanted to cry when he didn't. I kept licking. He was hard now. Beautiful cock. I squeezed my tongue inside his fly and tasted his musky balls. It wasn't my fault that I liked it. He made me do it, you see.

"Writes like a fucking hypocrite," Evan mused. A literary thought! Good. That always got him riled up. His cock got even harder and he said, "Afraid of himself. He's just like you.

But this kid, it's his dad who he thinks is God. Thinks he's watching from the grave. You two, you have a lot in common…and you're going to fuck him."

My heart skipped. "No," I said. I fell back, fear in my eyes. I looked up at Evan, then down at his boot. Sweat burned my forehead, and I waited for the delicious pain. Waited for the kick to my already-swollen face. It was going to come. My hard little dick kicked in anticipation. *When was it going to come?* I closed my eyes and waited.

"He's 18," Evan said, eating again. "He'll wait for you. And you'll fuck him like I fuck you."

He's just like you.

As I lay on my rug on the floor, my leg jumped like a dog's while those words turned around me and stifled my dreams. There's no reason to understand me. I can't even understand myself. I eat, I shit, and I watch situation comedies that aren't funny, just like everyone else. But Evan. I wanted to understand him. He was different from the rest. A strong fellow, tough and good-looking. In many ways he had nothing. No power in his position or his life, and yet he had control of everyone around him. Blow jobs in his office from staff and students alike—it was all too easy for him here. He was bored. Mouth open, I tasted it in his spit when he cleared his throat and said my mouth was his cunt. Now he wanted to extend his power. To feel it reaching through my empty shell. My hands were his hands. My cock was his too. It wasn't me who'd manhandle that 18-year-old boy in his dorm room with the door locked. It was Evan.

Maybe I'd enjoy it. But I wasn't responsible.

The hallway smelled like a men's locker room. I made my way up the stairs and down the hall past a broken drinking fountain. A blond jock jerked his chin up at me to say "Hello" or "Hey, buddy." I looked away. Hard-rock music from the

'70s played through an open door. Not the room I was looking for. Not the number Evan had given me. I went farther down the hall and thought of the Master waiting at home, drinking whiskey. A little less bored. I had to get this right.

I stopped at Room 370. It was so quiet, I wondered if he was even there. But the time on my watch was right, just as planned. I guess everything was arranged. I'm still not sure. Anyway, I bit my upper lip, bones shaking through my skin. My eyes burned. I wanted to cry. Fucking hell, this wasn't the way I was supposed to be! I had to *submit*. Like Evan said, I had to submit to his strength and let it fill me. Submit fully to power. It was hard. So damn hard.

Wiping my palms on my pants, I made a small fist and tapped on the door.

Don't answer don't answer don't answer don't—

"Just a sec!"

My mouth turned dry. I had a lump in my throat. I oinked like a pig, trying to swallow the fear. But I reached inside for Evan's iron will, gave into it. The door opened. Gray eyes. Thin, pale lips. Redneck haircut, curly in the back, shoulder-length. A waft of air from inside smelled of pot. My heart thumped in my neck. Body tense. He said "Hello" and I didn't answer. My hands shook. It built up inside, the need to surrender through force. I couldn't breathe, and either I'd do my job or I'd have a heart attack on the spot.

So I pushed him.

"Fuck, man, wh—"

I punched him. My hand was still in a fist from knocking. I had to do something with it. What a surprise, though! I hit him right in the jaw and he reeled. I dare say his feet came off the ground before he spun back and landed on his hands and knees. Like ballet.

Or modern dance.

I kicked the door shut. He was yelling, getting to his feet. I tackled him to the floor, one hand full of his hair and the other over his mouth and nose.

"Shut up," I said in his ear. "Shut the fuck up, boy."

But *I* didn't say it. Hell, I was just an empty bottle with a note stuck inside. So it was Evan who butted this boy's head into the floor to break him. A nasty thump. The sound vibrated through floor and I felt it. Nice.

The college fuck choked and gasped through my hand. Sensuous noises. I couldn't believe my erection. I wanted to dry-hump the fucker through my pants. But he struggled to get up, lost his balance, my weight pressing into him. We tumbled. A sweaty skirmish of popping buttons, torn shirts and lust-anger, fingernail scratches on our skin. He got his mouth free of my hand, but he didn't scream. Not at all. He wanted it. He wanted me to *get* him. I broke free and pulled back far enough to kick his throat. I had on sneakers. Not exactly like boots, but a kick to the throat, man—it's still a kick to the fucking throat.

I panted, watching him. His body twisted around on the floor. He clutched at his sore spot and blinked his watery eyes. After a few seconds he looked up at me. I'd have smacked him for it too, but he collapsed with his cheek on the floor. Broken. That fucking easy. He was like me, after all.

Evan had said I'd want to run away, and it was true. But he also told me, or maybe I thought it to myself: *What you want doesn't matter.*

"You pissed your pants," I said, voice shaking. The floor was wet. I smelled it. I rubbed my erection through my slacks, telling myself the hard part was over. But I didn't really know what to do next. Not with the sounds of young men passing by in the hall outside. It all scared me. That's when I saw the drool running from this kid's mouth. Like an instinct, something told me to get down there with him and kiss the boy.

Just kiss the boy, Evan. Yes. Like that.

His tongue licked at mine, lips locked. Evan never liked when I kissed him back. But I liked it. Everything after that came easy.

I pulled him up. I shoved his limp body over a desk. A cellophane box of mint cookies crumpled under his face, a soda bottle spilling over his homework. "Easy, man," he wheezed, almost inaudible.

"Shut up," I said, pulling down his pants.

"But it doesn't have to be like this," he pleaded. "Evan told me you'd come."

"Shut up!"

"Evan told me—"

"Shut up!"

I kicked his feet apart as far as they'd go with his pants around his ankles. I could have told him who I was. I could have said who I'd become. Big and strong, hairy arms and good-looking. All man behind my puny flesh. But I didn't tell him. I showed him. Just as plain as the way he showed me his sweet, pimpled ass, all pooched-out and round as he lay coughing over his papers. He thought this was all a game. Thought he could persuade me to leave and say it really happened when it hadn't. But I wouldn't disappoint him that way. I wouldn't make him wonder how painfully good it could've been.

I cupped his balls and squeezed. "Don't fucking move," I said, and I let him feel my nails. His body shook. Little gasps came from his chest, and his balls tried to get away. It's like they thought they could escape up into his belly, but they couldn't. I had to laugh. "You don't need them, anyway. I'll rip them off if I have to."

"Yes," he said. "Yes, Sir."

I liked it. Balls in hand, I felt the power. I also felt for his anus with my thumb and stuck it in. A moment of extreme tension, and then his muscles relaxed. He even groaned with pleasure. It was a taunt to me. So I curled my thumb and tore my hand away.

"Aah!"

"How about that!" I spat at him. "You like that too? Huh? You gonna groan for me some more?"

He nodded his head. And I got my cock between us, purple head throbbing. I think it would've burst like a balloon at the prick of a needle. I dreamed of running across the room and landing in this college boy. Instead, I opened his ass cheeks, I spit on my cock, and I slung my hips back. This would do, and he was shaking again, the smell of piss on his thighs and rising from his pants. Better than cologne. I edged closer. Got my cock head against his sweet little hole. He opened just a little, and I pushed the tip in. I waited for him to tighten up. Like a sweet little kiss. Then I thrust so hard his head hit the wall.

"No."

"Shut up!"

You know what fucking is. I don't have to tell you. I mean, I rutted this guy raw, and I never gave him the satisfaction of knowing he'd made it to the end—I pulled out, came on his floor, and had him lick it up while I watched.

But you know the taste of come. You're like me. You know what it feels like to blow your wad and to taste someone else's. So let me tell you something you don't know. A fantasy.

I never wanted to die. It's a sin to want that. I learned that life hurts, and so what if I enjoyed the pain? It wasn't my fault. But sometimes when I was with Evan, I'd wonder. I'd wonder what it would be like if the moment before orgasm—that stretch of seconds where I'd teeter over the edge with my eyes all squinted up and my brow twitching, my ass tight and balls about to burst—I wondered what it would be like to spend that moment just knowing, just outright fucking knowing for sure, that I'd die when I came.

I'd enjoy it. I mean, any orgasm, even the last, has gotta feel good. Anytime you prepare to shoot a load of white ribbons into the air or inside someone, it doesn't matter if there's a war or your father is dying in the hospital with cancer. For that moment, the *coming* is all that matters

So what if you knew? Just like in those cults in the '80s. What if you knew, as sure as the sun would rise tomorrow, that the breath following release would be cut short. Boom. The end.

And as this skinny college lad curled into a ball with his back against the wall, his head on the floor and his feet above his chin, masturbating over his open mouth for my final amusement, I thought, *What if I knew the end would come in an hour?*

It took an hour to get back to Evan's. He wore a red leather jacket and red leather briefs with a steel zipper up the front. He sat on the couch with his hairy legs in front of him, feet on the coffee table while he talked on the phone.

"It's like that in Middle America," he was saying. A regular broken record, this poet. "Holier-than-thou, repressed fucks," he said. "No one here's strong enough to give in to their desires."

He was killing time, waiting for me. I knew this because the blinds were drawn and the coffee table was scattered with candles and cigars, a whip, and a ball of orange-yellow twine. A pretty ribbon for my hair. Some razors. A stiletto. Things that hurt. Things that could kill.

And as sure as the rising sun, I knew only one of us would leave this place alive. My fantasy would come true.

He hung up the phone, nodded for me to stand near. I did. I looked down at my feet. He asked if I'd done my Master's bidding. I summoned my courage and laughed. Right in his face.

His body came to life. All that shit spilled from the table as he kicked at me and missed. I'd stepped back. The place smelled of Chinese carryout. The knife and the ribbon landed near my feet.

"I'm Evan," I said slowly. "I'm Evan, and don't you fucking forget it."

I lifted my chin, Looked into the devil's eyes, and let his rage fill me. Wonderful! Better than I ever imagined, and I drank it up. All those unspoken words—like thunder in a vacuum. Maybe our souls met through our eyes. Something like that. Something like...

Something like *transference*.

I think I watched from a distance. I remember it like a movie, seeing the two players projected onto a screen. Which one was Evan now? I wasn't sure. The one with the knife, I guess. Holding it like he meant it and wrapping twine around the other's throat.

"I'm Evan now," said the one with the knife. "I'm Evan now."

Of course, I didn't kill him. Not really. I had no reason to. I knew his secret death fantasy, so I didn't give him the pleasure. But I hurt him. And I used his body like a rag the way he'd taught me. It's almost troubling, but I think he sort of liked it.

Ah, but none of that matters now. It's hot and sunny every day. I moved here just a few weeks ago. Here, to Atlanta. Not a bad scene in these parts, for those of you who don't know. I didn't waste a night, and I've already got two boys who never call me by my name. They call me *Sir*.

And me? I don't call myself anything. Like I said, I don't understand much about me, and I don't really care. I just obey. I obey Evan's will from inside me, taking what he wants and spreading his power. It's not up to me. Not my fault if I like it.

And I like it a fucking lot.

A Boy and His Wolf
A (Mostly) True Urban Fable for Hard-Core Fags at the End of the Millennium
By horehound stillpoint

horehound stillpoint is a poet and a pervert, and his stories are not quite like anything else we've ever read. We all know, or hope, that wild promises lurk within the darkness of surrender. stillpoint drags us down the road of excess, to the place where a crazy transcendence burns.

The boy sold his soul for leather, and God never said a word.

This young man (who wanted to remain nameless) traded his freedom for belts, heavy metal handcuffs, a chrome-plated dog collar, and yards and yards of rope. He was tied to a pole in the middle of a basement-cum-dungeon-cum-temple of renunciation.

A man called Wolf picked him up, walked him home, and then they went to church.

One hundred candles burned and 200 crystals glittered in the dark temple of the Wolf. A ten-inch dildo, "Black Bob," sealed the boy's mouth off from any idea of a kiss. Its eight-inch circumference choked his screams and made him swallow many hallelujahs.

Over closed eyelids, Wolf taped condoms. Heavy-duty, extralarge Leviathans, which the Master had filled with fresh ejaculate many moons ago, then tossed into the freezer. Before applying them to the boy's eyes and covering it all with the leather hood, Wolf pricked each rubber with a needle 13 times. The frozen semen thawed, leaked out, and dribbled down the boy's cheeks.

The come turned crispy in time.

This strapping young body wrapped in leather for three days and three nights produced a river of sweat that was Biblical. He also produced an ocean of come that was preverbal.

The tears, though, the tears of the boy were not his own but seeds of the past.

One weekend with Wolf rolled back 5,000 years of civilization.

Barely 18, new to the city, this kid was homeless and penniless but not without assets. His Olympic legs, prime-cut butt, Coke-can cock, and jet-black eyes stopped traffic everywhere he went. Young, wild, and cocky, he thought he was ready for just about anything. He was right. Men could suck his dick and spit him out and he wouldn't bat an eye. They dumped their loads up his ass, then dumped his ass altogether, but he could take it all. He wanted it. Needed it. Loved it, all of it.

Wolf wasn't bad either. Walking down the street, he seemed to be pure animal, scruffy, with hungry eyes and a rolling gait. The energy he exuded had a lone and dangerous spark.

This was only one weekend, among many, for them both.

The stereo down there raged ear-blistering feedback, then segued into snippets of old Sinatra. An hour of machine noise, brutal beats, then half a cut by Dusty Springfield. Just enough to make him yearn for more. It got so the boy heard summery melodies in the midst of white noise and a horrible buzz under the surface of "One for My Baby (And One More for the Road)." In periods of silence he still heard indescribable washes of remembered sound. Music would never hit him in the same way again.

Electrified tit clamps were set on an alternating pattern of stimulation and pain. His nipples were on fire. His nipples were bleeding. His nipples were coming in what felt like psychedelic explosions. For a long, long time his nipples were the center of the universe.

The boy felt as if he were being turned into the mother of his own enlightenment.

Time became irrelevant. All the external cues for the passage of time—light, food, sleep—had been displaced. Liquid nutrients dripped into his veins via an IV hookup. Most of the bags, laced with LSD, morphine, or cocaine, served a dual purpose, making sleep as unimaginable as sunlight. (But no speed. The boy's single demand on Wolf had been the promise not to use that one drug, which he thoroughly hated for reasons of his own.)

The other drugs were more than enough to turn 72 hours into a thousand lifetimes.

He died and was resurrected over and over again that weekend. Having his nerves twitching and twisting in the changing winds of pleasure and pain made the boy come alive to a whole other zone.

His real skin, his permanent skin, was this black leather. The soft pink illusion of heat and blood was like some childish toy, like a doll, to be tossed aside, or put away, especially in church. Big boys had more serious matters to attend to. Big boys could take it all—swallow screams as well as hallelujahs—and this boy was as big as they come.

He could not get any air inside the black leather hood nor could he exhale. If he had needed breath, he would not have survived his weekend with the Wolf.

Heat emanated from within and without. Sweat ran out of every pore; sweat rose up in his boots; sweat had nowhere else to go. And sweat was not the only thing that reeked inside this skin of leather.

Zippers here and there made everything accessible to the Wolf. A zipper would open up and all of a sudden the boy would feel a nine-inch dick rub up against his thigh. The Wolf's cock was heavy and fleshy, and it uncoiled like a snake. It was a busy thing too, with many tricks. Sometimes hot piss would trickle, then stream down into the boy's boots. Sometimes a different zipper was used, and piss flowed down his back, ran like a river over his butt, or swamped his chest. Wolf must have drunk gallons of liquid, because his output was astonishing. The recipient of all this steaming funk experienced moments of delirious panic, thinking that drowning was not only possible but imminent.

Just when the boy had adjusted to "Black Bob" being a permanent fixture in his mouth, Wolf pulled it out. That young mouth, usually so hungry, was stretched and taxed and sore and grateful and overwhelmed. Those lips, always cherry-red and porn-ready, were purple and puffy and sexy as hell.

Wolf kissed him half to death. He spit missiles of saliva into the back of the boy's throat. He plucked one of the boy's pubic hairs and forced his little soldier to swallow it. The Master worked the ropes momentarily loose enough to knock his disciple's legs out from underneath him, and the boy knew he was in for it. Wolf proceeded to fuck his young mouth into a bloody pulp. He pumped sideways into the boy's cheeks and he pumped deep all the way back to the base of the boy's tongue and he fucked the roof of his mouth raw and he rammed the teeth once in a while for good measure. Every square inch of that flesh was shot with come, and even that was not enough. The Wolf whipped those overworked lips with the head of his dick again and again and again, as if the future of Earth depended on it.

The boy learned: What felt like hot and horny fun for a couple of minutes or ten minutes or twenty minutes became something altogether different if it continued, unmercifully, for two hours, three hours, four hours. You surrendered or you were dead meat. Even if you did surrender, your body was still dead meat, but you...you were blissed out. No. You were *bliss itself.*

. Total surrender.

Ecstatic revelations.

Understanding that this was probably a once-in-a-lifetime event, both man and boy went beyond all known limits. Wolf had always depended on his sturdy prick, but this perpetual hardness and unquenchable need amazed even him. The volume of come was most astonishing of all.

Again and again, the Wolf opened a zipper, pumped his dick, and shot his loads onto supersensitized boy flesh. Once the jism was smeared in good, that zipper would be zipped up and another one undone. The boy's body marinated. His heart overflowed. He got drunk on the smells of piss, sweat, and come.

Unseeing, unhearing, untasting, unfeeling, unthinking, unlearning the last 5,000 years.

And those young shoulders, wrapped around a rigid pole in a dark basement, carried the weight of this rough-and-tumble manhood magnificently.

Words lost all meaning. Ideas didn't mean shit to a tree. The boy was not his thoughts or he would have gone mad that weekend for sure. Out of body, out of mind, the two of them sailed out beyond this world.

Buddies in high dungeon.

A hundred thousand hallelujahs would not have been enough.

The flood of come-spit-piss-shit-sweat scrubbed the boy clean.

A hypoallergenic steel rod—the size of a number two pencil—was inserted into the slit of the disciple's cock. He moaned, he whimpered, and Wolf was patient but persistent. He played the boy's cock like it was a violin.

A catheter tube was also inserted, from time to time, and Wolf siphoned the piss out of the boy as if stealing gas from a '57 Thunderbird. A noble theft. Devoted interception.

Another stainless steel rod, this one with a little kink in the shape of a lightning bolt, was slowly twisted into that same tender shaft. The spatulate handle made for easy turning, and Wolf spent hours playing with that handle. The tiniest turn, the merest push, and the boy saw stars, supernovas, and galaxies spinning into other dimensions.

Fortunately, the Master could play many instruments at once. After all, the young butt under his dominion could not be ignored for even a moment. Those tight mounds of boyish beauty needed much care, much fondling, and much fucking.

Wolf gave him enemas, to keep him clean and ready. He used his entire store of butt plugs, working his way up in size and weight. That boy hole was never empty. In between the plugs and the dildos, the Wolf attacked that rosebud with everything he had: fingers, toes, his tongue, his nose, and finally, most definitely, his dick.

He mixed Tiger Balm in with his lube so that the fire in the boy's butt hole could have lit up the night sky. He plowed the field and laid to waste any last pockets of resistance. He hammered and flailed and went suddenly so gentle that all the breath in the world seemed to wait for the next hundredth of an inch. Then he rammed home as if everything depended on this one seedy and inevitable act.

He fucked him silly, he fucked him raw, he fucked him so that he would know, once and for all, why he had been born.

In the midst of this supreme butt fucking, the boy had visions of his alternately burning and pampered asshole, as the eye of a hurricane, the source of all heat in this world, and the center of the Milky Way.

Another 100,000 voices singing "Amen" would not have been enough.

In the temple of renunciation pain was unconnected to suffering. Skin did not constitute a boundary. And this world was never born on the tip of a cocksucker's lips.

In the end the boy was beyond even rapture.

He was gone.

Pure.

Love alone remained. Spread like butter and fucked to shit, the nameless boy discovered who he was. The Bible of his balls could testify till doomsday, and God would never say a word. His tears—all tears—were fruitless seeds from many moons ago, thawing and drying up.

Thawing and drying up.

Wolf untied his arms and took him down from the pole. After removing the outer leather skin, the Master slapped his pupil's ass and sent him on his way.

Alone, empty, shining, and dark, the boy had tasted the end of all knowledge. He knew who he was. He knew everything and nothing. The no-thing-ness of the universe. Bliss. Not as a feeling. Not a sensual experience. Just the raw awareness that is more subtle and more pervasive than time or space.

With his soul shredded, tooth and nail, he left the basement saying over and over to himself: "Love is a Wolf. Love is a Wolf. Love is a Wolf."

A Beating
By Karl von Uhl

We've read a lot of revenge fantasies; this one stands out. It's nasty, uncompromising, and pretty damn sexy too. Karl von Uhl taps into the vengeful streak in each of us. After all, there's nothing like righteous anger and a hard dick.

"Evening, Ross," I said. I had planned a simple night out, even dressed simply—leather pants, vest, no shirt, sap gloves, engineer's boots, and jacket—to ensure a night of socializing. The bar was pleasingly dark, and the music's mechanized pulse was insistent and sensuous.

Ross stood at his customary spot, wearing a white T-shirt, torn jeans, and combat boots, a strip of black rawhide circling his neck and dangling midline down his chest. He had recently trimmed his Vandyke. "Good evening, Sir," he said, catching my eyes briefly, then lowering his gaze deferentially to my boots.

"Are you having a good night?" I asked, looking at his close-cropped hair, sleek and lambent in the blue light from the bar.

"Yes, Sir, after a difficult week, Sir," he said, raising his head but keeping his eyes lowered, obeisant.

"Sorry to hear it was a difficult one, Ross. Would you get me another?" I said, handing him my empty bottle.

Ross was an excellent boy, a fine example of what leather can do for a man. He was obedient in the best sense of the word, humble, appreciative of a strict code that is paradoxically liberating. In a world where meaning is popularly forced,

Ross was reliable, reveling in the dance of graceful, pleasing causality and respectful indoctrination.

Ross returned, holding a bottle. "Sir, your beer, Sir," he said, never taking his eyes from my boots.

"Let's go out to the patio," I said.

A scream pierced the night's camaraderie. I looked to the exit, my reflexes alert. Abandoning Ross, I ran to the door and threw aside the heavy leather curtain. Just outside was a young crewcut blond with a bloodied mouth and nose and the start of a black eye. A man in black latex propped him up. "Where?" I asked.

"In a red Jeep," said the blond, his speech muffled with edema and a missing tooth. "Three of 'em. One that got me had a baseball cap and a 'Niners shirt."

"Call 911," I said to his companion. I went to find the vehicle, in hopes of getting a license plate number.

I strode quickly up the street and cut down an alley. There were headlights at the other end. I eased my pace a little but paid careful attention. About 60 yards ahead of me was a pool of darkness between the Victorians, their languid regularity divided by the corrugated sheet metal gate of a pipe-fitting and glazing concern.

I reached for my keys as if looking for my truck but kept approaching. A voice called out, "Hurry up, dude!"

"Shit, I'm going as fast as I can!" said a voice from the dark.

As my eyes adjusted I could make out a figure. Male, maybe 5 foot 8, slim build, a baseball cap clearly visible. As he leaned into the light, I saw a number eight stenciled on the back of his T-shirt. Steve Young's number. Running, I grabbed him.

"Shit!" he cried.

The Jeep's lights flared as the engine roared. From the Jeep, a shout, "Some fag's got Seth!"

"I was just pissin,'" said Seth, trying to squirm out of my combination half nelson and hammerlock. "Fuckin' let me go!"

"No," I said. I lifted him easily and slammed his feet against the corrugated metal bordering the sidewalk. His cock, still leaking, dripped on his pants.

"Guys! Guys!" he yelled. The Jeep yanked into reverse, backed out of the alley into the street, then roared off. "Fuck!"

"Shut up," I said quietly.

"Fuck you, faggot!"

I twisted his arm farther up his back. Seth yelped.

"I said, 'Shut up.' " Keeping hold of him, I said, "I saw what you did. Don't try anything." I released his right wrist from the hammerlock; he shook that hand a few times but otherwise kept motionless. I unbuckled my belt and slowly removed it. "Give me your hand." He didn't move. "I said, 'Give me your hand.' " When he did nothing I flexed my elbow up to increase the pressure on the half nelson to ensure keeping him in line. With the belt in my hand, I took his wrist again.

"Oh, God," he muttered.

"Give me your other hand," I said.

"Who the fuck are you?"

"Give me your other hand."

"I can't," he said. I eased the pressure, controlling how much he could lower his arm. I shot my hand forward, caught his left wrist, brought it behind his back, and lashed it to his right. After making sure they were secure, I took my hanky and, threading my left arm up through his in an awkward embrace, caught one end of it in my hand, twirled it, and tied it around his head, covering his eyes.

I took hold of his wrists. "Walk with me," I said, heading for my truck.

"My dick's still out," he said, strangling a whine.

"This is San Francisco. Who's going to notice?" I said. "Open your mouth." I stuffed in a glove to shut him up. I walked him stiffly to my truck, sat him down, and locked him inside. He sat still. No one noticed him on the drive home. Needless to say, I took a circuitous route.

"Are you a cop?" he asked. He was in the middle of my play-room, tied in a wooden chair that was missing a large part of the seat. His arms were behind him, ankles lashed to respective chair legs. He wasn't bad-looking, maybe 19 or 20, brown eyes, buzzed hair, a jaw that would turn square when the baby fat melted. His cock still poked out of his fly; he was uncircumcised.

I stood beside him. "Would it make a difference if I were?" I asked. I had converted my playroom from a storage area under my house, added a couple of floor drains, soundproofing, a workbench, and extended plumbing and electricity.

He was still clothed. A video monitor provided the only light in the room; images of Marilyn Chambers eating out her costar flickered past, the light but not its substance reflecting on the leather I wore. He stared blankly at the screen, his cock stir-ring to attention at the sight of a female tongue on female parts.

"You brought me here to show me porn?" he asked, scornfully.

"No." I put my hand on his cock. He flinched. I watched as the tension leaked into his stomach and chest, through his shoulders and down his legs. "What's the matter? Never had your cock touched by a man?" I asked.

"No," he said, flat and hard.

"Not even a doctor?"

"OK, a doctor," he said, sullen and sarcastic. "But he wasn't a faggot."

"How do you know?"

"He wasn't."

"How do you know?" I asked, squeezing a little. His cock fit easily in my hand, the pale flesh contrasting with my black glove. I stroked the tip of his glans lightly with my thumb. "I'm circum-cised. That's one difference between my generation and yours."

"Shit! You wanna suck it, suck it, faggot!" he said, his anger peaking.

Tightening my grip on his cock with my left hand, I punched him hard in the gut with my right. "Takes one to know one," I said. He breathed hard. "Another difference between our generations is that mine was more optimistic."

I stood and turned on the light above my workbench. Various floggers and whips hung from a pegboard above it; below were drawers labeled T/T, C/B/T, and so forth, containing clothespins, clamps, sterile needles, scalpels, the detritus of a life committed to power exchange; a place for everything and everything in its place. I grabbed a pair of EMT scissors.

"Your name is Seth," I said.

"Yeah. So?" he said absently.

"I want to make sure I know what to call you."

"And your name's Faggot," he said, candid and direct.

I slapped him hard, then yanked his T-shirt out of his pants and made quick work with the scissors, making sure to poke him in the throat with their rubber-coated tips and exposed his smooth chest and almost pinpoint nipples. A thin trail of hair slithered over the faint web of his abs and led below his beltline.

"Seth, let's get something straight. You think you know why you're here, but you don't. So shut the fuck up. I'm calling the shots. So shut the fuck up. And if you don't shut the fuck up," I said, walking to the bench and grabbing a belter, "you'll get this," and I struck him hard with it across his chest. It left an imprint, white at first, then pink, then red, a sunset of the shades skin can offer.

I set the belter down and changed tapes in the VCR. Two men in various stages of leather and undress came on the screen, accompanied by a synthesized rendition of Stravinsky's "Firebird."

"Watch it," I said.

Seth turned his head away. The belter slapped against his chest. "Watch it," I said. Seth kept his head turned. Twice the leather slapped his chest; Seth gasped and turned his head to the screen. One man sucked the other's cock. Seth had gone soft.

"The worst fag bashers are always gay themselves," I said. "I think that's the case here."

"I'm straight," said Seth, rallying defiance, watching one man gulp greedily at another's cock, seeking whatever nourishment was there.

"You don't believe that," I said, hitting his belly with the belter. A network of red and white lines crisscrossed his torso.

"Quit hitting me! It hurts!" he yelled.

Smacking him hard with the belter three times, I yelled back, "Do you think so?" I wrapped the thick leather strap around his neck. "You stupid, arrogant little punk! You think you can get away with fucking someone up? Not with me," I said, tightening the strap with my hands. "What did you expect at my home? Ugly plus-size gowns, tattered wigs, and show tunes? See what stereotyping gets you?"

Seth's breathing turned rapid and shallow. I looked at his crotch and saw his cock stir. "See?" I said. I dropped the belter and yanked at his pants; they were baggy and difficult to manage, but I soon had them over his calves. Underneath he wore pale red boxers. He sat expressionless as I pulled them down. His cock unfurled lazily, pointing along his leg, his balls drawing up against his body. "You're getting hard," I said.

"Fuck you," he said, quietly.

"I'd be the sweetest piece you'd ever get," I said, slapping him on his belly. "You don't even struggle."

On the video screen were the two men, one fucking the other slow, deep, and hard. Seth's cock twitched again, but he obediently watched. "You've never felt that? Never felt a cock up your ass?" I asked.

"Fuck no," he said, surprised that someone would ask.

"No teenage sex play with your cousins? No Boy Scout blow jobs?"

"Fuck you," he said, derisively.

"You're the one getting hard. That just proves my point."

I walked over to my workbench, selected a pair of adjustable alligator clamps, and removed the rubber tips. Seth tried not to change expression as the jagged metal teeth bit into his nipples, but apprehension crawled slowly through his face. "You can't fight the sensation," I said. "It'll happen. Every man has the same nerves." When both were attached I increased the pressure slightly. Seth clenched his jaw, fought shutting his eyes. With a gloved finger I stroked the underside of his glans, sliding my finger underneath his foreskin. With my forefinger and thumb I pinched his frenum and pulled it forward, seeing how far it could be stretched; it would pierce nicely.

"Is this what you always do?" he asked. "Hurt guys?"

"No," I said, "just you," and kicked the chair. The chain on the clamps jumped; Seth whimpered.

Back at the bench I fetched a razor and a can of shaving cream. As Seth watched the video I kicked the back of his chair hard. He screamed, spilling face-first onto the concrete floor. I walked over to a sink, ran the water hot, and filled a bowl. "Time for Daddy to teach you how to shave, son," I said.

The wide hole in the chair's seat framed his ass neatly. I wet his crack and slowly applied the cream. His legs tensed every time I brushed his hole. "Feels good whether you want it to or not," I said.

I worked the razor carefully around the ruddy corona of his hole. The hair came off in short, easy strokes. Seth held perfectly still, made no sound, though I could tell from his breathing he was still conscious. His legs no longer tensed when I touched his hole, now smooth, the satiny flesh glistening from being rinsed so many times. I kept shaving, following the line along his perineum, stopping short of his balls.

Using my foot as a fulcrum, I wrenched the chair back onto its four legs. Seth stared impassively at me, as though somehow he could evoke pity, his right cheek heavily abraded and swollen, dotted and streaked red and brown. Dried blood lent a matte finish to his complexion. My cock swelled, pushing against my pants, held fast by the leather.

"You're not watching the video," I said. He looked at the screen. Two new men: one, rusty-haired and bearded, was smearing the butt hole of another, blond and bearded, with Crisco. The rusty-haired one dipped his fingers liberally into the other's hole, his thick peasant fingers glistening, the hole accommodating eagerly. Four fingers disappeared, emerged, disappeared. Without warning, the entire hand went in; the blond man opened his mouth, moaning, delirious.

I picked up a set of clippers from my workbench. "Bet you never knew your butt hole could do that," I said.

"Let me go," said Seth quietly.

"What?"

"Please. Let me go."

I knelt in front of him. "On one condition, Seth." Clippers buzzing, I sheared the hair from his balls.

He made a face, a little disgusted. "And what's that?"

"Admit the truth. Admit you're gay."

He threw his head back. "I told you. I'm straight," he said wearily.

I slapped the welts on his stomach. "Watch the fucking video," I said. The hair around his semihard cock dropped away. I followed the trail of hair up to his navel. "You don't seem to mind this part, Seth."

"I've shaved before," he said, a trifle relaxed and assertive.

"Not for bodybuilding."

"No," he said, a little defensive. "You don't have to be a bodybuilder to shave. For swimming," he added, with a note of pride.

"Ah. I was a linebacker in college," I said. After a casual conversational beat, carefully measured for its awkwardness, I said, "So you're a swimmer."

"Yeah."

"Does shaving really help?"

"Some. Reduces friction. I get better times when I shave," he said with authority.

"Coach tell you to do it?"

"He says we don't have to but it helps."

"You know, I would have pegged you for a boxer."

"Nah, that's no sport. No finesse, no technique," he said.

His pubes were the merest stubble. I looked him in the eye. "Now, see? We can have a nice, civilized talk. And we can do it when we're both hard."

"I'm not hard," he said, affable.

"Look down, Seth." I grabbed his cock, fat against my hand, a little over six inches. "My cock is hard in these pants. It wants out, but I'm not going to let it out. I don't want to make yours shy," I said.

I jacked Seth's cock slowly. "It feels good. It feels good whether you want it to or not. And if I tug on this," I said, taking the chain between his nipples, "it feels even better." He gasped, and his cock jumped out of my palm, and stood stiff, pointing from his groin.

I stood, leaving him to the video. "You know," I said, grabbing a bowl and a box of dental alginate from a drawer in my workbench, "a study was done not long ago. About homophobic men and their reactions to gay porn. Virtually all of them were turned on by it." Seth watched as one man plunged his arm into the other's hole, the hairs on his arm slicked by Crisco, sweat, and butt juice. Seth's cock never wavered.

"So?" he said. "You're gay, right? And that first video you put on was straight porn. Does that mean anything?"

I waved my hand. "A wiser man than I once said that if you process too much, you get Velveeta. All I know is you're hard."

"But I'm not gay," he said.

"You're hard."

"You can get hard for other reasons," he said abruptly, frustrated.

"Like what?" I asked. "Stargazing?"

"No. From fear," he said, discomfited. "Or other kinds of excitement."

"No doubt you read that bullshit in your high school sex ed class," I said, dumping a measure of alginate into the bowl. "At least I have the guts to admit why I'm hard."

"I'm not shitting you," he said. "You ever see pictures of hanged guys? They all have bones."

"Homosexuality and necrophilia," I said. "This is getting interesting." I walked over to him. "You mean to say you're just afraid of me. Nothing more." He nodded.

I slapped him hard, then grabbed his throat. "You don't know what fear is, asshole. Fear is not knowing who your friends are if you tell them who you really are." I could feel his carotid arteries dance feverish and monotonous under my fingertips. "Fear is having no job security on account of who you really are. Fear is the needle in your head telling you a walk down an alley could end in death." The muscles surrounding his trachea were slack against my fingers; his throat would make an easy fuck. "Fear is thinking your life isn't yours." I slapped him again. His stomach clenched. "I have to go upstairs. If I come back and see you aren't watching that video, I'll kick your ass. Is that clear?"

Seth nodded, measured and deliberate. He learned quickly, was trainable, malleable; here was Ross in the rough. My cock throbbed, swayed by the power of an autocracy built for two.

Upstairs, I went to my refrigerator, grabbed a quart of milk and took a quick swig. From a cabinet I took a tall disposable plastic cup. I descended the stairs quietly, making sure Seth was doing as ordered. He was. "Good boy," I said, scratching his head. At my workbench, I began cutting out the bottom of the cup with an X-Acto knife.

"Is this all there is in these videos?" he asked.

"You want plot in pornography? Two men meet, they fuck, they're much edified, the end. Like Susan Sontag said, 'There's only one dirty story.'"

"Who?"

I kicked the chair. "Watch the fuckin' video!" The two men were joined by a third, a dark-haired and bearded man. The rusty-haired man on screen wrapped a thick leather belt around his arm and sank his hand and arm into the dark man's ass. Elbow-deep, he started pulling the belt out, gently plunging his arm at the same time. The dark-haired man squatted on the cheap foam rubber mattress, his mouth in an open grin, supported by the blond.

I fit the bottom of the cup over his cock, securing the edge with surgical tape. Seth's cock tapped against the inside, a drizzle of dick spit oozing along his foreskin. I tugged the skin down, exposing his moist glans, and tied a small noose of fishing line just under its edge.

"What the fuck's this?" asked Seth.

"Nosy bastard," I said, mixing a little water with the alginate. "Ever been to the dentist? And he made an impression of your teeth? I'm gonna make one of your cock." I took the end of the fishing line to keep Seth's cock centered and poured in the alginate, tilting the chair so that the alginate was level in the cup. Seth hissed as the cool liquid swelled around his cock.

I brought my face to his. "Keep it hard, asshole." I kissed his forehead, tasting his salt and musk, a faint trace of nicotine, an acrid bite of something metallic. "Boy's gotta keep his cock hard for Daddy." Sweat rolled down Seth's face. "Pretty boy cock gonna stay hard, keep it up for Daddy," I said. "Think of that boy's hole you saw in the video, stretching wide open, those fingers sliding in and out, all that grease and juice feeling good, slicking up your insides. Make that hole slick and smooth, keep your pussy ready and wet for Daddy, give that cunt to Daddy, make him happy, keep his hand warm and safe in your guts. That's what you wanna do. That's what you need to do, just open up, just give it up, and say what you want, open up and suck it up your pussy, your pretty little boy pussy, tell your Daddy what you want." Carefully, I reached down and increased the pressure on the tit clamps. Seth looked directly at me, perhaps hoping to divine a message from my eyes. "Feels good whether you want it to or not. It all feels good. Whatever Daddy does feels good, and you want to make him happy, make his dick happy, make his balls happy, 'cause Daddy makes you feel good way up inside, makes you feel good, makes you feel safe, makes you hope your dick'll get big as Daddy's." I licked my lips and inhaled Seth's sweat. "If you're bad, Daddy'll whup you. But then he'll make it up to you, kiss away that hurt with more hurt, see what hurt his little boy can take, and Daddy's boy does anything for Daddy. You know deep down you came outta his dick. He gave you life, and you're afraid he'll take it back unless you give Daddy what he wants, what you know he wants, what you want to give him 'cause you owe him so much."

Seth's eyelids were heavy, burdened, and his breathing was deep. The alginate was set. I grabbed the X-Acto knife. Seth twitched when he saw it close in on his groin. The plastic cup cut away easily; I nipped off the exposed end of fishing line.

"You may go soft now," I said, tugging at the mold. Seth panted. "I said you may go soft," smacking his head. Seth looked up at me, puzzled.

I grabbed a bottle of Liquid Heet from the workbench. "Damn shame I couldn't prepare for this scene," I said. "Sometimes I fucking hate improvising." I swabbed his balls with the reddish fluid. "It takes a minute," I said. I reached up to the clamps. "Take a big breath," I said. As he inhaled I removed the clamps. His moan stretched into a series of yelps as the blood rushed into the dented flesh. I dabbed his nipples with Liquid Heet.

"Fuck fuck fuck fuck fuck," he said, squirming in the chair, almost jumping.

"You soft?" I asked.

"Fuck yeah!" he said, spitting through his teeth.

"Fuckin' hold still!" I yelled. Seth continued whimpering, the menthol and camphor cutting into his scrotum and nipples.

I carefully lifted the mold away from his reddening groin; his cock slipped out like a slack eel. A few hairs stuck in the mold, but otherwise it was a good impression.

"Fuck!" yelled Seth.

"Shut up!" I responded, punching his stomach hard. Seth's mouth was agape, his eyes wild. His lungs would not swallow air. His chest and shaved belly heaved, hiccuped, yet would not draw. I felt dick spit leaking inside my leather pants, a familiar buzzing in my nuts. Seth strained against the rope and chair, the sinew thickly corded as only the fear of death can make it. He turned pale. I watched, knowing his brain was racing at infinite speeds, thinking, *I'll never breathe again. I'm gonna die. I'm gonna die.* Suddenly the air sucked in, filling him deep; his color returned, flushing his face and neck, as if he were a creature of black and white bleeding into brilliant hues.

"It still burns," he said, weakly.

I unzipped my fly and pulled out my cock, eight inches, longer but not as thick as Seth's, with a slight upward curve. I flicked my middle finger hard against the underside, stinging my frenum, a strand of fluid sticking to my finger. My hard-on subsided as Seth watched, whimpering from the heat still slicing into his nuts and nipples. A sudden spurt of piss, then another, flew from my cock, landing on Seth's face. As the stream grew stronger I sprayed him at his neck and down to his scrotum, nipple to nipple, soaking him good. "It'll cut the heat," I said. I left him dripping. Seth's head was down, as if he understood this as an act of marking territory, and he felt ashamed.

I turned on a hot plate on the workbench; a small saucepan on it held paraffin shavings. "Ever read *Deliverance*? Or see the movie?" I asked.

"I saw the movie. Long time ago," he said, a little vacantly, panting.

"Did you like it?"

"Yeah. It was good, I guess," he said, still trying to catch his breath.

"Squeal like a pig, boy!" I said in my best north Georgia redneck drawl. The paraffin melted slowly, disappearing into itself, opaque into transparent. "So what do you think it's about?"

"*Deliverance*?"

"Yes."

"It's about testing yourself against nature. Finding out what you can do if you have to. Kind of like Hemingway," he said, warily.

"And what instructor told you that?" I asked. "*Deliverance* is gay porn made safe for straight men. There are clues everywhere; in the beginning John Voight's character fucks his wife in the ass as some forbidden delight before he leaves with his buddies and in a couple parts really gets into describing Burt Reynolds's muscles and cock. The other guy, Ned Beatty's character, gets fucked in the ass by a couple inbred freaks, the only men twisted enough to want to fuck a man's ass for sport, but only when Jon Voight thinks he's absolutely powerless to stop it. In other words, all the vectors by which pleasure could have entered have been carefully and pointedly eliminated. And, in the book at least, in the end one of the sheriff's deputies is named Arthel Queen. Which means his nameplate reads A. Queen. What more do you want?"

The paraffin had melted completely. I took the mold of Seth's cock, carefully poured in the paraffin, and set it aside. I grabbed some lube and exchanged my leather gloves for latex.

I knelt in front of him. Over my shoulder he watched the rusty-haired man gliding his hands into each man, as the other two, the blond and the dark-haired men, kissed deeply as their holes were expanded and plumbed. I smelled my piss on him. I poured some lube into my right hand and slicked it through my fingers.

I reached under the chair and began massaging Seth's hole. The pucker was tight, but Seth didn't flinch. I smeared the lube around in small circles, smoothing out the folded flesh of his sphincter. Seth's balls drew up. "It's just a finger, Seth. I want to see what you're made of," I said. "Watch the movie. You know it can be done." I pressed my forefinger against the clenched muscle, vibrating it a little. The tip slipped in. "Feels good whether you want it to or not," I said, softly. I rewet my hand with the other one and kept pressing. "It's all muscle control. Let me in."

A squint flashed on Seth's face, growing more apparent as I worked my finger in. "That's it. Suck it up."

My finger slipped inside suddenly. Seth flinched, then relaxed. "Please. Let me go," he said softly. "You can fuck me if you want. Just let me go."

"I don't want to fuck you," I said. I began circling my middle finger around the other where it entered him and slid it quickly inside. Seth caught his breath.

"You can fuck me if you want," he said again, absolutely still.

"Last time I heard that it was from a Marine, who then told me I couldn't kiss him 'cause he wasn't queer," I said. Seth's prostate was easily palpated. I rubbed my fingers across it; his cock jumped and began to swell but stopped midway. "I want to see if you're one of the big boys, Seth. I want to see if you can squirt," I said. "Are you gonna squirt for Daddy?"

"I can't," he said. His sphincter clenched onto my fingers. I continued rubbing his prostate. Dick spit oozed freely from Seth's piss slit.

"You don't think so?" I asked, pressing hard on his prostate. Seth made a strangled grunt, dread focusing on his face and chest as though projected through a lens. I pressed again, rubbing up and down, maintaining pressure, insistent. "What we have here is a failure to communicate," I said, pressing ever harder, kneading the smooth wall of his rectum. Seth squeaked a few times, and his cock lolled up to his belly. He grunted again; his sphincter unclenched. His foreskin peeled back, and white fluid drooled from his cock. He shivered.

I pulled out my fingers and stood up, snapping the gloves off. Seth was choking back tears. I licked his face, licked the abrasions that were swelling and darkening nicely, tasted the salt. I dragged two fingers through the jizz on his belly, stuck them in my mouth, then stuck them in his.

"You shot quickly, Seth. A gift of youth," I said. I grabbed his head in both my hands. "Keep watching the movie," I said. Seth obeyed.

The wax casting was still warm but solid enough to be removed from the mold with a little coaxing. I knelt behind Seth this time. "Daddy's real proud of you. You can squirt like the big boys. Daddy's gonna make you happy," I said, smearing lube on the wax dildo. "You're queer for cock, boy, got a sweet boy pussy, sweet slick pussy for hard cock, fingers, anything." I positioned the replica's head against his hole. "Ride it out, boy, gotta ride it out like Daddy tells you, let it slide up your pussy, make that hole feel good." Seth's sweat drained onto my piss, renewing that scent, which mixed with the slight, dark undertone of Seth's shit. "Smell that, boy? That's your pussy opening wide. That's your hole taking whatever Daddy gives it. Smells like sweet fresh pussy." Seth kept his face forward, eyes on the screen, his shoulders trembling a little. "Sweet little queer boy I got. Sweet little faggot son." I swabbed a little Liquid Heet around Seth's hole and relubed the wax cock. "Sweet faggot hole. Boy's got a sweet slick faggot cunt," I said. Seth's hole relented, and the cock slid in to its hilt. Seth cried aloud, openly, trembling, whimpering, squeaking. "Sweet boy cunt, best faggot cunt Daddy's seen," I said.

"I'm straight," he said, a drooling, watery, lachrymal whisper.

"Of course you are," I said. I went upstairs to jack off, leaving him to expel the dildo on his own.

Shortly before dawn I returned him where I found him, transporting him blindfolded and cuffed, his cock inside his pants this time. I kept the wax cock.

Seth may believe what he wants about himself. I know I will.

Aegis

By D. Travers Scott

*We think this story is one of the best about queers we've read in a
long while. It may be one of the best stories about pierced, pissed-
on, tattooed queer boys in Doc Martens and torn jeans ever.*

Soon, Ian thought.

The razor glided across his scalp, leaving a smooth, pink
wake in the lather. A chill followed the razor's swath, cold air
touching exposed skin. In contrast, a warm razorburn glowed.
The hot-cold juxtaposition reminded Ian of raves: flushed ecsta-
sy-forehead heat against cold menthol jelly on lips and eyelids.

Hot and cold make tornadoes, he thought.

Stevik was steady, careful.

Ian shifted his concentration from top to bottom as the
razor made another pass.

Feet flat against the floor tiles, back braced against the goal-
posts of Stevik's legs, Ian held himself as still as possible. The
tattooist's knees jutted out through torn black denim, the cotton fray and kneecap hairs tickled Ian's earlobes. Ian's arms circled back around Stevik's calves, the hard swells from years of
bike messengering wedged solid inside Ian's elbows.

Ian focused on the tactile sensations underneath his fingertips and sweaty palms. Stevik had put him on a steady diet
of L-arginine, niacin, pantothenic acid, and choline to height-
en his sense of touch. Boots and jeans flooded his system:
rough canvas cord, cold metal eyelets, and supple leather,

smooth spots on frayed laces, and rough denim all wove against his arm flesh. Stevik's shins ran down his bare back in sharp verticals.

Focusing on these sensations kept Ian motionless. Stevik could work around a nick, but Ian knew he'd prefer perfection from the onset and wanted to give it to him. He opened his eyes. The sun, low on Belmont, shot orange verticals of August evening slicing through the windows of Endless Tattoo. Stevik's boots glowed black-red; the silver ring on Ian's fourth finger gleamed in bright contrast. The oblique light carved deep shadows into the inscription, BOY.

Ian fought a shudder. It would take several sessions to do a piece as elaborate as Stevik had promised, as elaborate as the work he'd done on Toad: the outlining, fill, shading, color.

Finally, they were approaching the home stretch.

Once Stevik had marked him it would happen.

"So," the pierced guy with dreads drawled, "who gave you the ring?"

Ian turned around, surprised.

"No one." Ian's eyes, burning underneath thick, furrowed brows darted around the club. They lit on the dreadlocked guy. "Gave it to myself."

The man held his gaze, unblinking. "Self-made BOY?"

Ian looked away.

"Someday—" Ian glanced at his half-peeled Calistoga label. His eyes danced briefly onto the pierced guy, gazed past him out into the pit.

"Someday, someone'll give me one to replace it."

The man curled out his lower lip thoughtfully.

Ian scowled into his bottle.

The man with the dreads rose, took one of his two singles from the counter.

"Yeah. Someday," he muttered.

Ian's eyes trailed his dissolution into the crowd.

"There."

Hot-cold prickles ran over Ian's clean scalp, down his neck.

"OK, Ian. I'm done."

Ian stared at the ring, and his pale fingers gripping Stevik's black laces. He didn't want to let go. He'd waited so long for this—and what would follow—he almost feared its arrival.

"Ian, I gotta get you into the chair to do it."

Ian tilted his freshly-shaved head back against Stevik's lap, looking up into his eyes. Stevik's brown dreads circled down around his face like curtains. His face was a series of long shadows and gleaming sparks from the stainless piercings: labret below the lips, Niebuhr between the eyes, septum, eyebrow. Ian traced them with his eyes, drinking in the details of the man's face. His black goatee curled down in a point; scars striped his eyebrows. Two dark brown eyes terrified Ian, their enormous potential energy, poised to spring deep into him.

Ian smiled.

Stevik's lips curled into a fond snarl.

He spat.

The hot saliva splattered beneath Ian's right nostril. His tongue stretched to gather it up.

"Fuck," Stevik sighed. "I get so hot thinking about marking you."

Ian nodded. He squeezed Stevik's ankle and laid his face against his thigh. He breathed in sweat, dirt, and crotch funk through the stiff denim, nuzzled the coarse fabric, sighed.

"I know," Stevik murmured. "Won't be much longer, boy. Not too long. And it'll be worth the wait. You'll have earned it."

Ian exited into the gelid night. LaLuna's neon tinted the wet street hypercobalt.

Town always looks like a fucking car commercial, he thought.

Assorted young queers drifted past with affected chattering, unlocking station wagons and Buicks, strapping on bike helmets, revving motorcycles, stretching into raggedy sweaters and backpacks.

Ian kicked around the corner, disgusted. Another wasted night. Tweakers, smoked-out groove rats, slumming twinks. Even at the freak convention he felt the freak. The kids, his peers, had all been babbling about the Psychotronic Circus coming down from Seattle, trashing a new all-ages called the Garden, comparing notes on which of the street kids arriving for spring were fags and which ones would fuck around anyway, for money or a dose.

And the older guys: trolling, married, shutdown, falling asleep...fuckfuckfuck.

What I'd give for one fierce guy.

He cut through the alley, staring at his black Docs scuffing the gravel, listening to the regular jangle of his wallet chain. Chink-chink-chink. Another regular beat, some industrial ambient dub thing. Mix in a little Violet Arcana, maybe, and it could've graced the clove cigarette smoke in the chill room.

Chink-chink-chink—

Juh-jangle.

The dissonant beat startled Ian. He stopped, looked up.

The dreadlocked guy, one hand supporting himself against a Dumpster, stood across the alley from Ian. Facing the club's rear, his suede jacket glowed a scabby red in the halogen streetlight.

The man looked over his shoulder. "Oh—you. Hey."

He turned, releasing a splattering piss stream against the mossy bricks.

Ian stood silent, watching the piss steam slightly, froth pooling around his boots.

The dreaded man stared back over his shoulder.

Ian didn't move.

The man's boot heels ground into the muddy gravel. He pivoted to face Ian. His piss stream, spewing a circular arc like a lawn sprinkler, rained across the alley between them.

Ian met his gaze. The man frowned.

Ian dropped to his knees, immersing himself. The bitter piss ran into his eyes, dripping from his forehead, shoulders, and chest, gathering and falling from his face in swollen round drops, splattering on the earth.

The man shook off the final drops, tucked, buttoned. Ian's jaw dropped, the dour drops hitting his tongue. His eyes burned; his T-shirt was soaked and cold.

"Come on," the man whispered.

Ian followed him out of the alley.

"We'll just aim for starting the outline tonight. Just see how far we can go."

"I can take it."

Stevik's hand sifted through Ian's hairy chest, calluses stretching out a nipple like fleshy caramel. "I know you can. I know you can."

He jerked out a couple of hairs from around the aureole. Ian stiffened, inhaled briskly.

"I'll give it to you," Stevik said. "All of it and more. You know I will. But not till you're mine."

Ian's hard-on thumped against his belly, disconsolate.

Stevik unlocked the door of the metal Quonset hut. Ian followed him deep into the high-arched space, filled with only a few chairs, a couch, some cinderblocks. Eight-foot Sheetrock walls set off a room in the far back corner. In the ceiling's dark recesses, rain splattered against the corrugated metal.

A light clicked on beneath the farthest wall. Ian shut the door behind him and twisted the deadbolt. He felt his way toward the light.

He stood in the doorway, blinking in the light. Stevik sat on the edge of a bed that descended from the ceiling on heavy wooden braces.

Stevik looked up, almost surprised.

"What?" Stevik stopped, holding one boot in his hand. "What do you want?"

"I—ah—" Ian struggled for a response. "Well, why'd you bring me here?"

Stevik rolled his eyes and yanked off the other boot.

"Why'd you follow me here?" he shot back, tossing the boot onto the floor.

Ian shrugged. He took a step toward the bed.

"Look!" Stevik barked, "I don't want to *touch* you, get it? Little fuck—I don't know shit about you, if you're even worth it. I just... You can stay here, tonight, if you want."

He jerked his thumb toward a pile of dirty clothes in the corner.

"There. Sleep over there if you want."

Ian stared at him. Stevik rolled away, still in his clothes, and jerked a plaid comforter over himself. He clapped twice and the lights went out.

Ian found the pile of clothes in the dark. He could smell them.

Ian climbed off the floor into the chair. He stared ahead at the screen Stevik had set between the chair and the store's windows.

"Bet you've been dreaming about my dick, every night all these months," Stevik said, rolling open his station's drawer.

Stevik pulled out a rustling sheaf of carbon papers. Ian had seen him working on them. It was the design, the tat for his scalp. Stevik hadn't let him see it finished.

"What it feels like, how it smells. You've only seen it pissing. You don't even know what it looks like hard, how it feels in your hand, all hot and heavy."

At the apex of the Broadway Bridge, Stevik told him to stop.

Ian stared at Stevik, a few feet before him, hands across chest. A curtain of vertical lights rose behind Stevik, a skyscraper-light mirage that made Portland look, at night, like the metropolis it wasn't. The verticals of lights were only expensive houses rising up along the West Hills, but it had fooled Ian that night, years ago, when he'd leaped off the freight train beneath this very bridge.

"Take your clothes off, jack off, and don't look at me."

Stevik sauntered over to the walkway's railing and leaned back.

Ian pulled off his T-shirt, unbuckled his belt. He was elated to have run into Stevik again but wondered where things would go this time. He kicked off his Reeboks, pulled down his jeans.

Just the boxers left. If someone comes along...

"I said don't look at me, dog shit!" Stevik kicked Ian's shirt out over the bridge's lane gratings.

Ian scuffed off his shorts. He leaned back against the cold metal girder, its single-file row of rivet heads pressing into his back like a formation of soldier cocks. He licked his palm and rubbed his shriveled dick, trying to coax a hard-on. He kept his eyes moving to avoid Stevik: the tiny scythe blades of moonlight on the Willamette River, the splintery wood planks of the walkway, the kitschy yellow lily of the Suicide Hotline sign.

A dull roar grew. Cold whiteness rose up his bare side; Ian kept a steady rhythm pulling on his soft dick.

A breeze whipped against him as the truck plowed by; the bridge vibrated against his back and ass and feet. Silence. Ian was raging hard.

Relaxed, he stared up at the stars. Orion guarded him above, bow drawn. Ian stared at his jeweled belt and came.

"Good," Stevik said. He was standing right at Ian's side, holding Ian's shorts.

"Here."

Ian slipped them on, his jeans, socks, shoes... He looked over at his tire-tracked shirt stretched across the grating.

Stevik set his jacket on the girder and pulled his own T-shirt off. "Here. Yours is trashed."

Ian swallowed and pulled the shirt over his head, Stevik

smell surrounding him.

"You don't always have to wait to just run into me, you know," Stevik said jovially as they descended the bridge. "You can just come by the shop."

Stevik sprayed disinfectant onto Ian's scalp, a minty-cool mist dancing across his raw skin as it evaporated dry.

"I bet you dream about it in your mouth, going down your throat, sucking it dry, swallowing all the come I can shoot out."

A sticky bar ran across his head, leaving residue. Ian smelled of Mennen Speed Stick, a cloying musk of ineffectual father-macho.

Ian waited across the street at Subway, watching Stevik work. He chewed pepperocini thoughtfully. Watching Stevik from a distance afforded him moments of striking lucidity, quite distinct from the blind heat saturating his mind in the man's close proximity.

This is so weird, he thought. It was one thing when it was so—casual, but now... *Fuck, Ellen's already rented my room out to that sculptor guy.*

He's never hurt me, though. He's never done anything I haven't loved.

"And your ass just itches, don't it? It hurts—don't it hurt so bad, the way you want it? You think of me up there, my arms crushing your chest, my tongue in your ear and my dick, that dick of mine you dream about just ramming away up inside your ass, plowing into your hot gut. Goin' in and out."

Stevik pressed the carbon against his scalp, the design transferring to the adhesive deodorant.

"Put some music on," Stevik muttered as they entered the long metal building. He wandered into the kitchen for a beer. Ian flicked on the living room light and rifled through the CDs.

"Wanna Sheaf?"

"Yeah, that's great." Ian hummed happily. Stev had never asked him to pick out the music before. Some old Front Line Assembly would be fun, he thought. Or maybe more mellow— This Mortal Coil or something. Or Coil—yeah, that'd be the perfect combination.

None to be found: Marc Almond, Everything but the Girl, Annie Lennox, Edith Piaf, Billie Holliday...

God, I've gotta unpack my discs soon.

Stevik walked into the room with the two brown bottles of Australian stout.

"God, Stev," Ian quipped, scowling at the track listing on *Billie's Blues*, "you got anything besides all this diva-queen crap?"

Stevik set the bottles down carefully on the floor. His fist plowed squarely into Ian's gut.

Ian collapsed to the floor, gasping.

"Put on the headphones and listen to that CD," Stevik seethed through grit teeth. "Don't go to bed till you get it."

He picked up both bottles and stalked into the bedroom, slamming the door behind him.

Four in the morning.

"Stevik."

Stevik rolled over, blinked.

"Can I go to sleep now?"

Ian was crying.

"Yeah."

Ian knelt to spread out his blanket.

"No." Stevik pulled off the sheet, stretching out in a black T-shirt and shorts.

"Get in here. You ain't gonna get anything, and don't cling on me all night, but just go ahead and get up here. You don't have to sleep on the floor anymore."

"You think of me fucking you and you get all weak, don-cha? Like your knees giving out."

Stevik peeled off the paper and set it on the counter. Ian stared at the ceiling, feeling the vinyl and chrome of the chair beneath him. Stevik spoke in a steady monotone as he set out his supplies. The ink bottles clinked against the individual glass wells as he dispensed and mixed the colors.

Ian waited on floor beside the chair.

"So you're Stev's new boy, huh?" The woman looked down at Ian, balancing her water bottle on the shiny black hip of her PVC hot pants.

"He marked you yet?"

Ian smiled, shook his head.

"Oh, so you're still in the, uh, trial run." She laughed. "He let you talk?"

"Yeah."

"But he told you to wait here for him, right?" She smirked. "Been gone a long time, hasn't he? I think he's up on the roof fucking my sister."

Ian bit his lip and tried to sound polite. "He didn't tell me anything," he said. "I just want him to be able to find me when-ever he wants. So I'm staying in one spot."

"Not bad," she appraised. She turned around to face the crowd at the far end of the Quonset hut. Stevik broke through, dragging a skinny bald guy under his arm, both howling loudly.

"Well, your wait's over, it looks like. He's bringing over the ex for introductions."

She looked back over her shoulder at Ian, eyebrow arched. "You must rate."

Stevik and the bald guy tossed her happy nods in passing. They planted themselves loudly before Ian.

Stevik slapped the bald guy's chest proudly. The guy's chest, arms, neck, and scalp were a myriad of designs. In the dim light Ian could barely sort out the intertwined images: an octopus sat on his head, tentacles creeping down the neck. Two figures hung down his pecs, crucified at crossed wrists just above each nipple. Geometric spirals rose out from the waistband of his black leather pants.

"This is what real skin looks like, boy. See this? This is real work! This is the kind of work *I* do when I *give a shit* about someone."

The bald guy beamed proudly, his blue eyes sparkling brighter than the glinting four-inch steel spike through his septum.

"Don't take all the credit, now!" The bald guy grabbed Stevik's crotch. He crouched down, confidentially, to Ian. "Stevie, now, he didn't do all this, mind you. But, eh, he got it all started."

"Look at this fag's shit!" Stevik yanked Ian's T-shirt, pulling it up over his head.

"See? He's a little lost tribal boy. Look at that. My!" He grabbed Ian's arm and stretched it up high. "A chain around his arm! Tough shit! And wait, there's more!"

He reached over and grabbed the back belt loop of Ian's cords.

"Stand up, fuck," he muttered.

He spun Ian around and pulled down the back of his shorts, exposing the dogpatch hair leading down to Ian's ass. Off to the left side, where the hair faded into pale fawn down, was an ankh.

"Wook! It's a wittle ankhy-wankhy!" Stevik sneered. "Itn't it twoo tweet?"

Stevik howled. His friend belched. Ian stood, patiently waiting.

"Toad," Stevik said to the bald guy, "this little turd wants me to mark him. He wants me to put my art on the same skin with all this other piss-ass shit." He snorted.

Toad smiled. "Now why don't you just, eh, cut out those old ones, eh, Stevie?"

Stevik laughed. "Nah, no scars for him yet. Maybe we get Ben to brand him someday. For now I want his skin clean."

Toad nodded. "Then you'll just have to cover."

They stared up at Ian. He held his head bowed.

"Look at me, fuck."

Ian raised his eyes to the short, dark man.

"You really want to get marked by me? Like Toad here?"

Ian nodded.

"I had to earn this, you see," Toad said with quiet pride.

"I understand."

"It was quite difficult."

Ian nodded.

Stevik and Toad exchanged glances. Stevik shrugged.

"Go let Toad fuck you, asshole. Head's clear."

Stevik jerked his head toward the crowded rear of his space.

"Keep the door open," he called out as Ian and Toad walked away.

Stevik shifted weight in the worn easy chair cushions, his boots propped up on the a cinderblock. He watched across the space till Toad's serpent-entwined arm shoved Ian out through the bathroom door, to the cheers of the crowd. They gathered around Toad, laughing.

Ian pegged his shorts back up. He looked around the floor by the chair for his shirt. It was soaked with beer and cigarette ash, marked in the middle with a bootprint where it'd been used to swab the floor.

Ian wiped the wet come muck off his face with the back of his arm. Sticky smears clung to his hairy abdomen.

"Sit down," Stevik muttered.

Ian sat, wrapping his bare arms around his chest.

Ian looked at Stevik's boots. He leaned forward.

"Touch me and I'll beat the living shit out of you, right here."

Ian froze.

"Christ, you stink."

"Like you wanna cry. You think about how bad you want

me inside you, how you want my dick head kissing your heart, my cock's shit-smeared blessing. You want it so bad you can't stand it. You think of it and you think you'll just collapse in a big whimpering, slobbering mess, begging for me to do it. Doncha? Doncha?"

He slapped the boy's naked stomach.

Ian nodded, dislodging tears that dripped onto his chest, trickled down the sides of his neck.

Ian heard Stevik tear open the needle package.

"But you haven't, have you?"

Ian shook his head proudly.

"No, you haven't. You're tough. You never even asked me for it, never went around with your ass in the air like some damn cat in heat."

Stevik ran his gloved hand down the side of Ian's face, wiping away the saltwater, the rubber dragging across Ian's lips.

Stevik kissed the clean scalp.

"You already got it, man. You already got it. Everything I'm ever gonna give you, you already got it."

Studying the Alliance of Professional Tattooists manual and the Oregon state regs, Ian imagined Stevik marking him. He imagined Stevik fucking him, till the two fantasies meshed.

The tat machine and Stevik's all-but-unseen, imagined, longed-for dick merged—the machine's rabbit ear screwed into the base of Stevik's pubis, its mechanism sticking out from the pubic hairs. The armature bar shot upward as the base of his shaft; DC coil, spring contact points, and base all curled into an electromagnetic nut sac. The rubber bands were black neoprene cock rings. A dark brown foreskin stretched out over the armature bar and sanitary tube; it skinned back to reveal a five-point grouping of liner needles arranged in an X, like five dots on a die, like a man spread-eagled. The red cock needles shot in and out, woodpeckering Ian's scalp through scaly layer, epidermis, into dermis. Stevik pushed his cock needles farther, standing above, Ian bowed at his feet. The needles mixed Stevik's pre-come ink with Ian's head blood, sucking the serum up into the foreskin tube through capillary action, Ian's capillaries got some action, filling with Stevik's #C Hard Black spunk. Stevik marked deeper, aiming for Ian's fontanels, poking through the skull joints' cart, past the blood-brain barrier. Ian's whole body spasmed, muscles fibrillating with abandon.

Ian's fantasy lost physical specifics at this point. He couldn't visualize or verbalize, only feel a destruction, absorption, union.

Stevik stuffed cotton wads into Ian's ears.

Ian looked over at the tat machine in Stevik's hand.

Time slowed down. Ian watched. Current flowed through the coils and the base of the machine. Electromagnetized, it pulled the bar down, pulling down the needles and opening the silver contact points. Opening the points killed the magnet, and the spring assembly brought the bar back, causing the needles to move up and contact the points, conducting current and repeating the cycle. Again. Again. A cycle of opposite motions and polarities, endlessly repeating.

The first of the needles broke his skin, the ink penetrated his dermis, hundreds of times a second.

The Endurance Game:
Part of a Memo Found Behind a Pentagon Shredder
By Richard Cleaver

You want edge play? Here it is, pushing the boundaries of "consensuality." Richard Cleaver's story can be read as a brilliant fable or as the truly twisted product of a sadistic mind. Either way, or both, it turned us on and knocked us out.

Eyes Only
To: Secretary of the Navy
From: Commandant of Marines
Re: Discovery of potentially dangerous secret society

Problem Statement

It has come to our attention that a secret network or organization potentially disruptive to morale and discipline in the United States Marine Corps has been operating clandestinely for a period of 18 months in the vicinity of several bases in the United States and abroad. What follows is a summary of the group's activities insofar as our investigations to date have revealed them. As it is a clandestine organization, our report must of necessity be fragmentary. We have uncovered two original documents, reprinted in full below; the remaining evidence is hearsay. Many details are lacking and much of what we suspect is unconfirmed; nevertheless, it is the opinion of this office that an aggressive campaign to neutralize this group is warranted.

Name and Organization

The group in question goes by several different names. Among these are the Pain Pigs, Bulldogs With Balls, the Crutch Club, and the Endurance Game. This variety of nomenclature notwithstanding, there is no doubt that we are dealing with a single network. We refer to it hereinafter as "the Club" or "the Game." The majority of players are enlisted personnel of the USMC, although it is rumored that policemen, firemen, and other uniformed civilians have recently joined. No officers nor members of other armed services are allowed.

The Game is reportedly conducted by two civilians known only by pseudonyms, evidently nicknames given them by the first marines involved. One, described as short, husky, and talkative, is known as Napoleon. The other is tall and relatively less talkative; he is known as Tall Guy, or more often simply as TG. We have been unable to discover the true identities of these two men, or even their places of residence; they have turned up in the vicinity of nine Marine installations in the continental United States and at Yokosuka and Iwakuni in Japan. They use personal ads and the Internet to make contact with willing marines and to arrange meetings of the Club.

Discovery of Documents and Resulting Investigation

The existence of this group was discovered by chance. An unfinished letter, or a partial draft of one (with neither salutation nor signature), was found in a wastepaper basket in enlisted quarters at Quantico, along with a typeset, photocopied leaflet titled "The Rules of the Game." These documents led us to open an investigation of the movements and associations of the marine most likely to have written the letter, a lance corporal from the Midwest who is a star boxer for the Corps. (So far he denies all knowledge of the letter or its contents. Questioning continues.) In the course of the investigation, we were able to obtain affidavits from two individuals: the former girlfriend of one of the participants and a marine who was approached to participate in the Game but declined, and subsequently cooperated with Naval Intelligence. Excerpts from their affidavits are given later in this memorandum. The letter fragment reads as follows:

> You guys will probably never get this letter since I don't have any address for you. But I had to write it anyway, because you changed my life. I got the rules of the Game [Note: presumably the document found together with the letter] from a buddy you know as Rusty—the redheaded bodybuilder whose left ankle you broke and dislocated in North Carolina about six months ago. He told me that he never realized before that putting himself totally in a stronger man's hands would give him the most intense hard-on he ever experienced, better than any sex he'd ever had with a girl. It was so hot he said that he was going back for more, and next time I saw him he showed me how all the toes on his left foot were broken and described how you broke them one by one, starting with his little toe, and how each time you made him beg for you to break the next one, and how he finally came like never in his life when you busted his big toe. I knew then, from what he told me and from reading the rules, that I had to try. I joined the Marines in the first place because I like to push myself to extremes, and this seemed more like the real thing than anything in boot camp or later training exercises.
>
> I would never have let another guy touch me if Rusty hadn't told me about you. But when he did I realized how much I wanted to let go and let another man control me, if he was strong enough to. And I figured any man hard enough to break

another guy's ankle deserves my respect. I guess you busted Rusty's good, from what he told me about the pain he went through from it and what the medics told him.

At first I thought I just wanted to show myself how far I could go and show you guys how tough a real marine could be. I knew I was tougher than Rusty. But you showed me more than I showed you. You taught me that facing pain, especially when you know it's coming and how excruciating it's going to be, then enduring it and breaking through to the other side, where pain becomes your friend, and not your enemy, is what makes a man totally a man. I guess I never knew what that meant until you hurt me so bad, or even that it was what I was looking for. Anyway, whatever I was looking for I found it, and I just want to thank you sincerely for giving it to me. The whole scene was so hot: two prime muscled marine bodies stark naked and straining against the ropes; the two of you in black leather so that sexy leather aroma was mixed with the smell of our sweat; the two witnesses in fatigue pants and T-shirts that showed off their arm and shoulder muscles as they stood behind you on crutches with their left feet in casts and their toes showing; silence except for the sounds of our soles being beaten and our groans and curses and screams. You saw my hard-on and you watched me come when I heard my own bones snap. While I was laid up in sick bay that first week, I beat off five or six times a day, and each time I replayed it all in my mind. I hope you found me worthy enough to play the Game again soon, so I can push myself even harder and go even farther into and through the pain than last time. I

got off crutches today, and they told me I might
only need to be in a walking cast for two or three
more weeks. When it comes off I

[*At this point the letter, handwritten on both sides of one
sheet of common typing paper, breaks off.*]

The contents of the leaflet are as follows:

The Rules of the Game

Challenge: It's time to quit talking and prove who can take
the most pain. We will conduct the following challenge match
to determine the answer. Victory will not be easy. We will continue until one challenger gives up, using the following words:
"I respectfully request you to stop torturing my foot, Sirs,
because this marine is too weak to take any more pain." These
words, repeated exactly, and no other, will end the torture. The
remaining challenger must then beg for more pain, using the
following words: "Hurt me some more, Sir, I haven't had
enough pain yet." Passing out from the pain will end the torture and result in a forfeit.

Setup and Procedure: We will torture only one of your feet,
and no other part of the body. Each challenger must name which
foot he wishes us to torture and must give a reason for his choice.
You and another challenger will be tied naked to horizontal
benches set end-to-end with the soles of your feet facing the work
area in the middle. If you crunch your abs you will be able to sit
up just enough to see the other's agony. When one of us is flogging your foot, you will count each stroke loudly and distinctly
so that the other challenger may hear—we will inflict an exactly
equal number of strokes at each turn, alternating challengers. If
you miscount or fail to count off, we shall start again, in which
case the other challenger will have to take an equal number of

extra strokes, so as to keep the total number strictly equal, guaranteeing that the one who breaks down like a baby has had no more pain inflicted on him than the real man. The two of us will change places at regular intervals, so each challenger has been tortured by each of us equally. This is to prevent any suspicion that one or the other of us was "harder on" his victim.

Preparation: We will begin by stripping you naked and preparing your foot as follows. First, your second toe and your fourth toe will be tied up and back tightly with rawhide thongs fastened behind the ankle and a short stick inserted and twisted until the toes are held in a painful position. Then a stiff wire brush will be used to sensitize the skin of your foot, including your sole, your instep, and all the soft skin between your toes.

Stage 1: Flogging with your toes still bound. From time to time, as your toes become numb, we will tighten the tourniquets simultaneously. We will beat the entire sole of your foot, laying down the strokes crosswise from heel to toe, each just above and slightly overlapping the previous one. We will use the following tools in order: a wide black leather belt; a riding crop; a wooden dowel about as thick as a pencil; bamboo ditto; thin bamboo; a rattan rug beater; a weighted leather paddle; a wooden paddle with large holes; and a rubber hose.

Stage 2: Clamps. After removing the tourniquets, we will bend your middle toe under your sole and secure it in this position with a C-clamp. This will be slowly tightened, forcing the toe against itself and straining the joints. Eventually we will remove the C-clamp from your middle toe and apply one clamp each to your throbbing second and fourth toes. We will attach a strong spring-loaded hand clamp (the kind that looks like those exercisers you squeeze) to your big toe and use it to twist and bend your big toe to a variety of painfully unnatural angles. If you haven't broken yet, there may be additional flogging with the clamps in place.

Going further: A lightbulb that has been burning since the start of the challenge may be applied to various parts of your foot for measured, and increasing, periods of time. A soldering iron may be applied to your toenails or to the skin between your toes. Hot wax may be dripped on your foot, then removed by flogging. Wooden vises may be attached to your toes, instep, or ankle and tightened slowly, crushing the part in question. From time to time these vises may be used as levers to twist and wrench your joints.

Be advised that we are not the least bit reluctant to break bones or tear ligaments or dislocate joints. Do not enter the Endurance Game if you are not prepared to end up on crutches. If you lose, but are good-looking enough, we may give you the consolation prize of having a cock shoved up your butt. But only if your butt is worth it. *Talk is cheap. Put up or shut up.*

Affidavit 1

[*This affidavit was given by the former girlfriend of one of the marines who participated in the Game. She came forward voluntarily and seems to have been unaware that the matter was under investigation. Apparently, she became suspicious when her boyfriend appeared with all five toes on his left foot broken— only two weeks after getting off crutches for a severely fractured and dislocated ankle—and ordered her to suck his broken toes.*

There is strong reason to believe the informant was motivated to come forward by jealousy and anger. It will be noted, however, that even the most unlikely points are corroborated by independent evidence.

The informant herself claimed to be motivated by patriotic sentiments and her conversion to a strict form of fundamentalist Christianity. She insisted that the latter motivation preface any and all use of her information and that she be recognized as "bearing witness against the Satanic scourge of homosexuality that is sapping the energies and moral fiber of America's defenders and placing the country in danger both from foreign enemies and the wrath of a just God who will not allow his commandments to be flouted." The affidavit is quite long and, with the exception of the direct quotation above, we will excerpt only the most relevant of the marine's boasts to her. The affidavit in its entirety is available upon request.]

Fucking right I went back for more. I had to. It's a rush; it's better than sex. Nothing makes me feel like so much like a man as letting somebody do his worst to me and taking it like only a man can take it, just suck up the pain. Marines eat pain! [...]

I cried when they broke my ankle, I admit it, but that was just a reflex because I didn't expect it. It doesn't count. Still, I had to go back and let them do it to me again and show them I wouldn't cry this time. Being on crutches is nothing, broken bones are nothing, pain is what makes it real, what makes you alive, or not pain by itself but seeing the pain coming and taking it anyway. It was even better the second time. I knew how bad I was going to be hurting afterward, and I knew I was going to be on crutches for a while, and they knew I knew, those sadistic fag bastards, but I came back for more anyway. You can face anything when you don't know what's coming, or rather when you don't realize what it's going to be like. I thought it would be like hazing in high school, when you moved up from junior varsity to varsity on the football or wrestling team. But this was a lot worse. They put me on crutches with a busted ankle, but I took it and came back for more. So I knew I earned their respect. I don't care if you don't respect me—a man's respect is all that counts in the Corps. [...]

This time I knew what was coming and I asked for it like a man and went them one better. Like when they finally broke my big toe. You may think because my toes are kind of long they'd break easy. But even though my three smaller toes broke easy, my second toe and big toe were hard work for them.

I've broken toes a couple of times, so I knew what to expect, sort of. It's not the same when you know it's coming, though; it makes it like slow motion, and the pain just gets sharper and sharper and you can't take your eyes off your foot when they're pushing that toe up and backward and it's so unnatural look-ing that you just know it's going to snap and it does.

Anyway, when they came to my second toe, it was that Napoleon guy doing me then. He shoved it up and back like the others, and since it's my longest toe it looks real breakable, but it didn't break. He kept pushing and twisting, and he had to really put his weight behind it, and even though he's kind of a fat guy, it still wasn't enough. So he took a C-clamp and bent my toe down under my foot and squeezed my toe in the clamp and started to tighten it down real slow. I could feel the joints start to give way, and then for some reason he decided just to leave the clamp on my second toe and go on to my big toe. He got this spring-loaded deal and attached it to my big toe at right angles, and first he just left it there and it was fierce, the spring, I mean. It hurt like fuck just hanging there while he went back to my second toe and tightened that C-clamp some more.

I was sure my toe was about to break then, the pain was outrageous, and it kind of traveled up and down my leg when he jiggled the clamp a little; he was trying to get me to break down and give without having to break my toe, I guess. There were tears in my eyes from the pain, I don't mind telling you, because I know you broads all like a man that cries. But I didn't make a sound even though I just about ground my teeth away to keep from screaming. I really wanted a bullet to bite.

Napoleon went back to my big toe then, and without any buildup or warning pulled it hard sideways so that it was at a right angle to my second toe, and then he gave it a twist, with that spring loader for a handle, and I felt my big toe pop out of joint. I swear I could hear the ligaments tear, but I still managed not to even whimper. Instead, I spat on the floor and started baiting Napoleon for not being able to break my toes.

"Break the suckers, man, I'm asking you to," I said. "I can take the pain. Go ahead, make me happy. Those toes are fucked anyway, you just dislocated my big toe, and I think you tore a bunch of ligaments in my second toe, and the rest of my toes are already busted. I ain't going to be able to walk on these feet after what you done to them. I may as well go back to the barracks with all my toes broke so that I can get some sick leave. Break my toes, asshole, break my damn toes. Go ahead, do it. Not man enough to do it? Faggot too weak to break my bones? Go on, snap my toe bones, man, let me hear them crack. Do it. I dare you. Do it. Break my bones; put me on crutches. I want it. I want the fucking pain, man. Go on, man, give me some *real pain,* wipe me out, see if you can make me scream!"

He didn't say anything, just went back to my second toe. But he didn't turn the screw to break it. Instead he grabbed the C-clamp as if it were a door handle and rotated it hard, and there was this sick

crunching sound, and then it was as if my toe was getting screwed off and this tidal wave of pain surged
through my foot and up my leg and I was shaking it
hurt so bad, but I ground my teeth together and nearly dislocated my own jaw. But I didn't scream, at least
not out loud, just sort of inside my mouth. Napoleon
was still holding my foot in his hand, and I opened my
eyes, which I had shut to fight the pain, and I could see
from the look on his face he was getting turned on
watching me bucking and writhing from the pain and
all my sexy muscles and my tattooed pecs flexing and
shit from the pain. I bet I was real hot to look at, just
like I am now on these crutches. That's when I knew I
won, because he was weak enough to show he was
getting off on looking at my buffed marine body and
not man enough to hide that he's nothing but a faggot.

Just when the waves of pain coming from my
second toe finally started to let up a bit, Napoleon
yanked the clamp off. Talk about pain! I nearly
pulled my shoulders out of their sockets then, trying
to fight back the agony. You can still see the rope
burns across my chest and abs, where I lifted my
whole body off the bench. He grabbed the vise on
my big toe and bent it viciously inward and down,
and I could feel the dislocated bones rubbing
together, and then he pushed my big toe up and
back and held it there just at the breaking point.

Then he grinned. I couldn't stand the sight of
that fucking homo grinning at me thinking he won
when anybody who looked at him could see he was
a sadistic fairy pervert not fit to touch a real man's
big toe, much less any other part of me. Made me
sick. So I threw up in his face.

When I did that he twisted my big toe and broke

it right then and there. It cracked, loud, and even a guy as tough as me couldn't help myself because the pain was unreal. I bellowed and swore and spat at him again just so he wouldn't think my screams were weakness, because marines *eat* pain!

Affidavit 2

[*This affidavit was given freely by an acquaintance of one of the club members, who had attempted to recruit him. The informant spoke freely once he was approached; repeated assurances were given that he would not be subject to any disciplinary action since he had in fact declined the invitation. Apparently he declined because of his buddy's remark that the loser in the contest would be subject to forcible anal penetration by one or both of the civilians involved, a penalty the club member seemed to think wholly warranted (we can only assume that he was not a loser, although he nowhere stated this). He referred to those who suffered this penalty as "proven pussies," or simply as "proven," and our informant has the impression that this phrase is a term widely used by members of The Club. This penalty was unacceptable to our informant, who apparently considered it at least possible that he would be unable to bear the pain described by his buddy. We only paraphrase those descriptions here. The tortures themselves seem to have followed the order prescribed in the Rules cited above. The affidavit in its entirety is available upon request.*]

Getting your soles beat hurts like a sumbitch, all right, just like I thought it would from seeing that scene in *Midnight Express.* Your feet are really sensitive, even when you think they're pretty tough like from going barefoot a lot or doing karate or whatever. And then Napoleon and TG make them more sensitive by scrubbing them with a wire brush first, and then they blow on them to see if they're ready. They don't start the challenge until you cry out from the pain of them just blowing on your foot. That tells you how bad it hurts. But it's sexy pain, the way your soles get all sorta electrified by the brush, almost like how your dick feels when it's first getting hard and the slightest touch just turns you on more. Then they start in with the flogging, and that's like no pain you ever felt, but it's a turn-on kind of pain, warmlike. I could see the other guy's soles after they'd been beating them for a while, and they were bright cherry-red. Then as the pain gets worse you start to get hard, see, and that makes you want them to keep beating your feet even though it hurts so bad you don't think you'll be able to walk after. The pain just keeps building, but your dick is getting stiffer and stiffer all the time, so you don't want it ever to stop. That's when you make mistakes, because they're making you count off each stroke out loud, and if you're late or lose count, you got to start over from "one." And you're getting so turned on by the way the pain just builds and turns into pleasure that you're distracted, like, and forget to count. Then they nail you. [...]

The rubber hose is amazing, although that thin bamboo hurts like hell too, and it makes a weird humming sound in the air where the rubber hose just makes a dull thud. That hose, it's got this double-whammy thing happening. First, there's the pain from the blow itself, real bad pain, sickening pain, and then a few seconds later there's like a pain echo. That hurts even worse, real deep in your foot, like almost as if your bones were exploding from the inside, and that pain goes straight to your balls, man, and it's literally blinding, just like in cartoons and shit, when the guy gets hit and sees stars. It's like a drug, man, the pain is so intense, but it's like it's connected directly to your cock. No, I didn't think I was into pain either until I tried this—I just did it to see if I could take it. I didn't realize it would be such a turn-on. Shit, it's better than the best fuck you ever had. And you're totally naked, man, so your dick is like waving in the breeze and that gets you even harder, and they can see you're turned on and that gets you harder too. Even my damn nipples were hard! Pain is a real rush when guys like those two know what they're doing. I'm telling you, man, you gotta try it. Trust me, it'll drive you wild. I'm hard just talking about it. Look, you can see my boner through my cammies. It's all I can do to keep from whacking off again right here and now. [...]

The worst pain, or maybe it's not the worst but it's the least expected so it feels worse, happens when they take the clamps off. You think it's going to ease up the pain and let you catch your breath or whatever, but what really happens is the blood comes rushing back into your toe or your ankle or whatever and that sends a whole new kind of pain through you and it's like the way the blood rushes into your prick when you get hard, if it's too much too fast it hurts but feels good at the same time, you know what I mean? Only this is even more intense. [...]

Another amazing thing, they had this big vise that they put on the sides of my instep, and when they started tightening it my foot just kind of folded in on itself lengthwise and it looked like all the bones was about to shatter and it hurt bad. But the fear, when you know what's coming and you want to stop it but there's nothing you can do but watch your bones give way, that's fear, man, but it's really amazing at the same time. Blew my mind. I couldn't believe my foot wasn't completely fractured, but then they loosened the vise, real slow, and it's like I said before, the pain of the blood rushing back into it was wicked, but the feeling was so sexual it was almost as good as coming. Almost better, because you could do it again right away. They did too. I was sure they'd break my foot this time, but they didn't, or the third time either, which hurt worst of all. When they were doing it to the other guy, because they do the same thing to both of you, he was kind of moaning and gasping and it may have been the pain, which is wicked, but it sounded to me like he was having some wild great sex and he was just about two seconds away from shooting the whole time. [...]

Only bones I got broke were my toes, but they broke all those, one by one, slowly. That was a trip, because they made me sound off on each broken toe and then ask for the next one. And if I wasn't respectful enough, they'd twist and wrench the toe they just busted until I nearly passed out. It was like getting a bayonet through each toe, man, it hurt that bad, but it was also like getting my balls licked too. [...]

The sexiest pain occurred when they ripped up my ankle ligaments, I guess because it took a while and the pain kept building and building. The pain was so awesome, I was sweating like a pig the whole time they were twisting my foot, and squealing like one too, or like a girl getting her cherry popped. Which I kind of was, I guess. Anyway,

they took this big vise and attached it just below
my ankle bones and then started squeezing that
soft tender place right there, like a pressure point,
a little bit back toward the Achilles tendon. The
pressure from the clamp just grew and grew, and
every so often they tightened it down another turn
and there was a new wave of pain. It hurt like fuck,
but by then I had just sort of given myself up to
them, and it was like that terrible pain was a hug,
even though it didn't stop hurting. It just kept getting more intense as they kept turning the screw,
but each turn felt better, like a hug does when it
gets tighter, and by now I was unbelievably turned
on, and then they started to use the vise handles
like levers, you know, and started to twist and bend
my ankle in all kinds of extreme positions. So combined with the pain from the squeezing there was
this feeling like my ankle ligaments were slowly
stretching and getting ready to tear, and I was so
turned on and kind of flying from the pain that it
was like I could feel the fibers begin to pull apart
and each one gave off a little spark of pain like fireworks, and the pain kept getting worse and making
my dick stick up harder than ever and it was fucking dripping all over my abs and I was afraid I
would come and ruin everything and then all of a
sudden I could feel the ligaments give way and
there was this pulling and ripping sensation and my
ankle got all loose. It felt so good almost like a
cramp letting up and then I felt my foot go out of
joint and I could hear my ankle dislocate and I was
on the brink and then the guy, it was Napoleon, I
think, gave a kind of twist to the handles and my
ankle popped back in joint and that's when I came

and at the same moment I could hear the other
marine's ankle break, it made a loud crack and he
screamed and choked out the words of submission
and I looked up overhead where the two phrases
are posted in case you forget them and read the one
where I begged for more and I knew then that I
won so that made me come even more and Jesus,
man, I'd never felt so *powerful*.

The other guy? He cried like a baby, man. I don't
think it was just the pain of his broken ankle, either.
When they untied his arms he grabbed that leg in
both hands like he was in total agony, and I bet he
was too, but then he took both legs and just lifted
them and said in this low, kind of choked voice,
"Go ahead, fuck me. Bust my asshole like you busted my ankle. I lost my manhood. I may as well lose
my cherry too." And TG and Napoleon just took
him, and he kept whimpering and part of it must
have been the agony of it, because they were not at
all careful about his broken ankle, but also part of
it was knowing he was a proven pussy now and not
a real man at all. If he were a real man, he'd have
taken it. So he just kept going, "Yes, yes," like some
damn cheerleader on her first time. When Napoleon
was reaming the guy's ass, he reached up and
grabbed his broken ankle, which was resting on his
shoulder, and it was totally swollen and starting to
turn purple, and he squeezed it with one hand and
with the other hand he grabbed the guy's all-blown-
up, twice-normal-size foot, and Napoleon like
crunched up the guy's broken toes, and all the time
he was fucking the guy, real rough, and then when
he was about to come, he like forced that broken
ankle sideways and made the marine come too.

That Napoleon, he's a man. I don't care if he is a fag; anybody who can take a straight marine like that and hurt him and make him beg to be fucked and hurt some more and then make the straight guy come in the bargain, now that's a man.

You gotta try it, buddy. I promise you, the Game will make you a man among men just like Napoleon and TG. What else did we join up for?

Remarks

We should note that both of the affidavits describe the challenge aspects of the Club, while the letter suggests that there are meetings of veterans of the Game (whether of winners only, or losers as well, is not clear) to share their "war stories." Although these bragging sessions may seem inadequate to permit description of this network as a "club," we have evidence indicating that veterans identify themselves to one another when transferred to a new duty station, perhaps employing secret signals or insignia for this purpose, and may occasionally plan "tournaments" or "playoffs" among winners. One NIS investigator heard rumors that a "World Series" was to take place at some future date, in the form of a double-elimination tournament. (See recommendations, below.)

Recommendations

There are those in this office who believe the fact that this group includes nonmilitary personnel and seems to be run by civilians justifies sharing our files with the FBI. The majority in this office opposes going outside DOD on this matter. The risk of leakage to the press and damage to the image of the Corps is considerable. It would provide considerable ammunition to antimilitary members of Congress and radical groups agitating for a so-called "peace dividend." As you know, it is already our policy to keep under wraps the existence on or near Marine bases of other unpalatable groups, such as the Ku Klux Klan.

A small minority believes that, given recent congressional limitations on our traditional endurance-building exercises, now characterized as "brutal," we should turn a blind eye to these activities, which appear to serve a similar purpose and are to all appearances wholly voluntary and outside the chain of command.

There is something approaching consensus that if a "World Series" is planned we should attempt to infiltrate it, using suitably handsome and well-built volunteers from Naval Intelligence; or if it is not planned, to conduct it ourselves as a means of either destroying the Club or bringing it under some degree of control by the chain of command.

The final decision is of course up to you, Mr. Secretary. My personal view of

[*Editors' note: The text breaks off at the bottom of a page here, and it appears that the remainder of the memorandum is irretrievably lost.*]

Cage

By Bill Brent

In "Cage" Bill Brent explores the far reaches of submission, skillfully taking us to a place where the concept of "self" has lost all meaning. It's a place some of us dream of but few of us have ever been.

I live in a cage. I hope I will never leave. I pass the days in darkness and silence. In truth, I do not know the days from the nights; all I discern is my own inhaling and exhaling. Nothing else colors my existence. It is completely black in here. Do I dream or sleep? The only way to know for certain is to taste the skin on my arm. For some reason I cannot duplicate that taste in dreams.

Sometimes I dream of my previous existence. The memories seem shadowy, forced, false. It was always a burden to be so conscious of self. Here I have no self. It is a relief.

I do not know where I am nor how long I have been here nor how long I shall remain. I only know that I do not have the choice to leave. I do have a keeper. I do not know when he will come, how long he will stay. Sometimes it seems minutes, sometimes it seems weeks.

When he comes I know that I am not alone in this world. He fills me with a boundless terror and rapture that I can only describe as a complete immersion. Every pore of my being is infused with him. I soak and wallow in a purity of extreme feeling. And still I have no self; I am pure feeling, without identity.

Is this madness? I don't care.

A small amount of food is provided on a regular basis. I know that my diet is monitored and that what is rationed is what someone has determined will keep me most fit for his use.

It is so delightful to be the tool of another. To have no plans for myself. I must be the luckiest man alive.

Sometimes I am slapped so that I may learn to be more alert. I do not question the motives, though. I am happy to be slapped if it gives satisfaction to he who slaps. Lately, though, I wonder if this is a good idea. Why am I important enough to be singled out for slapping? It makes me uneasy to contemplate this. To realize that my existence has an impact on others.

There are others here, though I never see them. On rare occasions I can hear their moans and cries, intensely remote, more distant than dreams. It is as if they are being kept in a building next to mine—a factory, perhaps, with thick concrete walls—that serves as a reminder that others still remain on this earth. It is a nagging reminder, though—a vestige of selfhood and responsibility and communication I would prefer to put behind me forever.

Sometimes I am obsessed with the fear that I may one day be forced to function again beyond these walls, out in the loathsome world of names and complications. When I cannot shake this thought quickly, I hear someone screaming, and then I realize it is me. But the noise exhausts me, and I grow quiet again. I remember where I am, which is nowhere, and it brings me peace.

I never see his face. Sometimes he slaps me, sometimes he punches me, sometimes he burns me, sometimes he whips me, but I never see his face.

Sometimes he blindfolds me and leads me from the cage. He presses me into a sort of slanted wall—smooth steel, cool, nice—and then he whips me. I hear someone screaming, and then I realize it is me. I feel something cool breaking across my back, and then I realize it is my own blood. The wall is lowered, or perhaps the earth rises. From high above I feel something hot stinging my

back, and then I realize it is his piss. I scream in the most delirious bliss. My entire body and soul tremble with the ecstasy, my
seed is ripped from the pit of my stomach, and I often collapse to
the floor. To receive communion from my Master, my own personal God, is humbling and profound. I do not feel worthy of this
attention, but if it satisfies him, then I am overjoyed.

Once he brought some others to piss on me. They were
women; I could tell by their scourging laughter, thin and high.
It was the only human sound I'd heard in weeks; it was a terror
and more torture than the scalding of their urine splashing into
my wounds.

I believe this is our game: The more he demeans and debas-
es me, the more I exalt him. Yes, it's easy to tremble before the
vicious man who carries the key to your cage, but why not?
Others fear an avenging god, but I would rather know a god
who makes himself violently present than some abstraction
who reveals himself to none. My God is no delusion.

He may not even be the same man each time. I don't care; I
can feel his power in many. In fact, I am sometimes visited by
several men at once. Once they tied me to a steel table and left
me for an eternity. Maybe six hours? I pissed myself—I couldn't
help it, I was there so long—and when they returned they
mocked me and lowered the table and relieved themselves on
me, laughing at the pathetic little lunatic before them. There
must have been six of them; I was pelted from more than the
four directions.

They can do anything they please with me, and I will endure
it. If they kill me, they kill me. It's only death. It's not as if I matter anyhow.

I am just a tool. A tool and a fool.

I remember how it felt to have desires. Lonely. Here I am surrounded by no one, yet I am never lonely. Almost never lonely.

Sometimes in dreams, I am a bat. I fly weightlessly through
vast corridors of black, relying on radar and instinct, feeding on

those smaller and weaker than I. Yet always, I end up glancing off a wall I cannot see, which reflects my limitations back to me. And I think, *This is how it works in the larger world. Those who fly high still have their limits. We spend our entire lifetime ignoring or defying our limits, but still, there they are. Our limits are the source of our loneliness and unhappiness. It is best to accept them and thus be free. It is best not to see.*

I taste the water, and it tastes like guns. It makes me think unaccountably of him. It must be drugged then. It makes me impervious to pain, or at least detached from it. Thus, I know he is about to arrive. I wonder which limits I am intended to surpass today. I drink heartily, gulping this water I cannot see. The blackness shimmers. It swims in on me from all sides, and it leaps inside of me like a vibrant fish.

Time slows to a crawl. Hours have passed, or so it seems, and there is still no sign of him. I grow restless, and I hate him for making me wait. I hate myself more for showing my weakness. I grow conscious of my desire, and it inflames me. I taste the skin on my arm. The tongue tastes salt; it feels the fine hairs. I feel my teeth sinking hard and deep into eager flesh. I taste my blood; it fills my mouth. I hear someone screaming, and I know I am not dreaming.

I have received communion from myself.

So this is the boundary I have surpassed today; I do not need him anymore. I grow quiet, exhausted, totally at peace.

I have never felt more alive.

Then, he enters.

Whose Little Boy Are You?
By Wendell Ricketts

When Rough Stuff *was first conceived, this powerful story, originally published in* Doing It for Daddy, *came to mind. Wendell Ricketts takes us deep into people's souls, where hard cocks and the burdens of the past combine in ways that are beautiful, scary, and as surprising as they are inevitable.*

The royal blue panel truck is heading straight for me, the solid field of its two wide walls broken only by the name of our afternoon newspaper in authoritative, gothic script. I'm in the crosswalk, but the truck is swerving wildly out of its lane, and I can see the driver's face. I don't think of trying to get out of the way. In fact, in the moment before the truck hits me, I have only one thought in my head: *Thank God! It's finally over.* If there were more time, I would run the last few steps to the grill of the truck, throw my arms back like the handsome shirtless Czech student standing before a Soviet tank in that famous 1967 photo, and leap.

And then the truck doesn't hit me.

OK, it was only a dream.

Oh, man, what a fucking cop-out. I'd be plenty pissed off, if I were you.

It wasn't a dream, but it is true that the truck didn't hit me. Maybe I was never in any danger. I do think a lot about mayhem, though. When I was in the deli getting my roast beef sandwich, right before I came out and faced down the truck, I was watching the handsome, geeky deli boy cut the meat for my sandwich in one of those enormous, semielectric slicers. He cinched down the hunk of beef and slid it back and forth across the blade; his other hand caught the slices as they fell, weighing them in his palm to see when he had enough. Can you imagine what I was thinking of?

"Portion control is the most important thing in food service." My Uncle Jess, who always talked about opening a restaurant but never did, used to say that all the time. He never got around to opening the restaurant because he was busy raising the two half-Vietnamese grandkids that his useless, alcoholic, child-molesting son Willis had dumped on him and his wife, Vera, before Willis went to jail. He was also busy dying from the doses of Agent Orange that he'd gotten on his five tours of duty in Vietnam.

He told great stories about Vietnam, my Uncle Jess. He made it sound romantic. When I was 8 and my pet rabbit had died and I was devastated, I wrote Uncle Jess a long letter about it and mailed it to him in Vietnam. There were so many pages that I sewed them together with needle and thread, bound along the left margin like a book.

Jess sent back one of the kindest letters I have ever received, about how life was precious and you had to savor it, but that you couldn't control anything and, when bad things happened, you had to take them in stride. He wrote that in the middle of the jungle somewhere, with the sound of rifle fire near enough to hear. I imagine he thought a lot about mayhem too, my Uncle Jess. But he helped me, about the rabbit.

Uncle Jess was a foot soldier, a grunt; he spent his time clearing villages and wading through rice paddies, trying not to step on punji sticks. He didn't want to be an officer—had no respect for them, he said. Uncle Jess never got any higher than sergeant. I think he liked to kill people. He thought the war was right.

When he came home between tours, he and Vera and my parents would stay up late, getting shit-faced. Uncle Jess was a fun drunk mostly; he liked to tell dirty jokes and sing songs about

poontang and tropical diseases that rotted men's dicks off. After
Willis went to jail and Jess had to retire and his lungs started to
give him pain all the time, he drank on purpose, and he wasn't
fun anymore. He would bark at the children and call them gooks
and half-breeds and bastards. But he loved those kids. When the
woman Willis had fucked, lived with for two years, and then
dumped wrote that she and their two sons were in a refugee camp
in Thailand, it was Uncle Jess who flew there and brought the
kids back. And it was Uncle Jess who made sure money went to
their mother every month for years, until she disappeared.

After Uncle Jess's ugly drunks got started, Vera would show
up at our house with black eyes, weeping. Everybody knew
where she got them, and she knew everybody knew, but she was
fierce and wouldn't let anyone say anything to Jess. "He's in
awful pain from his lungs, and Willis just about broke his heart.
I've loved him for 30 years, and I don't care if he hits me now.
He's not going to suffer that much longer, and I'm strong enough
to take some of whatever he's mad about. Maybe it helps."

I can hardly talk about Vera now. She and I used to go beach-
combing; she made lampshades from shells we found on the beach.
You could find shells in those days, on the sand right across the
road from their house. She was a big white woman, with family
from the Ozarks. She was the first person who ever fed me hominy.
For money, she took in ironing and kids, and it must have helped
to pass the time when Jess was away in Vietnam and all she had to
do was worry about whether he was going to get killed or whether
he was already dead and they just hadn't gotten around to telling
her yet. She had huge breasts and piles and piles of bleached blond
hair, but she wasn't even a little bit pretty. Jess was no prize, either,
come to think of it. Vera used to joke that he had a face like 40
miles of hard road. She wasn't smart, except that she decided early
on who she wanted to love and set her life to doing it.

There was pretty much only one thing Vera was an expert on
and that was taking care of children. She had a great lap, but she

wasn't much of a cuddler. I think she figured kids kind of had to take care of themselves, but she was happy to sit you down and play hours and hours of Crazy Eights with you if you could keep from squirming all over the place and not cheat. She had no patience for molly-coddled children. The kids she baby-sat wore some grownup's old T-shirt and a diaper, until they were old enough for shorts. She'd have laughed out loud at the idea of OshKosh B'Gosh.

Vera thought you ought to make a bird feeder out of an egg carton and Popsicle sticks and a truck out of pieces of wood leftover from Jess's workshop and a sand bucket from an old Clorox bottle with the top cut off. Vera never bought a single thing for a child to play with, and I can tell you that being at her house was a lot more fun than being at mine.

Vera loved being a mom, and I guess she was lucky because she never had to be anything else. I suppose she was also, officially, a housewife, but that word always makes me think of the kind of women who were in the *National Geographic* ads in those days, slim women in nice dresses, dusting the furniture in high heels. Those women had nothing to do with Vera. Vera sweated and smelled of sweat, and she wore stretch pants and stained shirts and had varicose veins. Stray pieces of hair were always pushing up out of her head like they had someplace else to go. She could iron a pair of slacks with a baby in her arm and supper on the stove.

The only kid she wasn't any good with was her own, Willis, and I think she just didn't know what to do about him. When she and Jess got the grandkids, Will Jr. and Jason, you could tell she was determined that nothing was going to go wrong with them.

She kept writing to Willis in prison, even though Jess told her not to. For a while she had Willis send his letters to our house so that Jess wouldn't see them. Anything about Willis just made him upset, and that made him drink.

You could tell it weighed on her, when Jess died, that they wouldn't let Willis out for the funeral, but maybe the way it happened was that Willis didn't really want to come. He'd tried to be what his daddy had wanted—a squared-away soldier, a good killer, and a patriotic American—but he was ruined inside, ruined the way Jess was. Maybe it was good that Jess was gone away to war so much; he would have been hell for Vera to live with day in and day out. Like Vera, there was only one thing Jess was good at, and that was being a soldier. Soldiers and mothers probably can't live together for long.

Maybe Willis's trouble was that he didn't have a woman like Vera; not everybody has what it takes to kill people for a job and not have any comfort waiting at home nor anyone to understand what you do for a living. I think it got to Willis—first the killing and then the fact that doing the killing didn't bring him any closer to Jess. The war gave them something to talk about: They could swap war stories over beers. But Willis had a lot of buddies he could tell bullshit to. He didn't have much of a daddy, though.

That part of the story has been told a million times before: Willis had no stomach for being a soldier or for killing, and that made him feel weak, and he hated himself for being weak, and he hated his father for seeing him weak. Something like that. When he started going after his kids though, that was different. It's evil, but it's pathetic at the same time. The kind of man who does that to his sons is someone who never expects to be able to stand on equal footing with a man or a woman.

Willis wasn't any good from the time he was in high school. Vera said as much, even at the time. He worried them both something terrible, but especially Vera, because Jess wasn't there to worry, and I don't think Vera wrote him much about it. She tried to send him cheerful news when he was overseas. The downside of that was that it was always a bad surprise when Jess came home, once or twice a year, and saw Willis again with no time to prepare himself for the changes. Because you could just look at Willis as a teenager and see how far gone he already was.

Willis terrified us younger kids, and I remember how we'd scatter to the rear yard when his nasty-ass black Camaro came flying up the driveway, spraying gravel, the radio blaring, and the noise from the muffler sounding like a plane was landing on the roof. Willis would come to a sudden stop within inches of the porch, slam the car door, and disappear scowling into the room Vera and Jess had fixed for him downstairs. He hardly talked to anybody, least of all to Vera. Sometimes he'd show up for supper when I was there, sometimes not. I don't remember that Vera ever called him up, though. If he did eat with us, he was silent the entire time and avoided looking at anybody. His eyes were scary.

Some kids get into a lot of trouble as adolescents but you know you're not just fooling yourself when you say they're probably going to grow out of it. I don't think anyone believed that about Willis. There wasn't much about him to make you laugh—none of the usual talk about how boys will be boys or the way he was full of the devil.

The kinds of things Willis did weren't going to turn into family stories that could be repeated years later, with a tolerant chuckle, over the remains of the Thanksgiving turkey. He hit Vera once, another way he was trying to be like his daddy; I heard her telling my mother about it.

Most weekends and many evenings, Willis worked on his car in the driveway. He never wore a shirt. Often it was just a pair of shorts made out of some torn-up, cutoff jeans. He'd lie on his back under the car, and I could look up the legs of his shorts, where they gapped open against the insides of his thighs, and see his dick. He knew what I was doing; he caught me staring right at him more than once.

The last time it happened was about a month before Willis joined the Army. When he noticed me there, standing at the edge of the porch and gnawing at my fingernails, he watched me thoughtfully for a moment from where he lay, then pulled himself out from under the car and stood in front of me, greasy and sweaty and bitter-smelling. At first he just looked at me with those flat eyes, like two grey stones under bad water, his white belly and pink nipples less than a foot from my face. Then he slid his hand down inside the front of his shorts and slowly and deliberately scratched himself. When he pulled his hand back, he held it out to me. "Wanna smell my fingers?" he sneered, then spit a thick ball of mucus into the dust between my feet.

I was 9 years old, and Willis knew one thing about me that was truer than what anybody else knew: I was obsessed with him. Even at that age I wanted not to give a shit about anything the way Willis did. I wonder now what would have happened if he had gone after me instead of waiting nearly ten years for his own sons to come along.

In order to play Daddy, you probably have to have had one. Otherwise, what do you play with? Not memory, not experience, certainly. You can play with the ideas in your head that others have put there, like the daddies on TV and in the movies or in books you read. But mostly they're not much good as fantasy material—either upstanding, deadly dull, and about as sexy as a jar, or else outright, broken-down losers. Take Willy Loman, for example. Now there was a flaming failure who left behind a couple of fucked-up sons who were never going to be able to get a hard-on without feeling ambivalent about it. I'd like to see the sequel to that play.

Hollywood and books have given us all kinds of moms, even monster moms, but they usually make sure to leave in the erotic charge. Sex is part of what makes those mothers monsters, maybe; their sons can't get out from under them and halfway don't want to. But full-fleshed dads are rare. Nobody likes to admit that dads want to fuck their sons. Or vice versa.

Anyway, the point is: my dad. My dad didn't like to wear clothes in the house, and he never closed the bathroom door. He was hairy and 62, and the shape of my chest is just like his. But I'm never going to be as tall as him, and my dick isn't ever going to be as big.

Why do you suppose my dad liked to have me come into the bathroom and sit on the john and talk to him while he was in the shower? Why did he get out and stand in front of me while he dried off, later moving over to the sink to shave, while I sat beside him, his soft cock pushing up against the tiled edge of the counter?

One thing my daddy taught me was longing.

But my daddy hated fags. I haven't forgotten the day, early in the year in which he died, when I called him up at work in my cracked and changing adolescent voice, and he said, "Who is this? You sound like a goddamn queer."

So does that mean he did or didn't understand what those mornings in the bathroom meant to me?

One of the problems with your dad being dead is that this is the kind of question that is never going to have an answer. Maybe he didn't know. Men do this to each other—flaunt their dicks and their naked bodies, tell each other horny stories full of lurid, exaggerated details, and the test is: Don't let this turn you on. The winner is the one who doesn't. That may have been something else my daddy was trying to teach me, but the lesson didn't take.

So if you don't have a daddy, or if your daddy dropped out early, you play with an identity informed largely by his absence, like the figure that stood at the foot of my bed once, perhaps a dream, the night after my friend Jack died 3,000 miles away and I went to sleep aching for his presence. Then, in utter darkness, I woke up to see the shape of a body, a figure made not of light but of a darker, denser blackness that slowly diminished into the ordinary colorlessness of my night bedroom.

Maybe it wasn't Jack, but it was what Jack has become—the hungry space where a person once existed; a void in air that sucks memory into it; an outline that disappears, perversely, the moment I try to focus on it, then reappears, perversely, at the periphery of my vision.

Periferia. That is where my friend Gino lives, in Rome: *le periferie*, what we would call the suburbs. He lives on the outskirts of town. What a language, Italian. One in which the cognates are just slightly wrong: *argomento* doesn't mean argument; *educazione* doesn't mean education. Gino lives on the outskirts of the city, alone with his small Buddhist altar in a room smelling of incense and the memories of his absent father.

When we make love, sometimes he calls out *Babbo*—Daddy—as I put my dick into him. Sometimes he says, in English, when I am fucking him, "Take me!"—a phrase he learned from bootleg American porn videos.

I'd rather he said *Babbo*, but "Take me" is closer to the truth: take me away, take me back, take me into my childhood dream of a man who could cover my entire body and engulf me, who could end the separateness that starts with my skin. Gino doesn't even mind that I've gained some weight since the last time he saw me; Daddies are bigger and heavier and hairier than you are anyway.

Gino's body is painfully thin; his cock—which is pretty huge—lies in the middle of a kind of platter, the wings of his pelvis high and sharp on either side like the ridges bordering a volcanic valley. His cock and the sudden tuft of black hair that grows in the middle of his chest are the only parts of his body that don't belong to a 12-year-old boy. *"Tu hai il fisico di un ragazzino,"* I said to him the first time we made love. *"Apparte che ce l'hai quel immenso cazzo."*

I think sex is simple for Gino. The script is very straightforward. His body is held, kissed, positioned, manipulated, entered; in the end Daddy wraps a slippery hand around Gino's dick and slowly makes him come. This is after Daddy has come himself, and he makes Gino hold completely still so that Daddy's softening dick stays seated deep in Gino's ass. If Gino can't control himself and moves around too much, Daddy doesn't let him come at all, makes him lie on his back with his hands and feet tied to the corners of the bed so that he can't hump the mattress or the bunched-up sheets the way he does sometimes even when he knows he's not supposed to. Even jerking off is easier for Gino; he has at least an extra inch of thick, tight foreskin to play with and never needs any lube.

But a lot of this is for my sake, not Gino's. He misbehaves because he knows I like depriving him.

It's even more complicated with Mike. After a few dates I had to stop seeing him; I didn't want to be "consensual" anymore, never mind "safe and sane." Mike couldn't say "Daddy" enough; he said it so much it started to sound like my name.

Mike didn't want to be tied up; he didn't want to be hurt. He didn't give up his ass easily either. None of that made me horny—it made me want to rip him the fuck apart. I stopped wanting to hear him moan in discomfort and started wanting to hear him scream in real pain. I stopped being satisfied with the squirming he did when I tied leather cords too tightly around his balls and started to want to see him in terror and genuine agony, yanking desperately at the ropes while I jammed hypodermic needles into the head of his dick or cut line after line into the flesh of his shoulders and arms. I wanted to make one clean slice across the palm of his hand and make him use the blood to jerk off.

And soon, I knew, I was going to do it—no asking and no turning back. And that was going to be the Bad Daddy coming out, not the good one that most boys want. It was the Medea Daddy who wanted to kill his children and lap up their blood. It was the Daddy who destroyed, not the Daddy who made everything better. I think Mike didn't want that kind of Daddy, but when you call out "Daddy", you don't ever know exactly who's going to answer.

"You must work out all the time. Your legs are like tree trunks." This is what my boy says to me, trying to be flattering. He knows nothing of my struggles with and against my body and its refusal to shape itself into a form I find at least tolerable, if not actually pleasing. He knows nothing of the way I pinch the skin along the insides of my thighs into crepey little folds as I lie alone in bed. He knows nothing about the days when I watch the reflection of my body as I pass shop windows and the reflective sides of bus shelters and hate myself with a loathing that is fierce and focused enough to start brush fires.

He doesn't know about the days when I catch a glimpse of myself in the mirror, out of the corner of my eye, and turn back abruptly to stare. "Who is that?" I say. "Who is that person in my clothes? Is that me? I thought I was taller. I thought I had lost some weight. I thought these pants fit me better." And I look and look, far into the depths of the mirror, as far down as I can see, unable to turn away because I keep thinking I've caught sight of the impostor. Or I'm gripped with apprehension and anticipation, certain that my real self, rippling just below the surface, is about to burst through at last—what I've always expected.

How can I be anyone's Daddy when I'm overdrawn at the bank at least once a month?

But my boy only wants to please me, and for this I am sometimes grateful and sometimes angry but always suspicious.

It's Sunday, the morning after a not entirely successful first date, and Reed wants to go to brunch. He has spent the night. It is late, and I am watching the day—and any possibility of work—drain away before my eyes. It is late because we've already spent nearly an hour and a half having sex that was, I think, more successful for Reed than for me.

I'm not ordinarily a fan of first-thing-in-the-morning sex, but Reed tells me he's never been fucked before, and I'm completely taken in by the possibility that it might be true. Intellectually, I doubt it's true, since last night I got four fingers into Reed's butt without a whole lot of trouble and was just about to slide my thumb in as well when he decided he was getting worn out. I had been kneeling beside him, twisting my hand around and around in 180-degree arcs, while he butted his head against the wall and sang a steady stream of sexy, guttural noises. Every once in a while he'd pause and quietly say "Ow" and then go back to his gibberish.

In the morning his butt opens right up again and within a minute I've got the first two fingers of my left hand buried to the hilt. With the other hand I'm trying to fit a condom onto my dick and get some lube to come of out of the container by the bed. You'd think it wouldn't kill them to make a condom that you can open with one hand, but no one seems to have mastered the technology. I suspect that people who make things like condoms actually spend very little time thinking about sex.

Reed is no help at this point because I've got him spread-eagled on the bed: hands tied to rings above his head, ankles chained down tight at the other end. He also mentioned that he'd never been tied up before.

Last night was supposed to be Reed's initiation into what he calls "leather sex," although there was no leather involved, unless you count my cock ring. When I first met him, though, Reed was talking about "sex magic," so "leather sex" was, believe me, an improvement.

Anyway, we didn't get very far before he started crying— actually sobbing—and he chickened out. When I told him to go over to the work bench and pick out the thing he'd like to get beaten with first, he came back to the bed with the thinnest slapper; I'm sure he thought it would hurt the least because it was small, but I gave him some significant welts before switching to the hairbrush, which raised a hot red glaze all over his ass and the backs of his thighs. Then I went back to the slapper and put a series of neat, pink ridges up and down his back, parallel to his ribs. Later he said to me, with a hint of reproach in his voice, "I thought only slaves got whipped on the back."

We didn't get much further than that before Reed started crying. It was all about how he'd been abused as a child. I've heard this before, and I wasn't even slightly impressed. People start doing S/M so that they can deal with their childhood shit, and then the ugly memories come up and the whole thing seems like maybe it isn't such a good idea anymore. Reed's daddy hurt him, and while

I hurt him he calls me Daddy. I admit, it can be confusing. After Reed calmed down a little, I made him give me a blow job because he'd already told me that sucking cock wasn't his favorite thing, and then we went to sleep. What can I say? Life is brutal.

In the morning it takes a while to tie Reed down because he keeps trying to move his hands and arms around in ways he thinks will be helpful, and by the time I'm done I'm not really into fucking him all that much anymore. Still, Reed's butt does have one intriguing feature: When I pull my fingers out, his asshole stays relaxed enough so that all I have to do is position my dick above it and more or less fall straight down. The sudden weight of my body knocks the wind out of him, and I imagine it hurts his ass a little, but the maneuver is renewing my interest in the idea. I pull my dick all the way out several times and try falling from different heights. I do a kind of push-up, with my hands on his shoulder blades and knees on the back of his thighs, and the most I manage is to go plunging down into his ass from about a foot above. I'm a little worried about hurting my dick—I read somewhere about someone who ruptured the spongy tissue on one side of his dick and wound up with a permanent right-angle bend about halfway down the shaft—but I'm also liking the sound of air being knocked out of Reed's lungs every time my body lands full force on his back, and I like the panting sounds he makes right afterward, and I like how my dick feels as it moves from the cold air of the room into the soft, hot interior of Reed's ass.

But even with all of that, while I'm fucking him I'm thinking to myself, *Am I having a good time? Am I turned on or not?* By the time I finally come—all that distraction means that it takes a while—we've both worked up quite a sweat. Reed actually sweats a little too easily. It doesn't seem like he's really earned it.

Reed takes a shower while I tidy up—winding the ropes into skeins, putting the greasy towels into the hamper—and by the time he gets out, I've decided to speed things up by skipping my own shower. Later that day, long after Reed has gone home, I bend over to tie my shoe and I realize that my crotch still smells like come and lube and the inside of Reed's ass.

His father committed suicide when Gavin was 16. The kind of men he was attracted to, Gavin said, were freaks, outcasts, like himself. He was attracted to a look, to the edginess of boys with shaved heads and fucked-up lives. He likes hanging out at a bar where he says a lot of communists and anarchists go. He said this, but I used to see him all the time in another bar, a regular old fag bar in the Castro with a lot of chain link and too little light. It was all about an attitude.

Gavin said he hated fags. He had a fantasy of going down Castro Street on a sunny afternoon with a flame thrower and an Uzi. He was 26.

He was pissed off because no one made him feel welcome; he wasn't at home anywhere. Home died with his daddy. The real one. "Everyone I love leaves me." This is what he sobbed, between bouts of puking, the first time he got drunk. That was years ago, in high school, on a bottle of cheap red wine his sister had sent him for Christmas.

He wanted to punish everyone who kept him from belonging. Everyone had rejected him. His father most of all, I guess. He wasn't worth sticking around for.

But the boys Gavin wanted didn't know how to stick around, either. The kind of guys who stick around don't spend their weekends at Club Anarchy or following the latest rave party. "Isn't it kind of hard to find a Daddy in a crowd of scruffy, sexy boys who don't want to belong to anything or anyone?" I asked him.

When Gavin was in high school, he came home one afternoon and found his father waiting for him. He was cheerful and talkative and hadn't been drinking. He kept touching Gavin on the arm and ruffling his hair. It was long past time for Gavin to have a decent tattoo, his father said, so they went out to the garage and Gavin's father drew a skull in blue on Gavin's right shoulder, one hand soft on the back of Gavin's neck, the other guiding the humming, buzzing needle. I imagine his fingers are thin and long, like Gavin's.

Gavin's father got his tattoo rig from an ad in the back of *Soldier of Fortune* magazine. He thought he might make a career out of it someday, giving a few tattoos away to his buddies at first—free advertising—then later charging for it. People did admire his designs, which he kept in a spiral-bound sketchbook that had a palette and a paintbrush on the cardboard cover.

But Gavin's father didn't always like finishing things as much as he liked starting them. After he'd exchanged words with a couple of friends, who wound up driving into town to get the color put into tattoos that Gavin's father had outlined but could never find time to work on again, the tattoo-artist idea soured. But he kept the rig, and every so often he sent away to the company that made the needle, and they'd send back fresh ink in a small box from the UPS.

At the back of the skull on Gavin's shoulder a space has opened, and flames shoot out in red and orange, like a kind of aureole. The eye sockets seem to glow. After all these years, the lines are still clean. It's a sexy tattoo, the kind of drawing that sullen teenage boys make on the covers of their notebooks and on the white sides of their Converse high-tops. It's all about an attitude.

Three days later Gavin's father went back to the garage, put the barrel of his rifle in his mouth, and fired it through the back of his head. What Gavin thinks of this now is that his father wrote his suicide note on Gavin's shoulder.

Gavin didn't like calling me Daddy much, which was OK with me. But he did want to be treated like a little boy. One night I took him out of the closet and ungagged him. I untied the rope that was around his ankles so that he could stretch a little. And I sat him on the bed with his hands still tied, his elbows still trussed together, nearly touching, and fed him supper with my fingers. He sat there chewing, calmly looking over my shoulder with his dick hard and twitching.

Later I paddled him for spilling food on himself and before

he went to sleep he said "Thank you" instead of "Goodnight."

Gavin tells me that what he really wants to do is open up a store where he can sell the leather jackets and cock rings and bondage equipment he makes. The tips of his fingers are permanently stained from working with leather and dyes, and his palms are rough when he covers his hand with lube and wraps it around my cock and moves it up and down. It feels like my cock is being licked with a cat's tongue. He never has to do it long before I'm spurting all over his fist.

But when his shop was famous, Gavin said, then he was going to get his revenge. He'd start selling firearms and switchblade knives and anarchist books on how to make pipe bombs at home. He'd sell pamphlets on IRA sabotage and on Nazi interrogation techniques and how-to manuals on seducing children. When the time was right he'd invite the press to come have a look at what S/M was really all about. "And they'd eat it up with a spoon," he giggles, one of the only times I've seen him smile.

I don't even know how to react to this. The S/M "community," whatever Gavin thinks that is, was the closest thing he had to a place to belong, and he said he hated it. I think that's how it was with him: He couldn't let himself have anything that really mattered. What I knew was that he tortured himself better than anyone else could, and one of the results of that was the constant disappointment he found men to be. They kept insisting on loving him, because Gavin looked as though what he needed most in the world was love, and it kept being the wrong thing to do.

Anyway, the truth was, Gavin was no more likely to pull off his revenge fantasy than his father had been to make anything out of his tattoo business. I think the real problem was that Gavin didn't actually want anything he wanted.

But I thought he was probably right about how some little Geraldo wannabe, all on fire with the idea of an "exposé," might react to Gavin's shop. On a TV movie the other night a woman was murdered in a garden; her dying body fell into the rose bush-es and was later dragged off and hidden in a basement. Early in the movie, before all the facts of her death are revealed, the coroner examines the scratches and small punctures and tells the detective, "Just a wild guess, but maybe she died in some kind of S/M scene."

Scars. Damage. Gavin is a grotesque. You can see it in the way he walks, lopes actually, tilting to one side, his arms too long for his body and swinging in counterrhythm far from his torso. His eyes are perhaps too dark and widely set, almost Asian, they seem to crown the sharp peaks of his cheekbones, where the skin is stretched tight and shiny, like a concentration camp victim.

He never looks me in the eyes, which means I can study his face at leisure. I do this even when he is asleep, because then there is always something about him that I want to know. Unlike the cliché, he doesn't look peaceful in sleep. In fact, his face is hard even then, the jaw set and angry. He twitches in the bed and can never stay in one position for long. It makes it hard to chain him to the bottom of the bed at night. He gets the chain kinked and usually wakes me up complaining that his leg has gone to sleep and could I please reset the chain.

He is always cranky when he wakes up like this in the middle of the night. He doesn't ask politely, and I am tempted to slap him a little for the demanding tone of his voice, which implies that I must have chained him up wrong in the first place. But I don't, because what I think mostly as I watch him sleep is how little peace he's had in his life, the way everything is a struggle, and the way the chain around his ankle embodies that struggle and the way he is angry at both of them: his life and the chain.

This boy is a lot of trouble. Friends told me he would be. He is angry with me nearly all of the time.

"Yeah, Daddy," I say as I watch the thin red welts come up across the backs of his thighs. "Yeah, Daddy." And I lift the crop in an arc, high above my shoulders, far beyond my field of vision.

I'm not sure exactly when things started to get out of control.

Was it after I had my fist up to the second knuckles in his ass and noticed the blood for the first time? Was it after he begged for my piss, and I let him suck it out of me, like an orgasm that lasted for minutes, holding my cock a few inches from his lips so that I could hear the sound my piss made, falling into his mouth, like pissing into a small hole in the ground. Or, later, after I straddled his chest, pinning his arms down with my knees and jerking off slowly over his face until I felt the come starting up my dick, and I dropped the head into his mouth, feeling—more than hearing—the first wad hitting the back of his throat.

But now he's sitting between my legs and I'm holding him, his back warm against my chest. My left hand plays up and down his flat, smooth stomach, the soft, boyish roundness of his pectorals, the skin silky and hairless, the muscles barely suggested beneath. I circle his neck with my right arm, his chin resting in the cleft of my elbow. He's got both of his own hands all over his dick and balls; his fingers and his cock and the insides of his thighs are slick with lube and shining in the candlelight. Out of his mouth is coming a steady stream of filth, the kind of talk he's so good at. I love watching him get himself off with sex stories; this time he's talking about having my fist up his ass, punch-fucking him. Sometimes he makes up stories about things he would never do, although this is not one of them.

He's starting to growl, his hands mauling his fat, pale cock. It stands up so straight and white, it reminds me of a grave marker, a missile on a launching pad. I'm tightening my arm around his throat, and that's making his voice hoarse too. He wants to come so bad, it's almost as if he's slamming an orgasm out of his cock.

"Oh, man, I wish I could have that big hairy arm going up my ass," he groans. "Uh huh, I do. You know I loved riding your arm. It hurt like a motherfucker, but I did it for you. And I knew you wanted to hurt me. You wanted to punch a hole in my guts, didn't you, Daddy?"

I lower my lips to his shoulder, brushing them softly against his skin and letting my tongue slide over the blue skull. "Yes, baby," I say, "I wanted to splatter your blood all over the fucking walls."

He's whipping his dick now with one hand, while he puts the other on my arm, trying to get me to ease up on his throat. I make my arm tighter and he chokes. "You tell me when, baby."

"Soon," he gasps. "Just a little while."

I can see the head of his dick swell, and I feel the muscles of his belly tense under my hand; his legs, against mine, are stiffening and relaxing in spasms as he pulls on his cock; his long, thin feet flex and contract.

The sounds coming out of his mouth now aren't words exactly: a moan, a chant, a stifled roar. "Now now now," he says, and I jerk my arm closed on his throat, squeezing the sides of his neck between my forearm and bicep. The first wad of come leaps out of his dick; his left hand flies up and tries to pull my arm away, but nothing could move it now. His face is red, alarming, and the veins in the side of his neck, in his temples, stand out; I think I can almost see them pulsing. Come is still shooting out of his dick and, with a shout, I lock his head in my arms and pull him against me with all my strength.

Now he's dragging at my arm with both hands, his body twisting and writhing. He's trying to say "Please." But it's too late to turn back now. This is what we said we wanted. "I'm holding you tight in my arms, baby. I've got you. Daddy's going to take you home."

Russian Roulette
by Wickie Stamps

Wickie Stamps, a former editor of Drummer, *writes smart, brutal stories tinged with a bleak sort of violence. The burned-out men in "Russian Roulette" run into each other somewhere near the intersection of Threat and Desire. Maybe you've been there too...*

I put down the piece of paper, remove my wire-rimmed glasses, place them on my desk, and rub the bridge of my nose. I've been writing for hours, getting nowhere. I glance out the open door beside my desk; my apartment adjoins a common space, a courtyard shared by several apartments that's actually just the tar paper–covered roof of the stores and flophouse below. The hour is 4 A.M. My favorite hour. I like the silence of this hour, the solitude, broken only by the screams and shattering of glass from the streets below.

I glance at my story, force myself not to tear it up yet again. My editor is waiting for it, like a vulture. The boxer Sonny Liston is the topic this time. Last month it was George Foreman. Last month went better. I wasn't belting back shots of bourbon. Or ending up sleeping in doorways, carrying on deep philosophical conversations with other drunks and dopers, all of us sitting in our respective doorways, thinking we're cool, smart outlaws instead of the drunkards we are, colluding in each other's self-delusions. I stare at my story, trying to see the words through my hangover. My stories. Endless adulation for real men, like Sonny and George, men like me who are always looking for an opponent.

I peer into the pitch-black courtyard, enjoying the cool San Francisco air trailing into my stuffy, cramped space. I assume that, at this late hour, the courtyard is unoccupied.

I am wrong. I hear the click of a lighter. In the moonlight I make out the shape of a man, leaning against the apartment building, his left boot resting against the wall behind him, propping him. Momentarily, the blue flame of his lighter highlights his face and I catch sight of the hard set of his jaw. He draws deeply on his cigarette, glances up, and looks me dead in the eye. I reach back through the past week's alcoholic haze and dredge up memories of this man that I'd passed in the hallway of my building. Night after night I'd stumble down the narrow smoke-stained hallway toward my apartment and he'd be there, on his way either into or out of his apartment—or room, as my building is really one step above a flophouse. Wearing short-sleeved workshirts, khakis, smoking a cigarette and usually turning the key to his apartment door, he'd look at me out of the corner of his eye, smoke curling across his face. Despite my alcoholic stupor, I'd never miss this opportunity to stare at his muscular forearms, covered in small, hand-inked tattoos; "prison" was written all over this guy. As I passed, often using the walls to prop myself up, he'd give me an angry look, sometimes even shaking his head in disgust. Me? I'd slither by, smile a shit-faced grin, and stare at his hairy, muscular arms and hard thighs, continuing my stumble into my charming hovel, my need to vomit overriding the desire to hit on my ex-con neighbor.

My neighbor snaps shut his lighter; the sound yanks me out of my reveries, back into the moment. In one smooth move he slips the lighter into his jacket pocket, takes another heavy drag off his cigarette, and, shoving himself away from the wall, walks loose-hipped across the deserted courtyard toward me. As always, he's wearing his faded khakis and work boots. He strolls slowly, deliberately, clearly someone who is seldom in a hurry or...easily intimidated.

Arriving at my open door, he takes a deep drag off his cigarette, leans up against the doorjamb, and glances around.

Empty Chinese take-out containers and bourbon bottles litter my abode. Smoke from his cigarette curls over his vein-covered hand, drifts toward his head. A look of disgust crosses his face.

"What a pigsty," he says looking around my trashed space; he adjusts his crotch, steps into my place, uninvited, drops his butt onto the thin, cigarette-scarred carpet, and grinds it out with the heel of his boot.

I am unnerved by this man's assumption that he can just walk into my home but am equally enticed by a man who has such disregard for his surroundings that he doesn't even think twice about dropping his butts where he chooses. Out of the corner of my eye, I stare at his boots. They are heavily scuffed, cracked, and speckled with mud.

"Like them?" he asks, staring down at his boots before looking me in the eye. He pulls another cigarette from his pack, bangs it on the back of his hand, and slips it into the corner of his mouth. There is an angry quiver in the right corner of his lip. He pulls out his lighter, lights the cigarette, and blows a few smoke rings.

I shift in my chair. "They'll do," I say.

"Prefer them with ashes?" he queries, dropping ash directly onto the worn, cracked leather.

I study his boots again, then look up at his face. Half-shaven, square-jawed. His dark eyes glisten in the moonlight. A patch of hair sticks out of the top of his blue Texaco shirt that has the name TOM stitched over the right chest pocket. For a few moments neither of us moves.

Suddenly, he reaches behind himself with his right hand and calmly pulls out a gun; in one quick move he grabs me by my shirt collar, balls it up into his fist, pulls me out of my chair, onto my knees, and out of my apartment into the dark corner right outside my door. My knees bang against the doorjamb, tearing my pants, scraping the flesh. He puts his right boot against my back, shoves my face onto the tar-and-gravel–covered rooftop. He pushes the gun against my temple. I look up through the cloud of smoke swirling around his face. All the air is forced out of my lungs; I can feel the warmth of my own piss spreading across my pant legs. I am incapable of making a sound. He looks down at me, a snarl curling across his lips.

My companion heaves me onto my feet and slams me against the brick wall so hard I hit my head. A warm trickle of blood drizzles down my forehead. I slowly slide to the ground. During my descent I put my hand to my forehead, pull it back, and stare at my blood smeared across my hand. I glance over at this man who in one smooth move spreads his legs wide, braces himself, and again points his gun to my head.

Click. In the dead silence of the night, that tiny sound shatters the silence, echoing off the walls. He's cocked the trigger! I cannot believe this is happening to me. My companion steps forward and kicks me deeper into the dark, cool corner of the building. I scurry back against the wall, covering my head with my hands. Using his boots, he kicks my hands away from my head, steps on one hand, and pins the other behind me. He pushes the gun hard against my temple.

Spin. The sound is endless as the barrel spins, boring into my head. I smash my face against this stranger's hard thighs, wrapping my arms around his legs. I think I whimper.

"Don't..." I sputter.

Click. He pulls the trigger. I do whimper. And cringe. And begin weeping.

Spin. He spins the barrel again. I try to pull away, my whimpering getting louder.

"You disgust me," he hisses, and spins the barrel again. I look up and see the hard muscles of his forearm holding the gun. He still has the cigarette in his mouth. I can see his dark eyes through the haze of smoke.

Click. He pulls the trigger again. I am openly weeping now, hugging my executioner, pressing myself against his rock-hard thighs.

Spin. "Oh, God, please…" I am sobbing so hard that snot is running down my face.

Pause. There is dead silence. *Pause.* He shifts his weight and momentarily loosens his grip on my shirt. I press myself closer to his body, my face pressing into his crotch, pressing against his cock. Perhaps…

Suddenly he yanks me to my feet, slams me up against the wall, pries open my mouth, and shoves the gun barrel down my throat. I retch, my throat closing around the metal. I taste gun-barrel oil dripping down my throat.

Spin. Time is endless. I can see his right forefinger pressing against the trigger.

Click. I stare at the face of my executioner. Hatred and pain twist each facial muscle. For a moment he looks directly into my eyes, then pulls the gun from my mouth, spins me around, and again slams me up against the wall, this time kicking my legs apart. I spread my hands across the wall, bracing myself.

Spin. Click. Spin. Spin. There are no pauses. There is no sound. Nothing exists except this man and myself. And his rage.

Spin. Click. Click. Click. I no longer have any hope; I am just waiting for my execution.

Blam! I hear the pigeons fluttering madly above us, fright-ened out of their sleep, fleeing their own terror. The smell of gunpowder fills my nostrils. I am aware that there is no differ-ence between this moment and the times when I kneel alone in empty churches. Defeated. Drunk again. And again. And again.

Suddenly I realize this maniac didn't shoot me; I am not dead. Although I do think I ejaculated.

My companion stands over me. I have collapsed onto my knees, am crumpled there, stunned. Slowly I raise my hand to my head. I think I have a slight head wound. I look up and see my neighbor, gun hanging from his right hand, his left bracing himself against the wall. He looks drained. And shaken. I, unquestionably shaken, rise slowly, using the wall to brace myself. I continue to stare at my own blood. I look at my would-be assassin. He's still facing the wall, gun in one hand, his other hand bracing himself away from the wall. I pull a handkerchief from my back pocket and dab my head, examine my blood. I determine I am not bleeding to death.

"Your drinking disgusts me," my companion mutters. He turns around and leans against the wall beside me.

"Well, that makes two of us," I reply. I dab my head again and look at this handsome maniac. He is totally out of his mind. "But I don't think I'm worth killing over it."

"I hadn't planned on killing you," he says. "Just scaring you."

I look at him incredulously. And chuckle nervously. "Well, you did that, darling. What were you trying to do, scare me sober?"

He crosses his hands in front of him, pouting. God, does he have hot forearms. His gun is now hanging over his left forearm.

"I hate it when you get drunk, that's all," he mutters and shuffles his feet. You'd think this guy had just fired a slingshot at a bluebird or something.

"Apparently."

"And I thought I'd teach you a lesson."

I chuckle again. I can't believe this guy is serious. But, I have to admit, after this I might think twice about drinking, or, at least, if I went out on a toot again, I'd make sure to use the back entrance and bypass this crazy bastard's place.

I looked up from my preoccupation with my own blood and noticed that my laughing is upsetting him. It dawns on me that he is serious.

"So you were concerned for me?" I look over at my companion, who by now is in a full-blown pout, chin down, his arms hugging his chest. He kicks the tarred roof with those lovely boots.

I chuckle again and put my hand out toward him, palm up. He stares at it, looking confused.

"The gun, you damned fool. Give me the gun." He pulls away and gives me a suspicious look. "Baby, give me that damned gun.

I promise you I won't take a drink for at least a few hours, OK?" He looks all hopeful. It's a look that melts my heart. My God, this crazy bastard has a crush on me, I think. Great, just what I needed: a 290-pound, muscle-bound, armed ex-con who hates drunks. "Give me that gun," I say firmly. He sighs, shuffles his feet and shoves the thing toward me, banging it against my chest. I take it gingerly, holding it between two fingers. I examine it, holding it away from my body. It's a heavy son of a bitch.

"It's the newest Colt .45 ACP," he says, looking sheepishly at the weapon.

"Oh, really," I say, my eyebrows raised. I can't believe this guy.

"Yeah, it's got a stainless steel slide and barrel on an aluminum barrel." His voice is excited, like a kid's. "I wanted the new FBI issue, a 1911-A1 .45 but..." he sighs, shuffles his feet and shoves his hands in his pockets.

"But what, baby?" I say, laying the thing in the palm of my hand and slowly flipping it from one hand to another.

"...but it's tough getting Springfield guns." His voice trails off and he gets real quiet. "It costs a lot of money and...stuff."

I glance over at my companion. His shirt is untucked on one side and one of his boots is unlaced. And, God, those forearms.

"Well, baby, maybe I'll get it for you for Christmas?" I look over; this guy eyes are all lit up. He thinks I'm serious. "But only if you are good, sugar," I add, and continue examining the weapon.

Slowly, I push myself away from the wall, take a few steps forward, turn, and point the gun at my handsome maniac. His eyebrows shoot up.

"Drop your pants," I mutter, slightly annoyed at my headache and the mess of my own fluids all over my favorite pants and shirt. My cute killer hesitates. I cock the gun, amazed that I figured out how to do this. I say a secret "Thank you" for all the cop shows I've watched.

"I wouldn't try anything, if I were you," I warn. I've picked up some dialog from the shows. "Turn around, face the wall, and drop your pants." I am totally impressed with the authority in my voice. Perhaps it's the gun. He stares me dead in the eyes. I know that if I don't push this guy, there is no way he's going to know how to give it up. "I said, 'Turn around, face the wall, and drop your goddamn pants.'" I feel the heat of my desire spread across my chest and crotch. He hesitates. I step forward, gun braced in both hands. He turns, faces the wall. "Put your hands on the wall," I say, searching my head for the words cops use in situations like this. He puts his hands against the wall. I step forward again, scared shitless, gun wobbling in my arms, the weight taking its toll. I take my left foot and kick his legs farther apart, press the gun against his back with my left hand, and reach around with my right and slide it down over his hard belly to his zipper. I can feel his cock, hard, pressing against the zipper. My body is pressed against his. I undo the button and slowly unzip his khakis. I feel his dick through his briefs. It's large, hot, and very hard. I press my hand against his shaft, then wiggle my fingers into his shorts, wrapping my fingers around his stiff rod. I lose my composure. Breathing heavily, I rest the gun against his back, lean my full weight against him. I squeeze his cock, rubbing my finger over the head, wet with precome.

"Turn around," I whisper, pulling back my weight. He turns, his shirt now untucked, belly hairs showing above his shorts. He and I both look down at the dick that I've pulled out of his shorts. His pants are down over his ass. I look him in the eyes, which is difficult, as his are averted.

"It's OK, baby," I whisper, my hand wrapped around his cock. "Why don't you hold your gun?" I say and hand my sweet criminal his toy. He takes it like a kid grabbing his favorite binky, dangling it at his side. He shifts his weight, spreading his legs, giving me more access to his crotch.

I drop to my knees, resting my face against his crotch. After a quick lick of his precome, I slide his cock deep into my throat, suppressing a gag. I position myself directly in front of my companion and start sucking on the sweetest cock I've had in a long, long time. My companion lays his hand holding the gun behind my head, bracing me. With his other hand he grabs my shirt collar. Despite a sore jaw and periodic gagging, I don't stop sucking until I hear a deep moan above me and feel my sweet killer's hot come pumping deep into my throat.

I pull myself off his dick, swallow his load, and rest my face against his leg. We stay in this position for several minutes. The deserted courtyard is getting lighter. I look up at my companion, sit back on my haunches, and wipe the come from my lips. He's leaning back against the wall, head turned up, body limp, his cherished gun dangling from his hand. I start chuckling. This has to be the strangest sexual experience I've ever had. I guess he hears me chuckling and looks down.

"What?" he says, pushing himself away from the wall, half-raising his gun.

"It's OK, baby," I say soothingly. "I'm not laughing at you. You are totally hot. I'm laughing at us and this situation." His shoulders drop and he lowers his gun. God, is he sweet. "But the next time you're upset with my drinking, you might want to try just talking to me about it." I look at this hot bastard. I sigh. "Or maybe not," I add.

He helps me get off my knees. I start walking toward my apartment, look back at him leaning against that wall. I wave for him to follow. I figure we could both use some breakfast.

"There was only one bullet," he says quietly as I slide some bacon and eggs under his nose.

"What?" I say, turning around, a pot of hot coffee in my hand.

"After I shot you, or pretended to, there were no more bullets in the gun," he says sheepishly and looks down at his eggs.

I laugh, walk over, kiss my crazy bastard on the top of his head, and pour him a cup of coffee. Then I remember...my deadline, and that vulture editor who's waiting for my story about Sonny...

Smoke

By B.J. Barrios

Unlike author B.J. Barrios, we're not into "serious stogie smok-ing." But this sweaty story of a nicotine-stained seduction turned us on big time. And, like the narrator, we thrive on the unexpected. Reason enough to include it in the book.

"You're mine now, boy," he whispered in my ear, as I heard the ratchet of the cuffs closing around my wrists. And I knew he was right.

At first the evening didn't seem very promising. After living in New York only three years, I'd begun to think I had exhaust-ed the supply of Tops that could handle a pig like me. I wasn't cocky, per se, it's just that I liked to play, and I liked to play hard, and there are only so many players in any given pool of people. I always made it clear to men that I was into full leather, heavy bondage, intense breath control, serious stogie smoking, tight gloves, tall boots, mean tit play, humiliating verbal abuse, complete uniforms, and layers of rubber. Not a lot of people in this town could run through that list with me, and those who could were mostly unavailable this particular Saturday night.

But hope springs eternal. So I got into my leathers and head-ed out to the Lure. I decided to wear my padded leather motor-cycle jacket, my padded leather touring pants, motorcycle boots, and tight black Damascus gloves. I didn't wear a shirt, despite the snowy weather. It would be (I hoped) hot enough in the bar, and I liked to show off the "treasure trail" of hair that went straight down my chest. At 25, 5 foot 6, and 150 pounds, I wouldn't have sounded like much—but in all that leather, smoking a maduro Magnum, and with my big, bushy stache and close-cropped beard—well, I looked at home in one of the nation's biggest and best leather bars, like I belonged there.

As I paid the cover and headed inside, I stopped short—I could have sworn I scented a Jeroboam in the air. But I couldn't see anyone smoking one of those mammoth cigars anywhere around me. I figured I must be smelling my own Magnum, though my cock knew better and was already at half-mast thinking about any man with balls enough to smoke a stogie like that.

I got a beer and wandered through the rooms. I was certain that there indeed had been a jerry in that bar recently, but I was damned if I could find the man smoking it. I nodded to some people I knew, stopped and said hello to others, but the rest of the crowd was enough to turn my cock soft again. I was disappointed; I could tell just by looking that there was no one there Top enough for me tonight. Oh, sure, there were plenty of men—some who looked ill-at-ease in their leathers, some who looked like gym bunnies in leather costume, some who looked really hot but lacked that subtle sexual power real Masters have that gets my nuts going.

I finally just propped myself by the door leading to the dark, cruisy corridor—my favorite spot in the bar. I finished my beer and my Magnum and decided not to light up another. I thought I would be headed home once again to read over my dog-eared copy of *Powerplay #6*.

I don't even know where he came from. I was sure he wasn't in the bar before, unless I just kept missing him. But all of a sudden, I *knew* I smelled a jerry near, very near. I was ready to turn around and look behind me when I felt his gloved hand grasping me firmly at the neck, keeping my gaze straight ahead. I felt the warmth from his stogie as it slid up beside my cheek, and I sucked in greedily at the smoke beginning to drift around my face. I had no idea what this man looked like, or who he was, but just the way he commanded me with his hand on my neck convinced me that I was ready to serve *him*, like the leather stogie pig that I am.

"You're mine now, boy." That's all he said; that's all he had to say, punctuating his claim of ownership by cuffing my hands behind my back. Before I knew it he was bringing me around with his hand and walking me toward the door. He was careful to keep control of me with just his gloved hand. I didn't even have a chance to see the man. He just saw what he wanted and he took it. I like that. A lot.

We were quickly in the chill night air. He stopped me and just stood there. I couldn't see what he was doing and was beginning to get nervous, my head finally overtaking my now-throbbing cock. And then his other hand, cupped, came around in front of me. He rubbed the still-warm-but-not-hot ash into my chest with his gloved hand while pulling me against his body. His stogie was all that I could see of him, glowing red where the ash had just been broken off. The sweet smoke swirled around my face but, in the breezy air, mostly avoided my efforts to suck it in. I reached back, felt around. All I could make out was the leather of his pants and a large basket. I was guessing that the pants were breeches, because I could feel a Sam Browne belt pressing into my back.

That's all I could find out because in another moment he was pushing me into a cab. I breathed in the cold night air to steady myself. I knew, if nothing else, I was in for a real adventure. I had just been taken by a complete stranger out of a bar and was headed God-only-knows-where.

I was scared. And I was rock-hard and dripping. Oink, oink.

Reality hit when I got into the cab. My head finally convinced my dick that what I was doing was stupid and dangerous. I was almost panicky, trying to think of a way out, or even just a way to get this guy's name.

But as he got into the cab, my cock took over again. He wasn't wearing just breeches or a Sam Browne—he had a whole fucking leather police uniform! His Dehners stretched up his calves to his knees, and I was ready to lick them clean. Then I would work my way up his leather breeches, black and tight with a yellow stripe down the sides. His belt held what he needed for the evening: his keys (oddly on the right. Was he a cop in real life? That's where a lot of cops wore their keys) and a handcuff case, now empty. I could see a leather shirt under his heavy leather motorcycle police jacket, and I glimpsed what might have been an AUA badge on his shirt. The gloves must have been Damascus—I could have guessed that from their tight, butter-smooth feel against my neck. Capping it off, he wore mirrored sunglasses despite the darkness. I could see my reflection in them. Mostly, I could see my desire for this Master reflected in them.

He was more than just a collection of leather too. I could tell he'd be just as hot completely naked (and I was hoping to have the chance to prove it). He looked older, mid 30s, maybe even into his 40s. His hair was short but not quite a buzz cut like mine. The flecks of silver in his dark hair and trim stache gave him even more of an air of authority. He wasn't a gym body, but I could tell he kept in shape. But more than anything he had a sexiness I couldn't pin down—there wasn't one particular feature about him that turned me on—it was him, *all* of him.

In the seconds after I took my first look at this mystery man, my head made another bid for control over my cock. I was starting to get scared again, but as soon as he gave the address to the cabbie, I relaxed. It was Mike's place. Mike was the hottest Stogie Master I knew, one who could handle me *any* time. But he was out of town for two days. I vaguely remembered him telling me that he had a friend that would be staying at his place. Things clicked. This was the friend, and any friend of Mike's was sure to be OK.

Mike lived in SoHo, so the ride was relatively short. The guy uncuffed me once we got out of the cab, though I could have told him Mike's doorman had seen worse. We went in and up to the apartment. Knowing that this guy wasn't a *complete* mystery pretty much knocked my head out of the running—my hard, dripping cock was doing all my thinking now.

He opened the door and pushed me ahead of him, into the apartment. He quickly followed, closing the door behind us. It was hard to see in the dark apartment, though I could tell where he was by the glow of his diminishing jerry. I heard him take off his sunglasses.

The next thing I knew, I was eating wall. He had my face pressed up against the plaster and held my body there by throwing his knee into my butt.

"Don't move fucker, understand?"

"Yes, Sir," I managed to say.

He turned on a few lights. I felt his hand on my neck again. His stache brushed against my ear.

"OK, faggot, you do what I say when I say it and you just might leave here in the morning with only a few bruises. Mike's bragged about you a few times and told me I should get together with you if I had the chance. Even showed me some pics he took of you, ass-hole. You better fucking live up to what he said about you, faggot, 'cause I don't have time for anything less than the best."

He backed away. I could see from the corner of my eye that he was headed over to Mike's comfortable leather armchair.

"Turn around." I did, slowly. He'd taken off his jacket. The uniform shirt looked great on him; it stretched taut against his massive chest, a tuft of chest hair poking out. The shirt was short-sleeved, emphasizing his large biceps and the short black gloves on his hands. I looked into his eyes—dark brown, with just a twinge of evil in them. "Well, fucker. I've been told you're a pretty good pig. Let's see what you're made of." He punctu-ated his statement by dropping an ash onto his Dehners. All he had to do was glance down at the boot. I recognized the com-mand. I almost leaped across the room and got on my hands and knees. I started licking and kissing the toe of the boot; I gave the ash a chance to cool, and then I went right for it.

It collapsed into a fine, hot dust in my mouth—a little salty, and I thought I could almost taste the Dehners in the ash as well. I kept worshiping his boot, both because he was so fucking hot and because it was helping me to get the ash down. I felt his other boot come down on my back, forcing me onto my stomach. I continued to make love to his Dehners, working my tongue between the laces, then all over the boot from toe to heel. When he let the boot off my back, I knew what I was supposed to do next; I started in on the other boot, and felt the Dehner I'd just spit-shined come down on my back.

Eventually he lifted his foot off me, and I knew he was through with me working his boots. I raised myself up and sat back on my knees, looking up at him, ready to receive his next command. He glanced down and inspected his spit-shined Dehners. I was hoping he had felt my tongue pressing hard into the leather. He gave a half smile. "Not too bad, faggot, not too bad at all."

He stood in front of me, his crotch brushing lightly against my stache. I could make out the shape of his hard cock through the leather. He reached behind my head and pushed my face into the leather. I was able to trace the outline of his dick with my tongue. I sucked and licked and slurped at his leather hard-on, chewing the breeches lightly and sucking hard. He stopped holding my head against the leather and pulled me to my feet. He must have been four or five inches taller than I am and damn did it feel nice to be looking up into his face, that stogie still smoldering in his jaw.

He took a long draw on his jerry and then reached up and removed the stogie from his mouth. I knew what was coming. I exhaled and prepared to eat this hot man's smoke. His gloved hand drew me into his face as he raped my mouth with his tongue and blew his smoke right into my lungs. I almost choked but fought off the urge. I held his smoke deep in my lungs while we made out. When he finished kissing me I arched my head back slightly and blew a stream of smoke up into the air where he could see.

"Nice, fucker. I like the way you take my smoke."

"Thank you, Sir."

He took another draw as we moved over closer to the wall. His gloved hand was suddenly at my throat, pushing me up against the wall, his knee in my hard, aching, wet, and slimy crotch. He exhaled his smoke into me again. But this time, instead of kissing me, he clamped his other hand tight around my nose and mouth, keeping the smoke inside me. With one hand at my throat and another over my mouth, I was ready to fucking explode. It wasn't long before I started struggling to breathe, to exhale the smoke that was beginning to burn my lungs. I looked up in his face, and he seemed to sense my limit. I thankfully blew the smoke out and gasped for air.

"I like to see fear, fucker. Like to see you struggle and fight. Like to make you feel my power over you. And I can tell just where your limit is by the look in your eyes. And the closer we get to it, the further we inch over it, the harder my cock gets."

"Yes, Sir!" Mine, for one, couldn't get any harder.

One hand still at my throat, his other holding his stogie, he moved in close to my face once again. After depositing a load of his stogie spit in my mouth—"Thank you, Sir"—he put his mouth to my ear, his stogie breath hot against my face.

"We haven't even started yet, fucker," he whispered as he slid the slimy end of his cigar around my tits. They, in response, became electric, broadcasting strong signals of pleasure to my entire body. "It's early, and I've got all fucking night and all of tomorrow too, faggot. I'm gonna work you until you collapse from exhaustion, and then I'm gonna use you as my boot rest."

"Yes, Sir. Thank you, Sir," I moaned. "I wanna be your fucking stogie pig so bad, Sir."

"You will, faggot, you will."

He quickly turned me around and pulled me into his leather-covered chest. He reached for my tits with his gloved hands, and I just went fucking wild. He knew *just* how to work them—

not hard, but easy, slow, soft. It was driving me crazy. The pleasure was getting to be so intense that I was having trouble staying on my feet. All the while he kept puffing on his slowly diminishing jerry; I was sucking in all the smoke I could, moaning from the tit play.

"That's enough fun for you, fucker. Good night." I wasn't sure what he was doing, but before I knew it, he had his right arm around my neck, his elbow just below my chin. I felt his big arm squeezing my neck. I tried to swallow and felt or heard or saw this buzzing...

The next thing I knew I was staring at his big fucking boots. It dawned on me that he had just applied a police sleeper hold. I'd heard Mike talk about the hold before. It felt weird but incredible. And—almost impossibly—it got my hard dick even harder. I eagerly lapped at his boots to show my appreciation.

"So the faggot likes feeling that cop power, huh?"

"Yes, Sir. That was incredible."

"That's right, fucker. Puts you right where you belong—at my feet."

"Yes, Sir!"

Clearly, everything about the sleeper hold was fast: It put me out fast; I must not have been out for long, at most 30 seconds, and I recovered fast as well. He reached down and grabbed my chin, pulling me once again to my feet. He started to feed me his glove. First finger. I could taste the smoke in the leather. *I bet he's smoked hundreds of cigars with this same pair of gloves.* Then a second finger. I was hungry for his gloves, for the smoke-filled leather. A third finger. And a fourth. He was damn near fist-fucking my face with his gloves. Then he took that hand out and started to replace it with his other. His wet and slimy glove began playing with my nipples again. I moaned, almost in a trance, while feasting on his second stogie glove.

He pulled his hand from my mouth and quickly clamped it

over my nose and mouth, forcefully sealing off my breathing. I looked into his eyes, and as I started trying to breathe harder and harder I could see how pleased he was with my struggles. When I started to panic he finally let go, a smile on his lips.

"Yeah, fucker. I fucking control your every fucking breath, faggot."

"Yes, Sir."

Again, he clamped his hand over my nose and mouth. Again, it was not until I was ready to panic that he let me breathe again. I was really getting off on the feel of his glove against my face. One gloved hand controlled my breathing while the other roamed over my body. Sometimes it would be at my neck; other times it would be tracing the trail of hair down my chest to where it disappeared into my leather pants. Then he'd grab my head, shoving my face harder into the one clamped tightly over my nose and mouth. All the while, fighting to breathe, I watched the pleasure in his eyes, filtered through the smoke curling up around him.

By this time he had a good inch or so of ash at the end of his stogie. He paused while I caught my breath. "Hold out your hand, faggot." I eagerly complied. "It's going to be a little hot, but don't you fucking drop it. Jiggle it around to cool it if you have to, but if you fucking drop this ash, I'll make sure your sorry ass regrets it." He carefully broke the ash off in my palm. I lightly jiggled it as it cooled. He went to the kitchen and returned with a cold beer. After about a minute he simply said "Now." I popped the ash into my mouth and started working on getting it down. "Open that fucking hole of yours, asshole." I opened my ashy mouth wide. He took a big gulp of his beer and spit it down into my mouth. A little dribbled down my chin, down onto my chest. As I struggled to swallow the rest, he rubbed the runoff into my chest and tits with his hand, then made me lick his glove clean.

"Thank you, Sir."

"Good boy."

"Yes, Sir. Thank you, Sir."

He finally finished his jerry. As he continued to enjoy his beer, he sat in the armchair and pulled his hard cock out of his breeches. Reaching into his shirt pocket, he took out a condom and rolled it onto his cock. Again, a look was all the command I needed; I fell onto his dick. I worked slowly and carefully at first. Exploring his whole cock with my tongue. Sucking, first greedily but gently, almost teasingly, on the head, then slowly but surely engulfing the entire shaft. His dick was not huge, and I liked it that way. It was just the right size for my mouth, and I went far, far down on it, until I could feel it pressing hard into my throat. I breathed in the musky scent of his crotch.

I continued to suck his cock while he finished his beer. Then he got up and said, "I think we're ready for the main event, pig." I just sat back on my knees and waited as he went into Mike's bedroom. I remember thinking that whatever he had in mind was fine by me. So I kneeled there, waiting and wanting.

I heard him rustling through what must have been his toy bag. He came out of Mike's bedroom, deposited a large pile of rope on the floor next to me, then went back into the room. After a little more rustling he returned with what looked like a large plastic drop cloth. As I looked on curiously, he unfolded the plastic—it was a huge plastic bag! The plastic was thick too, not thin like Saran Wrap or a cleaner's bag. I had no idea where he got it, but it was easily seven feet long and a foot and a half wide. He went into the bedroom one last time and returned with a gas mask—I recognized it was Mike's. It was Russian, not Israeli, rubber, fitting over the entire head without straps, and with a long hose just big enough to be plugged by a cigar. I had spent quite a few happy evenings in that gas mask, choking on smoke. I relaxed a little. I knew I could handle the gas mask...but I wasn't sure what he had in mind for the bag.

"OK, faggot, stand up and strip."

I got up and took off my gloves. As I started to take off my jacket, he stopped me. He gave me an evil little smile as he reached into the inside pocket of my jacket and took out one of my maduro Magnums. Then he let go and I got back to work. As I took off my pants, thin strings of precome stretched from my hard cock. I worked as quickly as possible, folding my clothes neatly and piling them next to the chair.

"Not bad, fucker. Mike was right when he said you had a nice little body."

"Thank you, Sir."

"Now turn around." I turned so that my back was facing him. I felt his arm reach around my neck and once again, in seconds, I was on the floor. As I slowly came to I realized that, in the few moments I was out and recovering, he'd tied my hands in front of me. He reached down and pulled me to my feet. Then he opened the plastic bag and scrunched it down. "OK, faggot, step into the bag." He must have seen the reaction on my face. "That's right, fucker. You're going to be bound, help-less, and sealed inside that plastic bag. We'll see how long it takes before you run out of air." I was a little scared but *very* excited as I stepped into the bag.

He worked quickly. He tightly tied my legs together, ropes at my ankles, just above my knees, and around my thighs. Then he wrapped rope across my chest, just above and below my vul-nerable nipples, and bound my arms to my sides, my hands loosely bound in front.

Before sealing me into my airless prison, he unwrapped the Magnum and removed the band. "Open your hole, faggot." I opened my mouth; he shoved the large cigar deep into my mouth and throat as I licked the entire length of it. He drew the stogie out slowly, leaving the end close to my mouth. "Nice. Now get it ready for me, faggot," he said. I bit a small, jagged hole in the end. He held up his gloved hand, and I spit the bit of tobacco into it. He thanked me by smearing it into my face.

He soon had the stogie lit and smoking. I strained forward,

wanting more of his smoke.

"So the piggy faggot wants my smoke, huh?"

"Yes, Sir."

"I'm gonna make you fucking regret you said that, asshole."
He stooped down and pulled the bag up around me. Before I
knew it, I was completely enclosed. He tied off the top with
rope. Then he hauled me up across his shoulders, fireman-style.
He carried my plastic-bound body across the room and threw
me onto Mike's leather sofa.

It was hot in the bag. I wasn't running out of air just yet. But
I wasn't sure how long it would take before I was gasping for
breath. I could see him beyond the plastic, could see the glow
of his Magnum, could almost see the smoke swirling up
through his stache. He reached down and started untying the
top of the bag; I figured he was through with this part of the
scene. Instead, he only loosened the rope. He picked up the gas
mask, detached the hose, and slipped one end inside the bag,
sealing the bag tight around it.

At first I wasn't sure why he was giving me air. I figured it
out as soon as I saw the first wisps of smoke coming through
the hose. "You're going to take *all* the smoke from this
Magnum, fucker—your whole fucking universe is going to be
my smoke—and it will be the last thing you remember if you
pass out." He punctuated this statement with more smoke.

At first I sucked it in greedily, eager to have this man's
smoke once again in my lungs. But the bag was starting to fill
up fast, and very little oxygen was getting in; he was careful to
clamp his gloved hand over the hose between long draws on his
stogie. It was getting harder to see him through the plastic, the
smoke, and the layer of condensed sweat forming on the plastic. But I knew he was still there because smoke kept pouring
in. As if to make sure I'd remember his presence, I felt him grabbing my chest through the plastic. Two tit clamps found their
targets. Even through heavy plastic, the clamps held fast and

tight and heightened every sensation.

Breathing was hard, and so was I. I could barely see my feet through the smoke. With the air getting stale and smokier, I was forced to breathe harder and deeper. I started choking on the smoke. Every time I did I could sense his pleasure at my increasing discomfort.

And still the smoke came.

It didn't take long before I was ready to pass out. I was choking, panting for air, getting nothing but smoke. I felt really dizzy, from all the smoke, from the lack of air. He must have known I was on the edge because right at that moment, I felt his hand grab my cock. My dick had started to go soft from the strain of the experience, but he worked it, lubed by my sweat and a pool of accumulated precome. Soon he was stroking a hard, wet, slimy cock. I couldn't hold on and I couldn't hold it in. I thought I was passing out as I felt myself come. He was right, the last thing I remembered seeing was even more smoke.

I came to, gasping and choking. I was still bound, still in the bag, but he'd undone the top and rolled the bag down so that its neck was around my throat. He gently slapped me back to full consciousness, his gloved fingers in my mouth. He soon replaced his fingers with his condomed cock. I sucked enthusiastically, wanting to show my gratitude for the most incredible orgasm of my life.

I could tell he was getting close. He pulled his cock from my mouth, ripped off the condom, and finished himself off, coming all over my cheek, using the head of his cock to rub his come into my close-cropped beard.

"Fuck, yeah. Good little fucking pig."

"Thank you, Sir," I panted in reply, still trying to recover from being in the bag.

He removed the tit clamps and helped me out of the bag. As soon as he'd lowered the bag, smoke came drifting out—it had been trapped in there while the bag was around my neck. I was wet and shivering. He went for a towel, cleaned off our come, and then tenderly dried me. And then we were making out again. I loved the feel of his tongue in my mouth, the feel of his leathered hands holding me tight into his leathered chest.

"You need a shower, boy."

"Yes, Sir. I think I do." He got a fresh towel for me as I pissed. The shower felt *so-o-o* good, though the hot, pulsing water reminded me that my tits would be pretty sore in the morning. I got out, dried off, and went back to the living room, where he was straightening up.

"Better, boy?"

"Yes, Sir!"

"Good. Now help me turn the bag inside out so it can air out and dry. And you can drop the 'Sir.' For now, at least. The name's David."

"*Very* nice to meet you, David." I helped him finish up with the bag. "My name's..."

"Yeah, I know your name," he interrupted with a sly grin. "I told you Mike told me about you."

I grinned back. "So how long have you known Mike?" We sat on the sofa and I snuggled up to him, enjoying the cool feel of his leathers against my warm, naked skin.

"I've been training with him for about seven months now," he said as he placed an arm around my shoulder.

"Mmm." My eyes closed in his leather embrace. "The two of you train boys together?"

He laughed and then looked at me as I opened my eyes in response to his laugh. He paused just a moment before speaking. "Nope. I'm Mike's new boy. He's been seeing me down in Philly for a while now, and I'll be moving in here with him soon."

"His *boy*? But..."

"Yeah, I know." He seemed to have a habit of interrupting,

but I'm not sure what else I would have said. I'd been convinced that this man was 100% Master. Then I remembered the keys on his uniform. "Didn't feel like it just then, huh?" he asked while flashing me his wicked smile. I couldn't help but smile back. "I was able to work you like that because I didn't have to get inside your head. I know what's in there because it's what's in mine. Top? Bottom? That shit's just for the mind. But this," he continued, grabbing my cock with one hand while his other hand tweaked my tit, "*this* just *responds*."

"Yes, Sir," I moaned in reply. He was right. "And here I thought only a *real* Top could handle me."

"I'm all real, whether topping or bottoming. It's all about power, boy. Mike has more power than me, I got more than you, and you got a hell of a lot more than most of the little shits out there."

Something about what he was saying was getting me hard, and it wasn't just because he'd kept his hands on my tits and cock. Somehow, I understood what he was talking about, and I liked the thoughts starting to run through my head. I reached over and unbuttoned his uniform shirt, sliding a hand inside, reaching through his pelt of fur to find the hard nub of a tit. "So you like spending time in that bag too, huh?" I punctuated my question with a hard squeeze of his nipple.

"Yep."

I squeezed his tit harder. My other hand shoved his hands away from my body. I clamped my hand over his nose and mouth. "What was that, faggot?" I watched as he started humping his groin into the air, enjoying the sensation of not being able to breathe. He struggled more and more, and I let him breathe again. I was hard, and I could see through his tight breeches that he was too.

"Yes, Sir."

"That's better." I smiled, he smiled, and we locked faces in a wet, sloppy kiss.

"Woof! Mike didn't tell me you had *that* in you, boy!"

"I didn't. Guess someone put it there recently."

"Well, Mike won't be back until Monday. You got plans for tomorrow?"

"Nope."

"Then let's get to bed. Tomorrow's gonna be a *long* day for both of us."

We went to the bedroom, and I helped him off with his Dehners. I was finally treated to the sight of his body as he stripped out of his leathers; it was as delicious as I thought it might be. I was half-hoping we might start up again then and there, but as soon as we climbed into bed, the light sound of David's soft snoring filled the darkened room. I couldn't sleep just yet—no doubt I still was wired from all the nicotine that had soaked into my body. I was doing a lot of thinking: replaying the horny memories of the night; imagining David in that bag; wondering what Mike would think of all this; hoping I'd get to play with both of them together; and above all, knowing that even if I *had* exhausted the pool of Tops that could handle me (which clearly I hadn't), there was a whole pool of bottoms left. And I was ready to dive in.

Blue Christmas
By Kevin Killian

Kevin Killian is a well-known avant-garde author whose stories are always more than a bit off-kilter. "Blue Christmas" is no exception. It's funny, creepy, and hot all at once, Dickens meets dicks. Filled with dead-end desperation and longing, it's a holiday card from hell.

Between his knees, up and down his long bare thighs Keith rubs the thick wool blanket, trying to stay warm. He's lying in his bunk using his right hand to beat off, in an absent way, part of his mind thinking this is going to be the loneliest Christmas any guy ever had. Outside the windows visible flakes of snow are sailing wildly all around the sky, and the setting sun lights up each flake in pastel colors, like the plastic pieces inside the barrel of a kid's kaleidoscope. Keith's bedroom has a western exposure, so the sun comes flashing in only at sundown; it's cold in winter. Tony hasn't said anything for about an hour. Tony sleeps in the bottom bunk, spends plenty of time there asleep, much more time than a normal boy, Keith can't figure it out, maybe he's dreaming of liberation, or home, wherever that is.

Keith's dick is firming up in his hands as he pulls its length up and down limberly, like stretching a piece of taffy. He thinks, *I'm yearning for the feel of someone's mouth around its thickness, some other pull besides my own moist hands.* It's a lurid thought, and one that drives him over the edge—literally. "Tony," he calls out to the bottom bunk. "You there? You conscious?"

"Mmm," Tony says out loud, in a tone of voice that sounds utterly bored. That's all the invitation Keith needs. Quick as a wink he spins his body over the edge of his bunk in a kind of skin-the-cat position, presenting his butt to Tony's face—the way monkeys will in the zoo. Being cooped up inside so much makes Keith feel, sometimes, like a zoo animal—that Parker and Legman are his keepers, which they are, of course. Keith hasn't been outside the walls of this house since his 18th birthday, four years earlier.

Tony kind of squirms or flinches, then raises a tentative hand to Keith's swinging bare butt, which keeps looming closer to his face, like a pendulum, only to draw away from him again, then come back in, closer and closer. Keith's cock and balls tumble down over his asshole, like some mighty waterfall at the mouth of the Orinoco. Keith's thinking Tony is from some South American country or another, maybe he's familiar with the Orinoco, with the way its mighty headlands release a white and green torrent of foam over a stony gorge. Maybe this visual echo will stir some atavistic longing in Tony's fuzzy memory, or so Keith hopes. "What country are you from, Tony?" inquires Keith, panting, his head upside down, tongue sticking out to give Tony the right idea, all the blood rushing to his head so that he sees Tony through a red haze of heat and longing.

"Peru," Tony says. "But that was in the old days, my friend." Back before he came to the States and met Parker and Legman in Youth Tutoring. And way before he came to live in this house with Keith and the other, luckier, boys—the boys who came and went. Tony reaches under Keith's balls and feels along the smooth line of his shaved perineum. When he does that it always gives Keith goosebumps—the kind that make him think, *If I were in love with Tony, maybe this would be superhot, but I'm not.* As it stands now Keith is in love with someone else. It's now December 18, one week to Christmas, and finally he gets Mr. Peru to apply his mouth, his big red lips, right around the head of his cock and to suck

Keith's shaft all the way to the base. Keith can see Tony's large brown eyes through the W of his legs, eyes begging Keith for more. His nimble fingers playing cats-cradle through the delicate hairs of Keith's asshole, then trembling in one by one as Keith thrusts his hungry, almost desperately hungry, ass muscles upon them.

Tony and Keith share a room, and Tony's the neat one. He irons all his clothes and sometimes Keith's too. He even irons his socks and underwear. Keith first met him in Youth Tutoring in Mr. Legman's class, and now they live in Legman's big old Victorian house at the edge of town. Here it is almost Christmas, and Keith is longing for one tiny thing, and he's got this...*sinking feeling* he isn't going to get his wish.

He is perhaps just about to come inside Tony's mouth when Tony shrinks back, his large, expressive eyes registering terror. Keith feels the familiar heat rushing up and down his wet cock, its head swollen like a Christmas ornament; then comes a sudden chill as Tony tears his mouth away from his cock and lets it dangle there like a—like a candy cane, all glistening with spit. Keith starts to complain—"What the fuck?"—but then he sees the door opening. The door without a lock or key.

God, why even have a door?

"Look at this," Parker says to Legman. The two of them are standing in the doorway: tall Parker and tiny Mr. Legman, a man so minuscule that when he was Keith's youth tutor at Vermont High, the kids called him "Bart" because he looked like a little Bart Simpson. Keith scrambles back to the top bunk, hauling in his hard-on, still wet from Tony's saliva and his own precome. "Did you see what I just saw?"

"Please, Mr. Parker," Tony begins, fumbling for words, his accent returning.

Keith clutches his pulsing dick, tries to stop the fix, but, wow, in an impressive arc a burst of come flows through the air like dripping seed pearls.

"Don't 'please' me, Tony," Parker says. "And Keith—button it up."

His face is an impassive mask. You can't see anything behind his cold face. Parker stands about 6 feet 5 inches tall and he's heavily built. He wears a beard, a black beard, just turning gray at the edges. His hair he keeps cut short in a quasimilitary way. He is left-handed but takes pains to disguise the fact. His big hands are pulpy as plantains, and in the twilight his eyes are a strange blue color, almost the color of slate, and they give nothing away. He used to teach English to Keith, but now he keeps him here, locked up in Legman's house, dependent on him for love, food, and everything else.

Tony is near blubbering. "Please, Mr. Parker, I was just hungry," he says, faltering. When he's scared or alarmed his English crumbles, his accent thickens like soup. Keith can hardly make out what he's saying and chalks it up to naked fear.

Parker says, "Tony, get up, get off your knees, try to be a man."

"Un hombre," Keith says helpfully to Tony.

"That's enough," Parker snaps at Keith. Tony keeps crying until Parker takes him outdoors to the snow. Keith lies back and watches, watches Parker haul Tony off by the ear. He almost envies Tony for being able to get out in the fresh air, though lying down on his stomach in the snow for an hour or more isn't Keith's idea of a good time. On the other hand, what is a good time?

Down in the kitchen Legman is making Christmas cookies, his ample waist cinched with a red-and-green apron that has a picture of a reindeer on it. Keith sits by the stove, warmed by the aroma of the fresh-baked cookies, pale brown Santas, stars, wreaths, bells, and angels that come out of the stove, pan after pan of them, laid out on greased tinfoil. When they cool down it's Keith's job to decorate these cookies with sugar and those little silver balls. And the tiny pastel balls of flavor people used to call "sprinkles" when he was a boy. (Or "jimmies" if they were chocolate.) It's a test of Keith's patience to sit in the kitchen, waiting for the cookies to cool off, waiting for the very first bite.

"*Dragées*," Legman says. "My mother called the silver balls *dragées*. She was a Quebecoise."

"And a nut," Keith says. "If she hatched you, Legman, she was a nut supreme."

Legman cracks a smile at that. He and Parker always appreciate a good sense of humor, a well-timed wisecrack. What Legman really appreciates is the way Keith fucks his tiny little ass, which is about the size of two marshmallows mushed together and not always easy to aim at. *Coat a little chocolate on his butt, and you'd have about two ounces of heavenly hash,* thinks Keith, who fucking hates Legman and can't think of a good word to say about him, not even at Christmastime. For Legman is the one who enforced the edict about no shoes.

So Keith goes barefoot year-round, like John Boy Walton, on the cold, bare hardwood floors. On TV everyone wears Nikes or Adidas or Ferragamo shoes. Legman and Parker explain that in the early '90s they let one boy have one pair of shoes and he'd run away. *If they don't have shoes, they don't run away, and maybe that's so,* Keith thinks. But that's all he wants for Christmas, one pair of shoes. When he tries visualizing a scene, though, tries to picture himself unwrapping a present under the Christmas tree, he can't see a thing. This is gonna be the bluest Christmas of all.

Later that night Keith helps Tony get warm again, huddling over his cold blue body like a blanket. "How romantic," Parker says, watching Keith cover Tony, trying to bring back the spark of life after his night in the snow without his clothes. The following day, which Keith thinks for some reason must be a Tuesday, Legman ushers in a boy, tells Keith to take his coat. Neither Keith nor Tony has ever seen this boy before, but he is a welcome stranger: blond, with short hair that bristles over his forehead, and big eyes the color of prunes. He is hella high on something and very loose, like he might slither into a puddle if not held up. Keith nudges Tony in the ribs, jerking a finger to indicate the old high-tops this kid has on his feet. "They're mine," Tony makes his mouth move to say, without a sound. "Fuck you," Keith replies, all very sotto voce. "This is Stewart," Legman says, propping him up against the sideboard. "Stewart is going to perform some science experiments with us."

"Is he my Christmas present, Legman?" Keith says.

"No, Keith," says Legman, abstractedly.

"Because, as I keep telling you, I want some shoes."

Stewart is some kind of speed freak, Keith guesses. Just by looking at him you know that he has the same kind of substance-abuse problems most of the Youth Tutoring boys do. And probably problems with self-esteem and absent parents, or he'd never have fallen into Parker's clutches in the first place. Stewart has rings around his eyes like a raccoon's and long, skinny arms throbbing with veins. He tries to speak, but the words kind of get lost halfway up his throat, on the way to his larynx. "Don't say nothing," Keith tells him. "Already you might as well, you know, abandon hope."

Stewart quiets down as Keith inches his hands down his chest, feeling the many motors of his blood and heart racing but in neutral. Stewart's breath smells like charcoal, like many meth users'. Like a bag of old charcoal one drags out of the garage at the start of a new barbecue season, not sure if one can choke one more use out of it. Parker sits in an armchair near the fireplace and spreads his long legs, significantly. He taps this one spot on the inside of his thigh. That is his signal for Keith to come and suck his cock for the benefit of the digital camera.

"OK, OK," grumbles Keith.

"Watch this," Parker tells Stewart, who sits next to Tony on the couch as if stunned, as though someone has hit him on top of the head.

This is the part where Keith has to lick the flannel of Parker's gray pants until he gets him stirred up. Then he must mouth the big log thing through the flannel. Flannel tongue, Parker calls him. Eventually he gets Parker's pants open—all with his teeth and lips and tongue—and gets his face fucked, while the camera's red-and-green lights blink on and on like a Christmas tree. Parker's strong, meaty hand winds itself around the back of Keith's head and shoves the young man's mouth all the way down into his lap. Cock hits the back of Keith's throat. He starts to gag and sputter and tears come to his eyes, but they both know how much they enjoy this. They'd never say it out loud, though. Sometimes Keith even wishes Parker would choke him with his dick once and for all; he's that devoted to the big man.

Meanwhile, Tony starts to caress Stewart, murmuring Peruvian endearments and swear words into his ear while tugging at the seam of his running shorts. Stewart keeps slapping Tony's hands away, but he must know this is a losing battle and, maybe, he likes it a little. Tentatively his lips meet Tony's. "Cold," he says.

"*Muchas frias*," says Tony, his eyes lowered. "I'm starting to feel things in my fingers and toes, *muy bien*."

Parker, close to coming, has pulled Keith off his dick. Now Keith pushes aside the brief leg of Stewart's running shorts, while Legman holds him down on the leather couch. Inside the crack of his butt, the skin is white as the powdered sugar Keith had traced onto the warm Christmas cookies, a white with pink and blue swirls underneath. "Stewart," Keith says, "let me lick your asshole for awhile." Overpowered, Stewart closes his ass tight, so its cleft bumps the bridge of Keith's nose, but Keith doesn't mind. Viewed up close, the muscles in his ass look like great mountain planes; watching his ass clench reminds Keith of an old film he'd seen on the creation of the world. His tongue leaps out to lick the crack. Keith figures, *In for a penny, in for a pound.* The smell alone is enough to make him hard. He glances briefly at his own erection and sees it jutting out properly. Pointing north-northeast. With three fingers he strokes the velvety shaft of Stewart's limp cock, and he begins, with increasing pleasure, to mouth

Stewart's wet, slippery ass. From the outside of his lips, he can feel analgesic, as though something in the skin itself was encouraging him to stop nuzzling, to start actually chewing. Like it's a meal he can eat. Stewart is responding, slightly, moving away, then closer, and in Keith's hand, Stewart's cock is unfolding steadily, like a hot-water bottle you'd fill with water or one of the old-time collapsible suitcases Legman keeps in the shed.

"Merry Christmas," says Parker.

"I want some shoes," Keith mumbles. He slides his hands, palms down, along Stewart's butt, shiny with saliva, and approaches the wide-open asshole with six of his fingers.

"Stewart has some shoes, don't you, Stewart?" Parker asks.

The boy's face strains as though trying to think.

"No talking," says Legman.

"Well, let him answer some questions. What's your favorite color, Stewart?"

"Green," Stewart says to Parker, just as Keith gets in.

"Who's the president of the USA?"

"Bill Clinton," Tony replies. He's been boning up on questions about the government for his citizenship exam.

"Not you."

"Clinton," moans Stewart, as Keith climbs up and down his back, his hard cock thrusting into Stewart's asshole, over and over. "You got a condom on that thing?"

Keith couldn't remember, though he doubted it. Instead of replying, he licks Stewart's right earlobe, knowing the rush of sound into his eardrum will, at the same time, confuse, delight, and silence him.

Parker says, "Complete this common Christmas phrase. 'Chestnuts roasting on an open fire...'"

Tony stands up. "'Yack Frost nipping at my toes.' Can I go to bed, *muy cansado*, Mr. Parker."

Stewart turns his face a little, and Keith can smell the charcoal on his breath. His large, dark eyes are filled with questions.

I love him, Keith thinks, *and the whole world will know it.* He whispers in his ear: "Can I borrow your shoes?"

Stewart's whole body shakes. Was that yes or no? Over his shoulder Keith glances at Parker, who nods slightly. Another signal.

Legman must have gone out, for now he comes back, just as Keith pulls out of Stewart's dripping butt and presents his spurting dick for the camera's facile eye. "Cookies for everyone!" Legman announces. He looks so...fem in that apron. It's hard to keep a straight face.

"I'm embarrassed," Stewart confides to Keith.

"These guys don't know embarrassed from a hole in the ground," Keith says. "Come on, cheer up. Life ain't so bad, and these cookies are fucking awesome. Now how about those shoes, bud?"

"What'll I wear?"

"I've got some in my room," he lies. "Let's swap."

"I guess." Stewart takes a cookie and puts it in his mouth, just lets it sit there and looks disgruntled while Keith kneels on the floor and takes off his shoes, like Mary Magdalene washing the feet of Jesus. It's like waking up on Christmas morning and unwrapping the greatest present in the world. "Stewart," he says, "I want to tell you two things, real quick. I love you, and you're not a bad fuck, but cut down on the meth. But I guess you'll probably have to anyway, huh?"

"Oh," says Stewart, tucking his bare legs under him, staring away. "And what's the second thing?"

"Look, everyone," Keith says, bouncing to his feet. "I've got shoes on." They were too big but just right for walking out the fucking door. "Merry Christmas to all and to all a good night..."

Dirty Pictures
By Tom Caffrey

The things we'll do when we're in the grip of an obsession! Tom Caffrey's sly, sexy story is about a kind of power we all know, the power of our dicks over our better judgment. It starts out in the gutter. Or maybe it started long before that...

I work as a garbage man for the city of New York. The paper pushers who write our job descriptions like to call us "sanitary engineers," like we somehow take people's discarded newspapers, crusty cat food tins, and broken television sets and turn them into machines for studying the motion of the stars or something. But what we really do is go around in the dead hours before dawn, scavenging scraps of other people's lives and hauling them away to a big landfill out on Long Island where they're buried in mass graves cared for by flocks of screeching gulls. It's not a real pretty job, especially during the long, hot stretch of a steamy New York summer, but it's a living.

Most people never notice the men who scrape away the city's daily coat of grime while they sleep. We're the invisible ones who come out after midnight and disappear before the noon sun reaches its high point. I've been doing this work for almost seven years now—almost a quarter of my life—without anything special to speak of happening to me. I've even gotten used to the daily ritual of getting up at 4 o'clock to make it to the truck yard by 4:30 and going to sleep when most people are coming home from work to begin their real lives.

Then, a couple of months ago, something happened that turned my usually routine workday into something much different. I was at the end of my haul, working down 17th Street toward Eighth Avenue. I only had one final row of buildings to attend to, and I couldn't wait to be finished. The city was broiling in a midsummer heat wave, and even in the early morning the temperature was already hovering near 80. I was sweating like crazy, a big stain soaking the front of my blue coveralls from throat to crotch. I couldn't wait to pull my wet, stinking clothes off and stand under a hot shower for a good long time.

I was thinking about how good the water would feel on my aching muscles when I picked up a cardboard box sitting at the curb and got ready to toss it into the back of the truck. I was swinging it into the jaws of the big crusher when something fell out and fluttered to the ground. Catching the motion out of the corner of my eye, I put the box down and bent down to see what I'd dropped. It was a Polaroid picture, and when I saw what it was a picture of, I almost dropped it again.

Framed by the thin white lines of the border was a shot of a naked guy. His head was cut off where the top of the picture severed his neck like the blade of a guillotine, but the rest of him was perfectly clear. He was a big guy, with a thick chest and muscular arms and legs. His body was covered in black hair, and his fist was wrapped around a huge cock. He was squeezing it tightly, and the big head was red and swollen. His other hand was stretching out his hairy ball sac.

I just stood there staring at the picture, unable to take my eyes off the headless man. It wasn't like I'd never seen a naked guy before. It was just that I never expected to see one fall out of the trash I was hauling. I mean, sure, I come across a lot of discarded porn mags, but this was a real surprise. People are usually pretty careful about throwing out pictures of themselves, like whoever finds them will have control over their souls or something. I rarely find actual snapshots of people, especially ones where they're playing with their dicks.

I was even more surprised when I realized my cock was starting to get hard from looking at the snapshot. I could feel it stretching inside my overalls, pressing against my stomach. Fumbling nervously with the cardboard flaps, I opened the box and almost shot a load from what I saw. Inside were dozens of Polaroids, all of different nude guys jerking off. Some were standing up and some were lying on beds waving their cocks at the camera. Some were bent over, their fingers shoved up their assholes. There were even a couple with two guys in them, where one would be sucking the other's cock or sticking his dick up the other guy's butt hole.

None of them had faces. There were just bodies and, in the case of guys sucking, mouths filled with thick pricks or ripe balls. There were armpits being licked by eager tongues, and at least one shot of just an asshole smeared with globs of lube, the hair swirled around the opening in wet strands. The bodies were fat and thin, black and white and brown, hairy and smooth, young and old. And their cocks were all different too. Some had big fat monsters that swung heavily between their legs. Others had small, thin pricks sticking out from their bodies. It was as if someone had crept into bedrooms all over the city and captured what he saw there on these tiny windows of film.

There were also some used rubbers in the box, scattered among the pictures like the discarded skins of strange animals. The thin blue-and-white sheaths were wrinkled and wet looking, the tips filled with dried come and the outsides streaked with faded lines of lube. I reached out and touched one, feeling the softness of the rubber under my fingers. When I picked it up the end swung down heavily, and I realized that the thick liquid that swelled out the tip was a recent load. Whoever the box belonged to must have put it out that morning and had a good time before he did it.

I riffled through the box and pulled out a handful of photos, stuffing them into the pockets of my work pants. I also put the used rubber in there, tying the end off so that none of the come would leak out. I could feel how hard my cock was when I put my hand in my pocket; I gave it a couple of quick jerks. I tossed the box with the rest of pictures into the truck and hit the button that brought down the big steel sweeper. I watched it crush the box, spilling out a feast of headless naked men who were quickly swallowed into the belly of the truck. My cock ached as I thought about the pictures in my pockets. I couldn't wait to get home and look at them again.

I finished the rest of my route in record time, depositing the truck at the yard and racing home. I didn't even bother to shower once I got there, pulling off my sweaty clothes and dropping onto the bed as soon as the door was closed. Spreading the pictures out across my chest and stomach, I looked at them while I jerked slowly on my tool, the cool breath of the window fan tickling my overheated skin in thin ribbons. My dick was rock-hard from all the anticipation, and it felt like steel beneath my fingers, warm steel pulsing with blood and desire.

As I moved my grimy hand up and down my shaft, I picked up each picture and looked at it, imagining what was going on when it was taken. My favorite was a shot of a man sitting in an old red velvet armchair. His legs were spread, his knees hooked over the arms of the chair, and in his hand was a long, straight dick. His balls were smooth, and his bush was clipped short. His stomach was wide and flat, the muscles bunched into heavy ropes. His chest and belly were covered in light blond hair, and I could see that he had his head thrown back. His free hand was between his legs, and he had two fingers shoved up his hairy hole, spreading it wide for the camera.

I tried to picture what the guy who took the photos looked like while I cranked on my meat. I imagined him telling the man in the chair what to do. I could practically hear him saying "Stick your fingers in that hole" while he snapped the shot. Did he jerk off while he watched? Did he fuck the guys when he was done shooting them? Picking up the used rubber and untying the end, I fingered it while I brought the feeling in my balls to a fever pitch with my hand. The weight of the man's load against my palm was reassuring and arousing, and I thought about him shooting it. I could almost see the photographer stroking himself off while his models posed for him, his hand jerking furiously on his crank.

Tipping the condom upside down, I let the contents splash out onto my chest. The come was cold and wet against my skin, but it felt so hot to have another man's load on my body that I didn't care. I rubbed the unknown man's jism into the hair on my chest and belly while I finished myself off. My fingers were sticky with his juice and my sweat as I massaged him into my balls and slid him into my hairy asshole, and I shot my own load all over my stomach. My balls tensed as volley after volley blew out of my cock and slopped over my hand and onto the pictures still lying on my stomach.

There was come everywhere, from my neck to my crotch. Drops of it stuck to my thighs and ran down my sides until I couldn't tell if it was mine or the man's whose rubber I'd found. It didn't matter, it was the hottest jerk-off session I'd ever had. My prick was still throbbing long after I'd finished coming, and the feeling of being covered in spunk was enough to make me want to blow all over again.

Picking the come-drenched pictures off my body, I wiped them off as much as I could and stuck them in a drawer for later use. Then I showered, lathering up and jerking off again while I thought about the mysterious photographer and what he must be like. I had to see him, and I decided that I'd go back to the building that night and see if I could find him. I knew it was crazy, but the tugging in my balls every time I thought about him told me I had to do it.

That night, at about 11 o'clock, I found myself standing across the street from the brownstone where I'd found the box that morning. The heat of the afternoon had never died down, and the air was thick and dry as bone in my lungs as I stood looking up at the three floors of windows, trying to figure out which ones belonged to the guy I was looking for. I was glad he didn't live in a big building, where it would have been impossible to find him. This way, I only had to eliminate two of the floors.

The lights in the second-floor apartment were out, so I concentrated on the other two. The windows on the first floor were covered by blinds, and those on the third were wide open. I stood for about half an hour waiting for some kind of a clue, my dick hard from nervousness and the excitement of doing something totally unexpected. My mind raced with all the reasons why I shouldn't be there, and I fought them down by waiting for the building to open up and give me some sign that I wasn't out of my mind. But the brick walls seemed determined to keep their secrets safe within, and nothing happened that would help me make my next move.

I was just about to give up and leave when I saw one of the first floor shades go up. An elderly woman poked her head out, leaning on the windowsill and looking up and down the street. With her thick glasses and rolls of fat billowing out from her sleeveless house dress, she didn't look like she was responsible for the box of delights I'd discovered there that morning. *OK,* I thought, *that means he must be on the top floor. Now how the hell do I get up there?*

Moving around to the side of the building, I found the fire escape. By standing on a trash can, and with no small amount of difficulty, I was able to pull myself up to the first level, grunting and straining as I hauled my body over the edge of the platform. *This is fucking nuts,* I thought as I sat there trying to get my breath. *I'm going to get arrested for trying to spy on some guy, and I don't even know for sure that he lives here.*

But the memory of the pictures and what they'd done to my cock kept me going. I crept slowly up the fire escape to the second floor, stopping to peek in the window. The room inside was completely empty, and from the faint patterns remaining in the dust that covered the floor, it looked as though no one had lived there for quite some time. That meant the third floor apartment was my only chance. I scrambled up the remaining stairs and found myself outside the window. I sat there for a minute, making sure no one in neighboring apartments saw me while I worked up the courage to look in the window.

Like the front windows, the side ones were also curtainless, as well as being pushed open halfway to let in the breeze. All that separated me from the room inside was a thin screen. Peering around the corner, I was able to see directly into what was obviously the bedroom. A light was on, and I could see clearly what was inside. There was a big bed pushed up against one wall, and an armchair opposite it. I recognized the chair as the one from the photos, and my dick jumped sharply in my pants. I'd gotten the right place.

Now that I was actually there, I had no idea what I was doing. I couldn't just open the window and go into the guy's bedroom. But I also couldn't bring myself to leave; I was too curious now to go without seeing what he was like. Before I could decide on my next move, I heard voices from the other room; someone came into the bedroom so quickly that I barely had time to dip my head below the windowsill before whoever it was saw me. I was scared to look up, in case the occupants were looking out the window, so I just lay there listening to what was going on, feeling my cock through my pants, my heart pounding in my chest.

"Take them off," I heard an authoritative voice say. "I want to see your dick."

The command was followed by the muffled sounds of someone removing his clothes. I heard his shoes drop to the floor as he removed them, then the appreciative murmuring of the same masculine voice that had ordered him to strip. "Nice cock," he said. "Get it hard." I heard footsteps as he walked across the floor, then the sharp slap of a hand against skin. "Nice ass too," he growled. "Can't wait to see my dick stuffed up it."

Hearing what was going on was too much. I couldn't just lie there listening. Lifting my head, I nervously looked over the bottom of the screen. What I saw almost made me come in my shorts. Standing with his back to me was a tall man with short black hair. He was naked, and through his spread legs I could see the head of his dick hanging over his balls. He was holding a Polaroid camera and barking orders to a man kneeling on the bed. The man, a smooth-skinned Latino guy with a big uncut prick, was slowly stroking his cock. His foreskin was sliding over his engorged knob while strings of precome flowed out and slid over his shaft.

"Looks fucking hot," the dark-haired man said, snapping a photo. "Now play with your asshole."

The Latino guy turned around and pulled his ass cheeks apart, showing the pink center of his pucker. He slid a finger in until it was right up to his knuckle, then began to fuck himself slowly while the other man took pictures. As he snapped one after the other, they fell like leaves from the camera, piling at his feet. From where I knelt on the fire escape I could see that none of them showed the Latino man's face.

"That's great," the black-haired man growled. "You've got me so fucking hard I can't wait." He put the camera down and moved toward the bed. His cock was stiff, and he pumped the thick shaft quickly as he moved in behind the Latino man. Then, in one quick thrust, he shoved his whole dick into the man's ass until his balls were banging against his butt.

"Oh, yeah," he moaned. "You can take the whole fucking thing, can't you, you little slut."

The Latino man squirmed against the bed as the big man impaled him on his cock, hammering away at his hole until his dick was sloppy with sweat and juice from the violated ass. The big man put his hands on the other one's cheeks and pulled them wider, forcing himself inside in long, angry thrusts. He was groaning and throwing his head back with each movement.

Watching the two men fuck was getting me really worked up. Pulling my fly open, I pulled out my tool and started man-handling it, jerking off in rhythm with the dark-haired man and pretending it was my ass he was screwing. Within a few minutes I was ready to come, which was a good thing, because the big guy yanked his dick from the Latino man's asshole and started jacking off. With a few strokes of his hand, he came. Long jets of come streaked over the prone man's back, landing in wet stripes on his skin.

Seeing the big stud come made me shoot my load in a blazing rush. I squeezed my cock head as it spat out a blast that splattered against the bricks of the wall. My balls tensed as jism flowed out of them and dripped onto the slats of the fire escape in heavy drops, emptying onto the street below. A low groan escaped my lips as I gave in to the pleasure wrapping my body in its grip.

It must have been just loud enough for the man inside to hear, because he jumped off the bed and ran to the window. Before I could even move, he had thrown up the screen and was reaching out for me, his big hand closing around my wrist. "What the hell are you doing out here?" he demanded angrily. I was so scared I couldn't answer him. I just knelt there on the fire escape, looking up into his beautiful dark brown eyes.

When I didn't answer, his eyes moved down to my prick, and he smiled slightly as he took in my slimy cock, still held tightly in my hand. All I was conscious of was the way my breathing seemed to have stopped and how his fingers felt clamped around my wrist. To my horror, I was still rock-hard.

"I think you should get inside," he said, pulling me toward him. Nervously, I scrambled over the windowsill and into the bedroom. The Latino man was still on the bed, and he stared at me as I stood awkwardly in the center of the room. The dark-haired man pulled the screen closed again, then walked over to stand in front of me. "Do you always spend your nights jerking off on fire escapes?" he asked as he gripped my chin in his hand and forced my eyes up to his.

Again I couldn't say anything. Everything else melted away as I concentrated on the way his fingers held my face and how his eyes bore into mine. While I tried to get my tongue to work, my skin burned where he touched it, filling me with a sweet pain that gripped my balls and squeezed tightly. I felt as though I'd done something forbidden, seen something I never should have seen and gotten caught. It made me feel slightly dirty, like when I was a kid and I'd look at the magazines in my dad's underwear drawer and jack off, afraid the whole time that he'd walk in and catch me, half hoping he would.

Only this time he *had* walked in, and I knew I was going to pay for it. When I didn't answer fast enough, the man moved his hand down and grabbed my cock by the base, pulling up on it until I cried out. "There," he said, smiling, "I finally got a noise out of you. And you seem to like it too."

I could feel my face filling with color as he continued to tug on my balls and I gave in to the feeling. I did like it, and he knew it. His strong fingers encircled my cock and balls and squeezed tightly, filling my prick with blood. I tried my best not to gasp, but when he pinched the swollen tip of my dick in his other hand, I almost came. He laughed. "Take your clothes off," he ordered, letting go of my pounding cock.

Hurrying to obey him, I tore at the buttons on my shirt and clumsily pulled off my boots and jeans. When I was naked I stood with my hands behind my back, waiting to see what he would say or do. He sat on the bed the whole time, his eyes on my face as the Latino man buried his head in his lap and slurped on his big dick. He didn't seem to be in any hurry and allowed the Latino to take his time tongue washing every inch of his cock. Then he pushed him away and stood up.

Coming toward me, he let his fist move along the length of his dick as he walked, stroking it slowly and fiercely, as though pumping it full of life. When he was right in front of me, he stopped. Taking my hand, he moved it so that his cock was against my palm. My fingers closed around it, and I felt him tense so that the hardness swelled against me.

"Do you like that?" he asked. I nodded, feeling the warm flesh under my fingers as I pulled on his shaft.

He pulled away suddenly, leaving my hand empty. "That's only for good boys," he said, grabbing me by the back of the neck. "It seems to me you've been a bad boy. A very bad boy. And you know what happens to bad boys, don't you?"

I swallowed hard, knowing that I had to answer. "They get punished," I whispered.

He pushed me toward the bed. "That's right," he barked. "They get punished. Now suck Tony's cock."

Tony leaned back against the pillows on the bed and spread his legs. His cock was stiff, and I remembered that he hadn't come yet. As soon as I was kneeling on the bed between his thighs, he grabbed my head and sank the entire length of his dick down my throat. It tore at the sides as it roared down my gullet, but I was so worked up I took every inch of him. He was uncut, and thick ooze poured from beneath his taut foreskin as I teased it with my tongue.

I sucked on Tony as best I could, wishing it were the dark-haired man's tool I was servicing. Behind me, I heard the whirring of a camera as he started taking pictures of me sucking Tony's dick. Thinking about all of the photos I'd found in the box and knowing that now he had ones of me made me even hornier. My lips slipped up and down Tony's spit-soaked shaft rapidly as I coaxed him to coming.

Suddenly I felt a stinging pain on my ass, followed by a red-hot burning sensation that seemed to roll over my skin like water.

Before I could figure out what it was, the pain came again. Tony's cock jumped in my throat as I tried to pull away and see what was causing it, but I felt a strong hand push my head back down.

"You stay where you are," the dark man's voice ordered. "It's time for the punishment bad boys like you deserve."

The slapping came again on my ass, and I realized that I was being spanked with a belt. Each blow on my tender ass pushed me onto Tony's cock, and I swallowed him hungrily as the beautiful warm pain sank into my muscles repeatedly. I tried to absorb it by sucking harder on the cock in my throat. There were tears in my eyes, but it was the most amazing sensation I'd ever felt. It was the same way my father had punished me as a kid, bending me over and slapping my ass until I cried. When he'd finally let me go, I would run from the room to the bathroom, where I'd jerk my dick and come, sobbing, all over my hand.

The strokes moved up my ass to my lower back, crisscrossing my skin in short, sharp lashes of pain that made my dick harder with every touch of the leather. I started to anticipate the next blow and let the force of it travel through me, drawing my lips tightly around Tony's prick at each slap on my skin. My ass cheeks were still on fire from the working over they'd received, and soon my whole back was tingling with the remnants of the belt's sting.

While he beat me the man continued to tell me what a bad boy I was. It felt a little strange, a man of 33 being called a boy, but it didn't seem to confuse my dick, which remained hard throughout my punishment. When I felt him move in behind me and spread my ass cheeks with his hands, a long pull of anticipation tugged at my balls.

As he sank one thick finger into my pucker, the man slapped me hard on the ass. "This is what happens to boys who look at things they shouldn't," he said, pulling his finger out and replacing it with the head of his cock. Then he slammed into me all at once, pushing himself deep into my ass.

Pushed forward, I felt Tony's stomach connect with my nose as his prick disappeared into my mouth. My asshole stretched wide as the man started to fuck me, and I was glad my throat was filled with Tony's cock so I couldn't cry out from the pain that seared my shitter. He hadn't even lubed his dick, and it was killing me.

Still, it felt wonderful to be used by him like that. His pictures had given me such pleasure, and now I was paying the price for daring to try to get more than that. His rough hands gripped my ass tightly as he savaged me, and the combined feeling of his thick tool pounding my insides while his fingers pinched at my skin sent me into a frenzy. I slobbered over Tony's cock as I satisfied my mouth with him, pumping his shaft mercilessly while behind me my hole was being tormented by the hottest, roughest fuck I'd ever had.

Tony came in a rush of jism that flooded my throat with warmth and sent me swallowing crazily to contain it all. Several thick gushes escaped his dick head before the flow slowed, and I gulped down every drop of it. Behind me, the dark-haired man saw what was happening and blew his own load in my butt, pumping faster and faster as his sticky juice streamed inside me.

It was all too much, being taken at both ends, and I lost control, spewing drops of come all over the bed as my balls gave up their heavy load. Tony's cock slipped out of my mouth, and I rubbed my cheek along his wet shaft while I moaned, sucking the last dribbles of come from his piss slit. My ass clamped around the still-hard dick invading my hole, and the dark-haired man gave me a final slap as I emptied myself beneath him.

When I was finished he pulled out of me and jerked me to my feet. Barely able to stand, I slumped against him while he pulled my head back and rammed his tongue into my mouth. He bit my lip hard while his tongue explored mine. Then he pulled away as suddenly as he'd come, and I dropped to my knees. Scattered on the floor were the pictures he'd taken of me.

One showed his hard pole piercing my willing asshole. Taken from above right before he started to fuck me hard, the photo showed him with half of his dick penetrating my hole, as well as the red marks on my back from his beating. My face was buried in Tony's crotch. Seeing myself taking in both of their thick cocks made me ache to have them back inside me.

"Take it," the dark-haired man said. "It's what you wanted in the first place."

Not daring to look up at him, I scooped up the picture. Then I quickly found my discarded clothes and pulled them on, still not looking at Tony or the other man, who watched me silently as I dressed. Come had matted the hair on my belly into sticky tangles, and I ran my fingers over it while I pulled my shirt on. I knew that I would not wash it off before I fell asleep that night, and the thought made me shiver as I tucked the photo into my pocket.

When I had pulled my boots back on, I turned to go. Neither man said a word to me, but both smiled as I walked to the window, slid the screen up, and climbed back onto the fire escape. It seemed the only proper way to leave. Taking a final glance at them as I started down the ladder, I saw the dark-haired man pick up his camera and begin shooting again while Tony, out of my sight, did something to himself.

Dropping the last few feet to the ground, I walked down the street as easily as if I were out for an evening stroll. But as I thought about how it felt shooting off on that fire escape, and being punished for it afterward, my dick stirred in my pants. It felt just like it did when I was a kid looking at those magazines in my father's drawer, and I knew that, just as I'd returned to those magazines time after time, I'd be back again for more of those dirty pictures.

Head Games
By Ken Butler

Ken Butler cannily explores the question of what we really want and what we're willing to give up to get it. This story builds sexual tension you can cut with a knife. We'll never approach software shopping—or monogamy—in quite the same way again.

I was standing at the software shelves when I first noticed him. I remember thinking he was attractive—tall, bald on top with dark fringe, wide-shouldered, thick-legged. He was trying to decide which fax-modem to buy; his jaw was set, and he reminded me of nothing more than a bulldog. Perhaps it helped that he didn't seem to have a neck; despite the short-sleeved, thin-striped dress shirt stretched across his torso, it was obvious he had at one time been a serious weightlifter. Muscles grew out of his shoulders and seemed to connect to his head not far below the ears. Those same muscles were prominent in his huge, hairless forearms, and in tree-trunk thighs that stretched the pair of gray polyester pants he was wearing.

Whew, I thought, *what a hunk of man.* He turned in my direction, and I quickly took something off the shelves, hoping he hadn't noticed I was staring at him. I looked down to find a calendar program in my hands as he spoke. "I run that. You'll like it."

"I already own it," I managed. "This is the upgrade. I'm trying to decide if it's worth 50 bucks." I looked into piercing green eyes as he took a step toward me, looking down at the box over the edge of his glasses.

"Yeah, that's the version I run." I took a moment to check out his crotch. The single nice thing about polyester pants is that they hug your crotch really well. I could tell he was wearing boxers (I guess that's two good things about polyester) and it was obvious he was well-hung.

"Farsighted, huh?" I said, tearing my eyes away from his crotch.

He snapped his head upward to meet my grin. "Yeah," he said, sheepishly. "I hate bifocals."

"My father sure hates his," I said, raising my eyes to the V of his shirt, where hairless bronze skin met my eyes.

His eyes narrowed. "Thanks for reminding me that I'm old." He walked back down the aisle.

"I'm sorry," I said, taking a step after him. "I didn't mean to insult you. I don't think there's anything wrong with getting older."

"That's because you're still under 30," he said, placing the box back on the shelf and walking away.

Hmm, I said to myself. *You sure blew that one. He was really hot.*

Now wait a minute, my rational mind argued. *You're taken, and you know it. Were you going to flirt with him?*

Nothing wrong with that, I shot back. *No harm done.*

(Unfortunately, I have these kinds of arguments with myself all the time.)

Uh, huh. You'd have ended up on your knees in front of him, and then *what kind of harm would have been done?*

Shut up! I thought. *Nothing happened!*

Oh, right. Weren't you lucky?

I can be a real prick with myself when I want to be.

I put the box back and wandered off down the aisle. I soon found the paper section and for a few minutes shopped for just the right hue and weight, finally deciding on a bright white for the presentation due on Monday. Dennis was out of town, and I planned to use the time wisely; by the time he got back from Chicago on Sunday night, I would have everything finished and be on my knees at the front door in my leathers, just the way he liked me.

I rounded a corner and nearly bumped into him. "Oops!" I said, narrowly missing his elbow, which was planted on one hip.

"Careful." The tone was guarded.

"Sorry." I walked past him, stopped at the binders, quickly picking out the size but wrestling for several minutes over the color. Black or blue or green? I couldn't decide but finally closed my eyes and reached for one. Green it would be.

"What was that?" he asked. My head jerked up to find him watching me, amused.

As I blushed I said, "I have a big presentation due Monday. It's got me spooked, and I couldn't decide on the color, so I just closed my eyes and let chance decide."

He chuckled. "Ah, the scientific method."

"Forgiven my faux pas?"

"Not yet."

A little chill ran down my spine as he continued to stare at me, boring those bright green eyes into mine. I actually felt my knees begin to tremble as I opened my mouth to speak.

"You don't have to say anything," he said, and he lowered his voice as he continued. "I saw how you were looking at me back there." He pulled on his cock through the fabric, and I nearly fainted. "You want some of this?"

I opened my mouth, but no words would come out.

"C'mon, kid." His voice was edgy, impatient. "I know you want it. All you have to do is say where and when."

I finally stammered out, "I'm sorry. I can't."

"Prick tease," he spat, looking down at the crotch of my shorts. "Your cock's hard," which was true. "Don't tell me you don't want it."

"I didn't say I didn't want it," I whispered. "I said I can't. I belong to someone else."

"Humph," he snorted, and stomped off down the aisle.

With shaky hands, I gathered the dozen binders I'd need and realized I would have to get a basket to carry all my stuff.

I walked down the main aisle, looking for the carts at the front door. He was paying for something but didn't look up as I passed within ten feet of him.

An hour later I'd finally calmed down and made all the decisions I needed to make for Monday. I paid a whopping total, praying I would get the account, if for no other reason than that Dennis would kill me if I spent this much money and didn't get it. I walked to my car, put the stuff in the trunk, and walked around to unlock my door.

"Let's try this again," he said.

I nearly fell backward in surprise as I looked up to see him standing beside me. "What do you want?" I said, the trembling returning in an instant.

"I told you, boy. I want to get deep down your throat."

"Forget it," I said.

"Not interested?" he sneered. He knew I was.

"I'm not so stupid to fuck up what I have for a ten-minute quickie. Now get away from my car door. I'm leaving." He stepped back, and I got in my car. I'd left the window down because it was so damned hot outside, and he seized the opportunity, leaning in and licking my left ear as I started the car.

"C'mon, boy. Make me feel good."

I hit the power button and rolled up my window, nearly trapping his head between the glass and the door frame.

"Bitch!" he cried as he stumbled back from the window. I put the car in gear and sped away, leaving him standing there.

I watched my rearview mirror all the way home, looking for some sign that he was following me, but as I pulled into the garage and shut the door behind me, I felt relatively sure I was alone and unwatched.

Two hours later I was deep into writing copy for the presentation, when the phone rang. I almost ignored it but finally decided that Dennis may have gotten a minute away from the other conventioneers.

"Yeah?"

"Hello, David."

"Who is this?"

"Polyester pants and a striped shirt ring a bell?" I dropped the phone, then picked it up and put it back in the cradle. A moment later, it rang again. I let the machine pick it up.

Dennis's recorded voice said, "Look, if you're selling something, get the fuck off our line. If you're related, leave a message. If you're a friend, you know why we're not answering the phone, so hang up and leave us to it!" My laughter in the background was cut off by the beep.

"Dennis has a sexy voice," he said. "The spelling of his last name is odd, don't you think? I mean, M-c-F-a-r-o-n is not the spelling you usually encounter..."

I grabbed the phone. "Who the fuck are you?" I yelled.

"My name is Frank."

"Frank who? How do you know who we are?"

"I have a friend at the DMV. I give him head, and he gives me names and addresses from license plates. A city directory fills in the blanks."

"Get the fuck off my phone. I told you I'm not going to do anything with you."

"Oh, but you are, David. You're going to meet me and do whatever I want you to do or I'll call Dennis and tell him we're doing lots of nasty things together. How do you think he'll take that news?"

"We aren't doing anything together. And we're not going to..."

He cut me off. "Does that matter? I can fake the details enough to make him believe it's happening. You're pretty good-looking, David. Dimes to doughnuts Dennis is jealous of you, especially since you said you 'belonged' to him. Masters are usually pretty protective of their slaves. Who do you think he'll believe? You or another master?"

"Please don't do this," I said, nearly in tears. "I don't want to..."

"It doesn't matter what you want," he said. "You don't have a choice. I'm going to have you, and you're gonna love sitting on my thick cock."

I hung up. The phone rang again immediately. I reached back and unplugged the cord.

I tried to work but was so upset that I couldn't concentrate. Then I began to worry that Dennis would call and not get the machine. Three hours later I was so frightened that I plugged the cord back into the handset. It rang and startled me so badly that I dropped it.

I picked it up and said, "Hello?"

"Hey, boy, what's up?"

"Dennis!"

"Why did you have the machine off, and where the fuck have you been? I've been trying to call for an hour!"

"I'm sorry, Sir."

"That's not an explanation. What gives?" *This is it,* I thought. *Tell him about the maniac and defuse the situation right now.* But I said nothing.

"What's your hesitation, boy? Hiding something from your Daddy?"

"No, Sir," I said, and fell silent again. *What's wrong,* my mind screamed. *Tell him!* But I lied instead. "I came in, listened to messages, then forgot to hit the button. I'm sorry, Sir."

"Well, why didn't you answer the phone?"

"I went out again. I forgot some stuff at the office supply, and you know how I am when I get in one of those places."

"David, it's after 10 o'clock."

"They're open all night, Daddy." *Why doesn't he believe me?* I thought.

Maybe because you're lying to him, you stupid shit, I shot back at myself.

"Oh," Dennis said.

We talked another ten minutes, then he said he had to get to bed. "Are you going too?" he said.

"No, I'm already behind on the proposal. I spent too much time at that fucking store. I'll probably work all night, then crash till 3 or 4 tomorrow afternoon."

"Well, I'll be busy all day, so I'll call tomorrow night at the same time. You be there, you hear?"

"Yes, Sir."

"Now, you know what to do, don't you, boy?"

"Yes, Sir." I began to speak softly to him, describing how wonderful it was to serve him, to work at making his cock feel good, and he moaned softly as he stroked himself. His breath became uneven as I described what I would be wearing when he arrived Sunday night, and he grunted as he came while I talked about his cock up my ass.

"I wish I was there to lick it up, Sir," I whispered.

"Hmm, yeah, boy, I wish you were too. I'd have done a lot more than jerk off."

"Yes, Sir."

"Good night, boy."

"Good night, Daddy." And he hung up on me.

I hung up the phone, a tear sliding down my cheek. The phone rang again, and I picked it up.

"Daddy?" I said, but he cut me off.

"I'm not your Daddy. But I am gonna be your Master. Now get your ass…" I hung up on him and unplugged the phone again.

I went to bed around 3:30 and slept until noon. I got up, dove back into the project, and made good progress until I realized I was hungry. I got a bite to eat, then took a shower. I was heading back to the computer when the doorbell sounded.

I walked to the door, looking out the peephole. He'd changed into a red muscle shirt, and I couldn't see down far enough to check out what kind of pants he was wearing, but I didn't care. I walked away, making enough noise on the ceramic tile floor that he would know I wasn't going to answer the door. The doorbell rang again and again.

I plugged the phone in and picked it up to dial the police. The thought of what I would say to them made me put the receiver back in its cradle. The doorbell rang, and I went back the front door. I always keep the storm door locked, and I was relatively sure he couldn't break it down—it's a security door— so I yanked the door open, hoping to startle him.

"Get the fuck off my property," I hissed through clenched teeth. "If you think I won't call the police..."

"Shut up, David. You won't do any such thing. You probably already went to the phone and then changed your mind. Otherwise, you wouldn't have opened the door."

My eyes fell to the ground, noting the running shorts he was wearing and the beat-up running shoes on his feet. There seemed to be no hair on his body, and I wondered idly if he shaved it.

"Look at me." I raised my head to meet his eyes, but they burned so bright I couldn't hold his gaze, and I looked down again.

"You're going to open this door, and I'm gonna have a good time with your hole. If you don't, I just might break it down, and how would you explain that to Dennis?"

"You know," I said, my voice shaking, "I know a lot of guys who'd be enjoying this. Slaves talk to each other, just like Masters do. Some guys get off on rape fantasies. I don't."

"Then why is your cock hard?" I looked down to see that he was telling the truth—the head of my cock was sticking out of the fly of my boxers. I began to cry softly.

"Please," I whispered. "Don't make me do this."

"You want it." His voice was low, his tone carefully measured. "You've wanted it since I grabbed my cock yesterday afternoon. Now open the door, David, and let me in."

I'll never know why, but my right hand reached up and unlocked the door. He slowly turned the knob and walked in, turning to shut the door behind him. By the time he turned back to me, I was on my knees, my head bowed.

He put a hand on my head, gently grabbing my hair and pulling back until my eyes met his. With his free hand he was kneading his cock through his shorts.

"You are to be totally passive, David. You'll do nothing of your own accord; you'll only do what you're told to do. If you so much as lick a nipple you've not been told to lick, I'll bruise your ass so badly that Dennis won't waste a minute throwing you out his front door." A tear slid down my cheek, but he let go of his cock, caught the tear on his finger, and brushed it away.

"That's it, boy. Give in to me." He released the handful of hair and let me bow my head again. My eyes were open, and I saw his shorts fall around his ankles. His shirt landed beside his foot; he stepped out of his shorts, then used a toe to pry off one shoe. Shifting his weight, he pried off the other shoe. My nose was assaulted with the strong aroma, and my mouth actually began to water.

"On the floor. Flat. Hands behind your back." I followed his order, and he slid his left foot under my face. I inhaled deeply, holding the breath until he spoke.

"Clean the top of that foot, boy." I opened my mouth and began to tongue his foot slowly, carefully. When it was clean he put his other foot beneath my face, and I cleaned that one too. My cock was painfully hard beneath me.

He barked, "Back on your knees. Keep your hands behind you. Face me. Open your mouth."

I looked up to behold his cock and sucked in my breath in wonder. *He could be a porn star,* was my first thought. My second thought was to be glad that Dennis was well-hung; otherwise, this cock would have torn me apart.

His cock was amazingly wide at the root, tapering out about nine inches to a still-fat head peeking out from under a thick flap of skin. Large testicles hung suspended in a loose sac, swinging back and forth behind his cock, which was hard enough to stand away from his body. He certainly gave lie to the notion that bodybuilders pumped up to make up for small cocks. As he took a step toward me, I wondered if he'd ever tried to stuff it into a posing strap.

My mouth fell open, and he put a hand behind my head. Pushing back on my forehead with his other hand, he adjusted his angle of entry as he shoved his cock down my throat. I took more than half of it before he stopped to pull out and look down at me.

"Your Daddy must be hung too." I didn't respond, and he grabbed his cock and guided it down my throat again. It was slick from the first descent, and he managed to get most of it down my throat on the second try. I gagged mightily, and he pulled back far enough to give me a little relief. Then he pushed a third time, and I had all of him.

We both held still a moment; I was afraid to move, and he seemed to enjoy just being inside me. Then he pulled back slightly, pushed forward and ground his pubic hair against my nose; it seemed to be the only hair on his body that he'd allowed to grow. I tried to moan in pleasure, but his cock cut off all sound.

Then he pulled all the way out and slid back in, hard and fast. I was not prepared for that and gagged, but he ignored me, pulling back and slamming his cock down my throat again. I tasted bile in the back of my throat, but he was relentless as he fucked my face. By the time he stopped to catch his breath, tears ran freely down my face.

He looked down at me. "I said, 'Hands behind you!'" One of my hands had begun to reach for my cock, which was painful in its hardness now. He slapped my face hard enough to get my undivided attention.

"I'm hot. You want my load?" I shook my head. "Fair enough." He slid his cock back down my throat, grabbing my head with both hands.

He fucked me hard again and stretched out my throat as far as it could go. After a minute he pulled back and shot all over my chest, the gooey stuff sliding slowly down to catch in my boxers. It was a large load; he let go of my head with one hand, using it to milk out every drop, smearing semen on my cheeks and forehead, sneering at me as he ran the softening shaft over my face.

Finally, he released me and bent to gather up his shorts and shirt. He dressed as I sat back on the floor, my hands still behind me.

When he was ready to leave, he said, "I'll be back tonight about 9. You clean yourself out good, or you'll be sorry."

"Dennis is supposed to call me at 10."

"So? Maybe you'll talk to him with my cock up your ass." He turned and let himself out the door, slamming it behind him.

I got up and went to the shower, soaping my chest to rid myself of him. Then I dried off and went back to the computer, trying to pick up where I'd left off.

By 8:55 I'd shut down the computer, taken another shower, shaved my ass, crotch and balls, and then cleaned myself out as instructed. I put chaps on over my slave harness, placed a two-inch stretcher on my balls, then slid a well-greased butt plug into place. I snapped a leather sheath over my cock, then slid my feet into my boots. It was the same stuff I wore when Dennis was coming home; I felt guilty but knew I had to get excited if his cock was going to fit up my ass. The knock at the door came right as my hall clock began to chime the hour. I took a hit of aroma and opened the door.

He tried to remain impassive, but I could tell he was impressed by what he saw. He stepped inside, magnificent-looking in a Gold's Gym muscle shirt and tight biker's shorts, the sheen from the nylon highlighting the bulge running down his left leg.

Shutting the door behind him, he said, "Strip me." I knelt and untied his running shoes, carefully pulling out the laces so that his feet would slip easily out of them, then stood and pulled the shirt over his head.

His chest could have graced the cover of a magazine, even though his skin had lost some of its tone. The bronze tan was even over the expanse of his chest, and the muscles rippled as he raised his hands over his head to allow the shirt to slide off. I hooked my thumbs in his shorts, kneeling as I pulled them to the floor. The movement pushed the plug deeper into my ass, and I groaned softly.

He stepped out of the shorts. "Tonight, you're to be as active as you were passive this afternoon. If I get the idea that you're bailing out on me at any time, I'll strap you till you're bloody."

I stood and attacked a nipple, licking and sucking on it as he raised an arm again. I dived for his pit and sucked in the few strands of hair that had been allowed to grow there, delighted to find some hair on him. Then he raised the other arm, and I walked around his broad chest to clean that pit too.

I tongued my way back across his pecs and then down his abdomen, feeling his cock hardening against my chest. As my knees hit the floor, he groaned and said, "Get your fucking mouth open."

I swallowed as much of his cock as I could. We groaned together, and I pulled back only long enough to lube the shaft with my tongue before plunging down on him again.

"Lead me to the bedroom." I crawled ahead of him, and he bent to wiggle the plug in my ass as I made my way down the hall. I'd stripped the bed and put on the leather mattress cover. The air conditioner was blowing full blast, and the room was cool, for now.

He fell back on the bed. The springs complained beneath his weight as he spread his legs and grabbed his cock. "Come here and make love to this." I ran my tongue up his left leg until I met his balls, sucking one into my mouth and rolling it around.

I repeated the action with his other nut, then sucked both large orbs inside me. He liked that and reached down to push my face away from him, stretching his sack tightly. I held fast to his balls, and he pulled on the skin until it was shiny with my spit, then grabbed my hair and pulled me back to his crotch. I inhaled deeply, whimpering in pleasure.

He used the handful of hair to guide me up to his cock. I opened my mouth and tried to swallow all of him in one gulp. He chuckled, moving his hand to the back of my neck and holding me down on his cock until my lungs screamed for air. When he let go I shot up off him for oxygen, then dived quickly back down, lest he think I wasn't interested.

We repeated that action several times, and tears smeared my face again. Then he pushed me off his crotch and sat on the edge of the bed.

"Get that plug out of your ass. I want in." I had put condoms and lube on the dresser; as I unsnapped the holding strap and gently slid the plug out of my ass, he ripped open a package with his teeth and rolled an extralarge condom down the shaft, grunting as the tight latex gripped his skin.

I got down on my knees in front of him and lubed the rubber, stroking it slowly with my hand to coat it evenly.

"On the bed. Flat on your stomach." I pushed myself over the edge of the mattress and slid onto the bed. I spread my legs as wide as they would go, then stretched my arms up over my head.

"Looks good, boy. Good enough to fuck." He knelt between my legs, positioning himself over me.

He must do this a lot, I mused as he settled his weight onto my back, because his cock slid neatly into my hole as he stretched himself out atop me. His cock was completely inside me before I realized it, and my cock strained painfully against the tight sheath that encased it. Buckles and grommets bit into my skin, but I didn't care. I welcomed all the sensations of his fucking of my ass.

He flexed his pelvis and his cock left, then entered me again. I cried out in pleasure, and he reached beneath me and stuffed his fingers in my mouth. I sucked greedily as he began to fuck me.

I was hot, really hot; I wanted him to fuck me hard with that big pole, but he was determined to make it last, cuffing the back of my head if I moved too urgently beneath him. I tried to thrust against his pelvis, but he let his weight fall on me, and it was all I could do to keep breathing.

Finally, he got to the point where he was ready to ride me. Placing a fist in each of my armpits, he got up on his knees and began to piston in and out of my burning hole. I started to weep from sheer pleasure, muttering, "Fuck me. Oh, please, fuck me," over and over.

Then the phone rang. I jumped, scalded by the sound alone, but he didn't seem surprised. After all, I'd told him Dennis was going to call.

The phone was within my reach, but he leaned over to grab it as it rang again.

"Please, no!" I whispered urgently. The phone rang a third time. One more ring and the machine would pick up.

He laughed. "I promise to be quiet." And he picked up the receiver just as it began to ring again, handing it to me.

I was panting, but I managed a "Hello."

"Out of breath?" Dennis was laughing.

"I was in the basement," I lied.

"Oh, really?" he said. "Sounds like something else." He spoke for a few minutes, telling me about the conference. Frank was still above me, his cock deep in my ass. I couldn't take a deep breath because of his weight and his fullness in my ass, and oxygen became more and more important as Dennis droned on about a speaker he'd heard.

Finally, I couldn't take any more. I held the phone away from my mouth, forced Frank up off me, and took several gasping breaths. Frank let me do that; then, as I put the phone back to my ear, he pulled back and slammed his cock back in to the hilt. The springs complained and, despite my best intentions, I groaned in pleasure.

"What the fuck was that?" Dennis said, instantly suspicious.

"Nothing, Daddy, I'm sorry."

"Are you playing with yourself, boy?"

"No, Sir." At least that was the truth—my cock was smashed beneath us, with no hope of my hand reaching it.

"I know you inside and out, slave, and I know what that groan means. Now get your fucking hand off your cock."

"I'm not playing with myself, Sir, honest." Frank chose that moment to stroke me again, and I caught the groan in my throat, making it come out as a cough. The springs gave me away, though.

"David, you tell me what the fuck is going on. I just heard the bed springs creak." He paused a moment, then spoke again.

"Is someone there with you." It wasn't a question, more of a statement to which he expected an answer.

"No!" I cried. Frank stroked me again, harder than ever, but I was too frightened to enjoy that one. I decided a big lie was in order.

"I'm sitting on a dildo, sir. The big one. It's taken me 20 minutes to get it inside me; I wanted to get it in before you called, but I didn't quite make it. I forced it in just a minute ago; that's why I groaned."

He paused. "And what about the springs?"

"I'm kneeling on the bed. I bounced up off it and the springs creaked."

He sighed, and what he said next knocked the breath out of me as surely as if he'd punched me in the stomach.

"Let me talk to Frank." I began a full-body tremble, and a sob escaped my lips as I handed the phone over my back to Frank, who was still thrusting gently in my hole.

"Hi, Dennis." He listened for a moment, then said, "Sure thing," and placed the phone back in its cradle.

"Dennis is pissed that you didn't tell him the truth. He wants me to get the dildo you lied about to him and shove it up your ass." He pulled out of me, my ass aching at his absence, and walked to the closet, yanking the door open with one meaty hand and reaching inside with the other.

He pulled out a dildo Dennis had bought for me on a trip to San Francisco. It had taken me weeks to stretch out enough to take its nearly four-inch diameter. We only used it as a prelude to his fist going up my ass; my trembling intensified as Frank pulled out a tub of Elbow Grease and began coating the pink monster.

I knew better than to resist, so I rolled over onto my back and lifted my legs, grabbing my ankles. Frank knelt between my legs, breaking open a capsule of amyl he'd found beside the Elbow Grease. I inhaled deeply at his command, and my head exploded as he placed the dildo at my entrance and began to apply pressure.

It took several minutes and many well-placed blows from Frank's palms on my tits and the globes of my ass, but I finally opened enough for the head of the dildo to slide in. My cock, rock-hard in its leather prison, expanded to an even greater girth, the sewn seam of the sheath biting into the side of my shaft. I screamed, and Frank put the capsule back under my nose as he pushed another inch of the dildo inside me. The phone rang again, and Frank handed it to me.

"Daddy!" I screamed in pain and pleasure.

"Boy, now tell me the truth. What's going on?"

"Frank has the dildo—a-u-u-ugh!—nearly all the way inside me, Sir! Oh, God! A-u-u-ugh! It's so fucking big!"

Frank pushed again, hard, and my prostate could take no more. With a yell that should have broken the diaphragm inside the phone, I came into the sheath, shooting out great gobs of semen that quickly coated my shaft. Frank grabbed me with his free hand and pumped, and my scream became a wail of pleasure. Still working my cock, Frank let the dildo slide back out of me slowly as I came down from the poppers and the intensity of my orgasm.

After a minute I realized that Dennis was still on the phone. When I could speak I croaked, "What was this, a setup?"

Dennis chuckled. "Not really. He's an old friend. He saw us at the bar not long ago and liked your look. He mentioned that he'd like to have you. But his running into you at the store was a fluke.

"He called my office and they told him I was in Chicago. He called my cell phone and dragged me out of a conference. I said yes. Is that OK, baby? I know you look at other guys but don't touch. I wanted to reward you for that. You're such a good boy."

"He scared the shit out of me," I said, then gasped as Frank slid his cock back inside me.

"Is he fucking you again with that big cock, boy?" Dennis's voice was almost a whisper.

"Yes, Daddy," I whispered back.

"Well, I think you know what you should do," he groaned, and I began to talk softly to him. He and Frank managed to come together, Frank growling as he filled the condom deep inside me, while Dennis yelled into the phone from the intensity of his own orgasm.

Then they were both still. Dennis said, "I still expect you to be at the door, in your leather, on your knees, when I get home tomorrow night."

"Yes, Sir," I said, my eyes filling with tears. "Thank you, Sir."

"And if Frank wants to be standing behind you, I won't mind."

"Yes, Sir."

"Good night, boy."

"Good night, Daddy." I hung up as Frank stretched out on the bed beside me. He pulled my head into his armpit, and my last conscious thought that night was a realization that I hadn't finished preparing my presentation.

Needless to say, I didn't get the account.

Like I cared.

Requiem for a Punk
By Thomas S. Roche

Nobody writes violent, sexy stories quite like Thomas Roche. This hard-boiled tale of a gunsel on the run is no exception. It is, like a Beretta, sleek, deadly, and rock-hard.

"I'm a dead man," Kenny moaned, raw terror in his voice. "I'm a fucking dead man."

He was wearing a torn white T-shirt, and he looked like he'd slept in the street. His black leather jacket was cracked and mottled with dirt and corrosion, and he didn't look like such a badass in that jacket now.

"Hey, relax," I told him, patting him on the shoulder and handing him a glass of Old Crow. He drank it all down in one gulp, his hands trembling. The sharp smell of his fear filled the tiny apartment. I sat down on the coffee table and squeezed his arm. "What the fuck is up? Why would Lucky Joe want to kill you? You're one of his best runners, Kenny."

Kenny was out of it, sobbing hysterically. I'd always known the kid would crack under pressure, but God help me, I'd vouched for him anyway. When I brought him in I knew I was gonna be sorry one day, but I just couldn't say no to that fuckin' kid. It wasn't just those fuckin' dopey, shit-stupid blue eyes that I could spend a whole year looking into; it wasn't just those big full lips or that tight ass of his or those tight jeans he wore. It was the way the whole package fit together into the finest punk piece of ass this side of the Hudson River.

Not that I'd had him, mind you. First off, the motherfucker acted straight as an arrow, not that I don't, but I saw not one hint that he swung the same way as I did. And besides, I don't mix business with pleasure unless absolutely necessary. And with Kenny I'd always figured it wouldn't be necessary. Now I was beginning to have second thoughts.

He just rocked back and forth and kept repeating, "Lucky Joe's gonna kill me. He's gonna fuckin' kill me. You gotta help me, Nick, you gotta fuckin' help me!"

I smacked him good, across the face.

He blinked at me, stunned, with those dumb-as-dirt blue eyes. I smacked him again, grabbed him by the shoulders and shook him. The kid just rattled back and forth in my grasp like an old rag doll. "Get a fuckin' hold of yourself, you pansy motherfucker!" I shouted into his face. "What the hell did you do this time, you fuckup? Did you screw around with the receipts?"

Kenny was silent for an instant, like he was getting his wits about him. "Just a little," he finally mumbled, looking embarrassed, his face turning red. "I didn't think anyone would notice. How the fuck did he figure it out? It was only $20, Nicky, how did they figure it out?"

Another smack, this time with my fist. Kenny groaned softly and sprawled out on the couch, blood leaking from his lip. I stood over him raising my fist, then thought better about it and just leaned down and screamed in his face. "You fucking stupid fuck! A dollar here, a dollar there, that's how Lucky Joe built his fucking empire, motherfucker! Micks and Polacks puttin' down their pocket change! You think he doesn't know that if you get away with it, pretty soon everyone'll get away with it and then he'll hafta fuckin' change his nickname?"

I stopped yelling at him, staring at his pathetic, shaking form on the couch. I instinctively felt in my pocket for my smokes, but I was wearing that ratty old bathrobe my mother gave me and there were none in there. Cursing, I stormed over to my little metal desk and looked in the drawer—pay dirt. Unfiltered Pall Malls. I shook one out and lit it. I was fighting the urge to wring Kenny's neck, but I had to admit it wasn't 'cause I was just mad. I was fuckin' scared for him. So help me God I still liked the little fucker; however many times he fucked up I wanted him worse than anything.

My own hands trembling with rage and fear, I took out a second Pall Mall, lit it, and handed it to Kenny.

"You know how deep you're in shit this time, don't you, Kenny?"

Kenny just sobbed there on the couch, "I'm sorry, I'm sorry, I'm sorry. You gotta help me, Nicky, please help me!"

"Take the fucking cigarette before I burn my fingers, punk." I said it with quiet menace in my voice.

Kenny obeyed, huddling on the couch, bogarting the cig like it was his last link to sanity.

"I didn't mean to take it, Nick, honest I didn't. It's just…it was a mistake, yeah, that's it, a mistake! Just an honest mistake!"

This time I smacked him so good the cigarette went flying across the room and landed on the carpet. I walked over and stomped it out.

"Come on, Kenny! I don't believe that shit any more than Joe's going to. Why'd you take the money?"

"It was…it was this prostitute, see…"

"Jesus fucking Christ," I groaned. "You stole a 20 from Lucky Joe Rossi so you could see a fuckin' chick?"

"Not a chick," he said sheepishly. "It was a guy."

That's when I started laughing, and pretty soon I was hysterical. Kenny just curled up on the couch and said, "I'm sorry, Nicky, I'm sorry."

I sat down next to him and patted his ass. "Well, whatever the fuck you're sorry for," I finally coughed, blinking with tear-filled eyes, "don't be sorry for that. Perfectly good reason to place yourself in grave jeopardy. I've done the same fucking thing for a few street hustlers myself, specially when I was young and stupid like you. Now if it'd been some fuckin' tart..."

Kenny stared at me, his eyes red-rimmed and incredulous. He sat up.

"Look, Kenny. Tell you what. You get some sleep. You're gonna have to lie low for a while, but that's OK; I got it all figured out. There's this place I got up in the mountains, about 6½ hours away. Nobody knows about it, not Joe, not Rocco, not anybody. I'm gonna set you up there while I come back to town and smooth things over with Lucky Joe. We'll have you home by the end of the week, OK?"

Kenny leaned back on the couch and he looked plenty damn fine in those torn jeans. "You mean it, Nicky? You'll help me out?"

"I'll fuckin' save your sorry ass is what I'll do, pal! Meanwhile, try to get some sleep."

A curious look passed over Kenny's face. It was one I recognized.

"I'm not much in the mood for sleep," he said, looking me over.

I'm a weak man, OK? I know it was exactly the wrong thing to do in that circumstance. But I reached out and grabbed Kenny's long feathered hair and pulled him against me. Then I pressed my mouth to his, tasting his tongue and reaching down to grab a great big hard-on through his worn, faded jeans. Kenny was hung like a horse, a fact I'd noted plenty of times when I'd seen him around the back room of Lucky Joe's restaurant.

"You know, some guys get hard when they're scared," I told him when our mouths finally parted, a string of saliva glistening between them. "I'm surprised you didn't come in your fuckin' pants."

"Me too," said Kenny, leaning forward and kissing me again. He reached out and undid the tie of my robe, letting it fall open. He reached out for my prick, which was rapidly getting hard.

"Jesus," he said with a little shiver. "You sleep naked?"

"Ever hopeful," I told him, and stood up, pushing his face down onto my cock. He went right to work and took it in his mouth, pumping back and forth as it hardened all the way. Kenny whimpered and took it down his throat like it was all he was meant to do in life.

"Oh, yeah," I grunted as I pistoned my hips against him, thrusting my cock harder as the pleasure built. It looked like that hustler of his didn't do all the work. But I wasn't going to let that little cocksucker get the best of me.

"Get your clothes off," I told him. "But leave the jacket on. I've wanted to fuck you wearing that fuckin' jacket since I first laid eyes on you."

Kenny looked a little embarrassed for a moment. But he obeyed me, grabbing his belt and unfastening it, unzipping, pulling down his pants. He was in such a rush to get undressed that he pulled his jeans off over his sneakers and climbed onto the couch with his sneakers still on.

He struggled out of the jacket and shucked his T-shirt, then put the jacket back on. I tossed off my robe and stood there naked behind him, working my cock. I looked up and down the rough outline of the worn leather jacket, loving how tight it was around his lower back, the way the black leather melded with the curve of his ass. I ran my hand up his inner thigh and reached between his legs, grabbing his balls and squeezing. Kenny gave a little whimper of pain as I squeezed harder and harder. Then I started slapping his balls, listening to the moans as Kenny's cock jerked in time with my abuse.

I wrapped my hand around his meat and stroked him while I formed a good ball of spit and let it dribble onto my hard organ. I climbed onto the couch behind Kenny and worked the spittle all over my prick. Kenny gritted his teeth as I nestled the cock head into his cleft. His ass felt good and tight as I penetrated him, and as it went in all the way, Kenny let out a low, rapturous moan. Then I gripped his waist, feeling the tight belt of the leather jacket, feeling my prick surge in response to its texture. I fucked Kenny good and hard, pounding him in long strokes while I reached around his body to work his shaft. He was the first one to come, shooting long streams all over my ratty orange sofa, and I got as much come as I could on my right hand and grabbed Kenny's hair with my left, leaning forward so that I could rub that come all over his face. He lapped at it, groaning as I kept pounding into him, and the sight of that boy with his face all glistening and covered with jizz was enough to send me off the edge. My cock spasmed and I shot deep into Kenny's asshole, shuddering as I released everything I'd ever had into that boy's lithe, well-muscled body.

By the time Kenny and I had finished a few more whiskeys in the darkness, both our cocks were hard again. So Kenny sucked me off, tasting the musk and shit of his own ass as he rubbed himself. We both came, and Kenny lay there on top of me. By that time it was almost light, and Kenny dropped off to sleep.

I eased myself out from under him and went into the bedroom. I sat on my bed and drank another whiskey, running over it all in my head. Then I got out a fresh pair of pants and a shirt, put on a sports jacket and slipped on my shoes. I went into the top drawer of my dresser and took out the twin .22s I kept in there. I made sure each was loaded and put one in each jacket pocket.

I had to pass Kenny on the way out, and his eyes fluttered open. His eyes suddenly got big and scared.

"Wh—where're you going, Nicky?"

"Hey, relax, I'm just going out to get more smokes. We're gonna need them on the drive up."

"Hey, you shouldn't have to do that—why don't I go out for you?"

I rolled my eyes. "Relax, Kenny."

"Then mind if I come with you?"

"Look, you stupid motherfucker. If Lucky Joe's looking for you, he's got my place covered. You're just fuckin' lucky you didn't get yourself sprayed with a Thompson when you showed up here last night! You are not going to set foot outside this fuckin' apartment until I bring the car around for you, OK? Be ready in 15 minutes."

"But—" Kenny started to mumble, and I shot him a particularly vicious look. He fell silent.

"Stop being such a stupid fuck," I growled affectionately. "You're gonna get yourself killed, and I'm starting to like that tight ass of yours."

I left him sitting there looking glum on the couch. I went down to the liquor store on the corner and bought three packs of smokes. As I walked, I looked around for a familiar black Buick, or maybe a Packard.

I found it.

I stopped in the diner across the street, which was just opening for breakfast. My stomach was rumbling, but I didn't stop for food. I went to the phones in the back and called Lucky Joe.

I brought the Caddy around back and parked it with the hazards on. The meter maid in the neighborhood is on Lucky Joe's payroll, so it was no big deal. I went up the back stairs to my apartment and let myself in.

Kenny was sitting on the couch with his jeans on and no shirt or shoes. He had my .45 in his trembling hand and he was pointing at me.

Goddamn it, I knew I should have taken the fucking thing.

"You called Lucky Joe," Kenny moaned pathetically. "They're coming right now to kill me."

I spoke in my most soothing voice. "Kenny, Kenny, put that fucking thing away. You ain't shot a gun in your fucking life. You aren't going to shoot me now."

"Oh, yeah?" he choked, and raised the gun. His eyes were red and tears were forming. "Try me."

"Kenny, relax! Put the gun down! Those fuckin' Colts have a way of going off, OK? Why the fuck would I call Lucky Joe?"

Kenny didn't put the gun down. "Maybe now that you've fucked me you don't give a shit!"

I laughed, inching closer to him. "That's bullshit. I'm not going to hurt you, Kenny!"

"Damn right you aren't," he sobbed. "'Cause I'm gonna kill you first!"

That's when I hit the ground and reached up for the gun. He pulled the trigger, but the stupid fuck had the safety on. I came up and kicked him in the balls, yanking the pistol out of his grasp.

I flicked the safety off, knelt over Kenny's squirming form, and stuck the muzzle of the gun in his mouth.

"You gotta take the safety off," I told him. "Now if I was gonna deliver you to Lucky Joe, why wouldn't I just blow your fuckin' brains out right now, motherfucker, and say you gave me a struggle? Then I could fuck your dead body for all anyone would care, asshole!"

My finger tightened on the trigger.

Kenny quivered underneath me, his eyes flashing "I'm sorry."

I pulled the gun out of his mouth and said, in the softest, most compassionate voice I could manage: "Get your fuckin' clothes on. We've got some driving to do."

My little show of dominance must have persuaded Kenny to roll over, because he didn't give me any more trouble on the way up. I even let him piss on his own, half hoping he would run away into the woods and get his sorry punk ass eaten by a bear. But he didn't.

Instead, he acted like we'd been best friends since childhood. By now I was convinced that Kenny was totally schizophrenic. But he gave me a blow job during one of our pit stops, so that kept me kindly disposed toward him—up to a point.

As we got closer to the cabin, I could feel the weight of the .22s in my jacket pockets, the bulk of the .45 Colt stuffed into my waistband.

I thought about Kenny's dying in the cold dirt of the mountains. I could almost smell his piss and shit and blood.

It was late in the day when we pulled off the remote mountain road and parked in front of the cabin. I fished in my pants pocket for the key and walked up the stairs. At the landing I waited for Kenny.

"Come on, punk, I ain't got all day." Kenny climbed the stairs wearily and followed me into the cabin.

Inside, it was dark. Kenny had just closed the front door when Rocco Morelli's voice, rough as sandpaper, said, "Hello, Kenny." Tony Brakes grabbed Kenny's arms as Rocco hit him hard on the side of the head, and Kenny went limp in Tony's arms.

"Afternoon, Nicky," said Rocco. "Pleasure to be working with you again."

I shook his hand. "Likewise," I said. "Listen, I want to be the one to do this fuckin' punk, OK? I got a bullet with his name on it."

"Be our guest," said Rocco. "For us, it's business—not pleasure. So be our guest." He laughed.

Kenny wasn't out for long. By the time he came to in the trunk of the Caddy, we were deep in the middle of nowhere and the sun was going down. We could hear him pounding against the trunk, trying to get out, but we didn't bother to knock him out again.

"He's thrashing around like a dying fish," chuckled Rocco, with a cruel twist to his lips. He tossed a cig out the window of the Caddy and lit another one.

"Yeah," I said. "Just like a fucking fish."

Kenny was sobbing as we made him dig his own grave. "Why are you doing this to me?" he kept asking. "Nicky, Nicky, make 'em stop! You promised you'd smooth things over with Lucky Joe for me! Please, you gotta give me a break! You can't just fuckin' kill me like this!"

About the hundredth time Kenny said that, Rocco started shooting. Chunks of dirt sprayed up inches from Kenny's foot, but none of the shots hit him. Rocco always was one hell of a shot.

"Come on, you fuckin' punk, shut the fuck up and dig faster. We ain't got all night!"

I was afraid Kenny might start spewing shit about what we did the night before, trying to beg for his life. And I knew that might cause me more than a little discomfort with Rocco and Tony. But for whatever reason—and I never really did figure this out—Kenny didn't say a thing about that. As much as he blabbed, he never did say anything about the fact that he had my cock in his ass less than 12 hours before.

So when it came time to do him, to put him in the ground, I guess I felt more than a little guilty.

"Just like I told you, boys. I want to put the bullet in this fucking punk's head."

"Be our guest."

Kenny stood sobbing at the edge of the hole in the ground, waiting for the impact of the bullets to push him into the grave. I lifted the .45 as Rocco lit a cigarette.

I sighted Kenny's head with the Colt, let the tension build as Kenny shook and blubbered.

"Just kill 'im already," grunted Tony.

I pulled the trigger of the .45 and one of the .22s at the same time. Kenny gave a yelp and disappeared into the grave. I heard him hit as the midnight wind whistled through the trees.

Blood was splattered all over me. I could smell the piss and shit. Bone fragments were scattered over the ground. I looked down with what I would have sworn was more than half a hard-on and felt Rocco's hands grasping at my ankles.

I looked down the barrel of the .45 and emptied it into Rocco's prone body. Tony was already dead.

Kenny, that pansy fuck, was lying in the bottom of his grave sobbing hysterically. I don't know if he thought he was dead or he'd just gone completely fucking nuts with the stress. I climbed in after him and pushed his face into the soft earth. I grabbed his jeans and yanked them down, then undid my own pants and wiped the slick blood and brains from Tony's head over my cock.

Maybe on any other night it would have disgusted the fuck out of me. But I was running a little short on mores tonight. I rammed into Kenny's asshole with all the force I could muster, and soon I was moaning and our loads were mingling in the soft dirt of Kenny's grave. He stopped his sobbing as his hard-on, covered with jizz, slowly dwindled.

I looked down at him with that weird breed of contempt you can only have for someone when you've completely fucked up your own life for them. For no good reason.

"Get out of the fuckin' grave," I told him. "We've got work to do."

"He's communing with nature, all right. Only one thing. What the fuck ever happened to Rocco and Tony? I had to do the job alone. Yeah. Yeah. No, I never got word from them. Jesus, you don't think…you don't think that, do you? No. No. Look, I'll keep my eyes open. No, it was easy; he died like a punk. All right. All right. I'll keep my eyes open. I just hope they show up. If those fuckin' east side motherfuckers whacked Rocco and Tony, I promise you I'll fuckin' make them pay. I'll find out who if it's the last fuckin' thing I do. You understand me, boss? If it's the last fuckin' thing I do, I'm gonna get the motherfucker who whacked Rocco and Tony. Yeah. Yeah. I know. All right, look, I'm gonna get some sleep. Maybe they'll show up. I'm sure they're fine. All right. I'll be in touch."

I eased the receiver into the cradle of the pay phone and went back to the Caddy. Kenny was almost done putting the gas in.

I settled back into the driver's seat and opened up the map.

Kenny finished up with the cashier and slid into the passenger's seat. He looked nervous.

"You OK, kid?"

He shrugged. "The sooner we can dump those packages in the trunk, the better I'll feel."

"You and me both," I told him, and found the spot on the map. "About 100 miles away. Just hope Lucky Joe doesn't decide to dig up your grave."

Kenny gave a shudder at that one.

There was no way to predict what shit was going to hit the fan first. I didn't know if I could make one of the east side bastards look guilty, give them a motive they never had, cook up incriminating evidence that didn't exist. Or if Lucky Joe would see right through my trick of mirrors and one night soon I'd been digging my own grave in the forest while Sammy or Johnny Numbers or Max the Knife pointed a .45 at me and laughed about how I'd pissed my life away for a faggot punk.

But until that night came, that fine, sweet ass of Kenny's was mine. And it was almost like he'd grown up the moment he fell into that grave—he had a different confidence now, a coldness he hadn't had before. Like visiting his own grave had made him different somehow. He didn't act like such a punk now. Maybe this is his requiem, then: his story, and my own, told in my scattered thoughts to the purr of a Caddy's engine, motoring down the interstate toward and away from twin destinies of sudden death. Requiem for a punk.

I pulled out of the gas station and eased onto the freeway, keeping the Caddy right at the speed limit through the endless fields of gold. The sun was starting to come up again, and the roosters were crowing.

But for Insouciance, There Go I
By Miodrag Kojadinovic´

Miodrag Kojadinovic' lives in the former Yugoslavia. Like his homeland, this exquisitely crafted story is brimful of casual cruelty, the smell of failure, and the will to go on regardless. Brutal things can happen in the most unlikely places...

"In the bathroom," I say. "Right now! You know you have to be punished." Just for a brief moment he hesitates, a look of dazzled disbelief challenging my authority, unprepared for this turn of events that is suddenly transforming him from a proud Capricorn into a he-goat about to be skinned on his way to Azazel. "Atone!" I whisper. "You can take it like a man."

His glance flickers away, slips over the plump girl's round face to the brightly lit kitchen (we can hear—but do not see—George banging the pans, getting the cheese pie ready) and back, down my midsection, focusing in on my high motorcycle boots. Two inches taller and a size bigger than his. Made for rainy days in England, not for sandy beaches on the isle of Cyprus like his. (Yeah, it's a class issue after all, and so what?) He swallows, not daring to clear the lump in his throat, and I know he is already broken. He looks me in the eye like a young puppy, tail bent between his legs, ready to roll onto his back.

I am aware that to sneak off and give me a quick blow job in his boyfriend's bathroom, Nebojöa perhaps has to risk his livelihood, and that gives the whole thing an extra kick. He, naturally, prefers staying at George's one-bedroom-with-den flat to traveling on a rickety train for an hour or so in the middle of the night, amid a bunch of drunken and abusive shift workers, to his parents' house in the outer ring of Belgrade's suburbs. Also, George has found him several part-time jobs, and though they are below what Nebojöa believes he should be doing, he's never managed to set any of his lofty plans in motion.

George's stepmother is the only niece of the last wife of Tito, the former dictator of Yugoslavia, and that has propelled George through the underworld of the Communist tribal lodges. A lonely child, he had been dressed as a girl into his early teens by his late Hungarian mother, whose identity he posthumously changed into Jewish. In the backward social structure of miserable Yugoslavia, it is easier for a sensitive gay child to believe he is persecuted as a Jew than as a "fag." But ever since his father aligned himself with a woman of the regime, it has been much easier for George.

Earlier this year he was accepted as a backup dancer at the National Ballet and has already established his own network of "contacts," encompassing all sorts of shady characters: an obese wig maker in his 60s whose seemingly inexhaustible supply of grass makes him the favorite pal of exuberant, inexperienced, provincial queens who have flocked to New Belgrade's residential developments from the sad, small towns of southern Serbia and the Dalmatian hinterlands; a well-built, tall, mustached but strangely sissy radio announcer who claims he can only get off by rimming military police boys (and is therefore quite often brutally beaten by men who believe they have to crush any suggestion that they could be faggots); a male-to-female transsexual who acquired fame on the local television when he underwent sex-change surgery in his-to-her 40s...

As Nebojöa turns to step into the bathroom, I prod him with a short whip. Traveling on Belgrade public transit, I had, of course, carried the whip in my favorite black leather doctor's bag from Amsterdam, heavily armored with brass buckles. "Strip!" I say coldly, almost wearily. Strangely, my slow, disinterested drawl never fails to enchant Serbian boys. I don't even have to pretend I am stronger than I really am; something vaguely aristocratic in the tone of my voice, something I have inherited from my maternal grandma, charms them into obedient slaves without much effort on my part.

Slowly, Nebojöa unbuckles his belt, pulls his jeans down; he stumbles, then manages to pull his left boot off. As he bends, I am startled to notice that his hair is thinning at the top of his scalp. Being sluggishly lazy as he is, in just a couple of years that shadow of a paunch will expand to merge with his flanks into a spare tire, although his body is not bad right now. He'll shed the remnants of hair from atop his scalp, a bald spot will come in its place to turn him into a Friar Tuck look-alike.

Now, however, the butt is still nicely rounded under his black underpants. As I pull them roughly down his thighs, I am, again, surprised; on an ordinary evening, in the banal flat of his seven-month lover, under patched black jeans, I touch not some cheap synthetic, as I first thought, but silk. Why silk underwear? Did he anticipate my exhibitionist escapade? Has he actually lured me into it?

"What do we have here? Girlie undies? One only has to peel that cheap macho veneer off of you, right, pussy?" This part is somewhat tough on me, with all my gender-equality, anarchist, and antipatriarchal leanings. But I've been around long enough to know: Boys just love it when I shove sexist slurs into their faces. Perhaps because beneath all pretense, behind all the masks, regardless of derogatory names for women's genitalia, they still remain intrinsically male. "But as soon as a real man is around, you know better than to play at being a man, eh?"

I pinch his nipples. His arms are at his sides, tense, he is about to grab my squeezing fingers, to stop the pain, but I stare him down. His look is that of a wolf whelp new to a pack, visibly hurt, yet too insecure about his own worth to dare rebel. I slap the round mound of his left breast with the nail side of my fingertips. My left hand pokes at the side of his upper lip, bares his fang. The other hand drops down to grab his balls and squeeze them. A tiny droplet of a tear dribbles down his cheek. I relish the moment.

"Where are Nebojöa and Mick?" comes muffled from behind the door, beyond the stage on which I am playing the only sexual role I know, the only one I've ever worked on—that of a cruel older brother. Now, you must not get me wrong. I am an only child and my one younger cousin and I met very seldom. I even believe, and now that we are both adults he has confirmed so, that I never physically tortured him. I was never a part of boys-only gangs as a child, only mixed ones (we did some relatively wild stuff, though), and the locker rooms, except for the short while when I trained at karate, were places I thought stank and nothing more. My desire to hurt springs from somewhere else, but I still have not found out where.

I take my whip from the back pocket where I shoved it earlier and don't even have to ask; he turns over gracefully, leans on the wash basin. The whiteness of his butt is in sharp contrast to his tanned thighs and loins. As I knew he was going to, he yelps when I first hit him. A crimson welt leaps across his left cheek to branch into the clenching crevice. I am standing to the side, of course, because the bathroom is way too small, and now that I've tested his limits, and proved him to be a crybaby, I can easily keep up a steady rhythm of less violent blows. He moans during the ordeal, but as he starts wiggling his now-striped arse, I am aware he enjoys it almost as much as I do. So I stop, pick him up like a bag of potatoes, and thrust him on the bathtub; his face visibly relaxes as his glowing skin touches the cold metal.

He is panting now, and it does not take long to have him sticking his tongue out eagerly. OK, here goes: I push past sharp teeth. They tend to get in the way; his yawn is rather small. I know that George's dick is long and somewhat thin, but this is ridiculous. Unless the two stay together for life, Nebojöa's going to have to do lots of mug-opening practice with a dildo.

There's a strange sound, as if a cat is scratching at the door, but George has no pets. Even the music is no longer playing. I have to come and quick! I pull out of the uncomfortable jaws, start jerking my own cock, and am relieved to feel his lips sucking on my balls— no teeth this time. A nice touch: He does not even work his own meat. I decide to believe it is because I did not give him permission, and the surge of control rushes from my perineum, around my prostate, up my spine to my right brain, and back down to erupt in gooey tassels spewing from the heart-shaped head of my cock.

As I walk out he is still fumbling with his buttons. George is icily civil and obviously upset. There are two new arrivals who are chatting with the plump woman. One makes an embarrassed remark about the noise we apparently made, but no one laughs. I feel utterly bored and out of place again. Soon the transsexual and two ballet dancers, a straight couple, ring up from downstairs. We had a date to go to a *thé dansant* at an overpriced bar downtown where hookers take their foreign johns for a sip of fake champagne, but I decide to excuse myself.

I say goodbye, and Nebojöa is strangely solemn as he walks me to the door under George's unflinching scrutiny. "He'll kick me out, but it doesn't really matter," he says, "I was gonna leave anyhow. This just relieves me from the responsibility of having to make a decision." In the door frame, in full sight of his boyfriend's angered look, I stroke his ear provocatively: "Oh, but you have made a decision. Nobody ever forced you to do anything you didn't want to do in the first place." And, as I suspect that what glitters in his eye is another tear, I turn to leave, asking absentmindedly, "Did it hurt? Does it still hurt?" and I'm half way down the corridor before he can answer. The black doctor's bag in my right hand swings to and fro.

Idol

By Lucy Taylor

*Can a woman write a great story about a gay pro wrestler? Yes,
if she's Lucy Taylor. In "Idol," hero worship is its own reward,
and nothing is quite as it seems. Be careful what you wish for...*

Conners felt his dick stiffen as the bronze god with flowing
white-blond hair made his way toward the wrestling ring. At 6
foot 5, 270 pounds, he could easily manage the five-foot python
slung across his shoulders. The reptile coiled around his powerful chest and over his shoulder, surveying the audience with
hooded, beady eyes and conveyed such blackness that Conners
briefly looked away. But not for long. He couldn't keep his eyes
off Darius. No matter how many times he saw the Python wres-
tle, he was always awed by the man—those slablike pecs oiled
to a sheen, sculpted deltoids, and laddered abs, a butt so perfectly tight and square it made Conners's balls ache to look at it.

If only, he thought. *If only I could know what it feels like to
get fucked by the hottest man alive. To bend over and feel his
dick slam into my ass. To belong to him and be his slave. Lick
his boots, let him tie me up, while he plows me till my butt
bleeds. Become so close that he and I are one.*

Conners thought of the scrap of paper in the pocket of his
leather vest, the list of dates and cities. Friday, July 15, the Coliseum
in Richmond, Va.; Saturday, July 16, the Civic Center in Roanoke,
Va.; Sunday, July 17, Dorton Arena in Raleigh, N.C. Three days to
get to Richmond in time to see the Python's next performance.

Unlike Darius, who flew first class from match to match, Conners drove a decrepit Mustang, which he fueled with gas by working odd jobs as he went along: cleaning up trash in the arenas; selling programs and wrestling souvenirs. Occasionally selling himself.

Shit work, sure, but he had to earn a living.

While he waited and lusted and longed.

And, sometimes, after a few drinks, talked too much about his adoration of Darius.

"You're fucking obsessed, aren't you?" said a trick he'd picked up after a TV taping of a cable wrestling show in Charlotte, N.C. The trick, an ex-con type with heavily tattooed forearms and skin that looked as though it hadn't seen sunlight in years, folded his dick back into his jeans and zipped up. "You're telling me you've arranged your whole life around following this steroid freak from arena to arena? Hell, I had a Deadhead girlfriend once who used to do that for Jerry Garcia. I *knew* she was nuts, and I think you are too."

Spitting the man's come from his mouth, Conners had explained that he didn't mind all the sacrifices, that if he could be with Darius only one time, it would be worth it. Still a little drunk from the boilermakers he'd consumed earlier, he told the guy about that song he liked to listen to, an old Carly Simon number called "Stardust," and how Carly sings about an unrequited love for a movie star whose "stardust is golden," how she's sure that just one touch and she'll be golden too, as golden as her lover, and...

The tattooed dude's shrill, derisive cackling had been the last thing that Conners heard before jumping into his Mustang, heading for the highway and the next wrestling arena.

Darius had reached the ring now and was handing down his living reptile namesake to his flunky manager, an ex-wrestler named McCoy, who waited outside the ring. With a smirk of disdain for his audience, he raised his huge arms and strutted and flexed. Lifting the amulet he wore around his neck, a small obsidian python, he kissed its ruby eyes. The crowd jeered and hurled paper cups and popcorn containers.

Jealous, thought Conners. Men and women both. Darius was a consummate heel and also the number 1 star of the World Wrestling League, beloved by the promoters for his ability to "put asses in the seats," as the saying went. Although Conners couldn't guess his age, he knew the man had been wrestling under one name or another for almost two decades. His spectacular physique and seemingly perpetual youth prompted the envious and inferior to concoct dark tales, weird rumors—that Darius practiced black magic, Darius drank blood—colorful but stupid wrestling hype, cooked up by burned-out bookers and believed by bumpkin fans.

But he'd heard other, more plausible rumors too. About how particular, how meticulously discriminating the Python was. He didn't choose a fuck buddy casually or often and sometimes "auditioned" for the right one from a group of three or four. Although he knew himself to be a hot-looking man, Conners only hoped that Darius would be attracted to his black hair and sapphire eyes and the hefty bulge that his tight jeans showed off to advantage.

Stardust, your stardust is golden...

He only hoped that Darius' magic would rub off on him, would make him golden too.

The crowd roared, and Conners came back to reality. Darius had just body-slammed Hangman Hughes over the top rope, sending him sprawling to the concrete. "Selling" the move so that he appeared to be dazed from the fall, the Hangman tried to climb back into the ring. Darius sent him flailing backward with a boot to the face. Leaping out of the ring, he upended his opponent and suplexed him onto the Spanish announcing table. Microphones went flying. Announcers scrambled to get out of the way.

The bell rang, and the gnomish referee scurried around the ring, waving his stumpy arms and calling for a disqualification.

In the midst of this Conners looked over and caught McCoy, stationed at ringside, ogling his crotch like it was an éclair on a dessert tray. The man's tiny scat-colored eyes were like drill bits hammered into his skull. McCoy edged over and leaned down. Spraying spittle into Conners's ear, he hissed, "Darius noticed you earlier. You hang around after the matches. He wants to try you out."

Late at night, with the matches over and the crowd gone home, the quiet of the coliseum made footfalls in the empty corridors sound to Conners like sharply struck anvil blows. As promised a basement door had been left ajar. McCoy, eyes beady as a lurking troll's, was waiting for him inside.

"This way," he said, and guided Conners down a corridor with doors that opened into a series of dressing rooms. They descended a stairway that smelled of beer and popcorn into a subbasement, then continued along another corridor to a locker room, where McCoy told him to strip and shower.

Conners's blood was thundering, much of it going directly to his cock, which stood already erect, the pink crown bobbing against his flat belly.

"Now don't take it too hard if you ain't the one Darius picks," said McCoy, leering at Conners's hard-on. "The Python's real particular. He don't have a man all to himself but once a month or so."

The revelation that he wouldn't be the only one made Conners's throat constrict with disappointment, but there was no time to respond. McCoy produced a key and unlocked a metal door. Inside was darkness. As Conners hesitated, McCoy's hand drove into the small of his back, shoving him forward.

Before Conners's eyes adjusted to the dim light, the smell assailed him: sweat and urine and the musky tang of come. And noises: the smack and grunt and panting of rutting males.

Then he turned a corner around a set of lockers and rocked back on his heels. There was a wrestling ring set up, and in it two naked young men, a blond who looked like a bodybuilder and a slender, dark-haired Hispanic. And in the center of the ring, resplendently, goldenly naked, Darius sprawled splay-legged in a leather sling that had been attached to some overhead cables. His mouth was open and his long hair hung down as the boys took turns directing streams of piss on him. Piss drops gleamed on his skin, glittered in his pale hair like a shower of opals.

"Go on, get in the ring," said McCoy, coming up behind Conners. "And don't forget, whatever happens here tonight, you ain't seen nothin'. Darius paid the night watchmen real good to let him use this place after hours."

Trembling with anticipation, Conners climbed into the ring just as the dark-haired boy, with his thick, bulb-headed cock, seized the sling and shoved Darius backward. Ass in the air, he swung on a collision course with the erect dick of the amply endowed boy behind him. Conners heard a wet thwack and saw the slicked meat disappear between taut, muscular buttocks. Impaled to the hilt, Darius groaned and stroked himself fast and hard. The swing reversed its direction. Darius hung his head back while the sequence was repeated, his pale, piss-soaked hair tumbling down in lank strands so that, to Conners, he resembled a degraded Zeus.

Darius raised his head and appraised those servicing him. In this light the fierce blue eyes gleamed pale silver, as though icicles had been plunged through his eye sockets.

His coldly seductive stare looked Conners up and down. "Ah, you at last. I've seen you ringside for months now. If you're half as depraved as you are dedicated, we may get along well."

Conners was more than ready to perform. The only thing that mildly flummoxed him was seeing Darius in the sling. From everything he'd heard, Darius's rep was as a consummate top man. To see the world famous grappler with his ass in the air, ready for reaming, surprised Conners but did nothing to diminish the hard-on throbbing against his belly.

As Conners approached the sling Darius's voice filled the arena, a rich, commanding baritone. "You'll start by sucking my dick and eating out my ass. Then you can lick the piss off me."

Conners positioned himself between Darius's elevated legs. Darius's magnificent cock was uncut and thickly veined, leading to a pair of heavy balls lightly furred with gold hair. He sucked the hefty knob into his mouth, relishing the tang of come on the crown.

He moved down, slurping juice across the heavy balls, then parted the perfect rectangular slabs of Darius's cheeks with his hands. The wrestler's asshole was a flawless purple rose, puckered and wet from earlier explorations by his other suitors.

Conners widened it with two fingers, probed it with his tongue. Hunger, at once terrible and thrilling, welled up and overflowed him. He wanted to eat his way into Darius's ass, up into his belly all the way up to his red pumping heart. He wanted to gorge himself on the sweet treasures of Darius's belly and chest, to burrow in and become one with his idol.

It was as if the force of his lust gave off a scent that was palpable even in a room that already reeked of sex.

Darius lifted his head and focused those cut-glass eyes on the other two men, who stood waiting expectantly for his next order. "You two get the fuck out of here. This one I'll keep."

The other young men sulked and glared but moodily complied as McCoy hustled them out the door.

When they were alone Darius fingered the stone python at his neck and said, "I noticed you staring at my little idol. A lot of people do. They think it's some sort of phallic god or a good-luck charm, but they're wrong. Why do *you* think I wear it?"

"Because it's a python," said Conners, feeling stupid. "And that's your name."

Darius hauled himself up and out of the sling and rested a heavy arm across Conners's shoulders. He seemed amused. "I got this many years ago from a man who wrestled pythons in North Africa. He was very beautiful, almost radiantly so, like an evil angel. He claimed to be able to channel demons through his pythons. Do you want to know what happened to him?"

Conners wasn't sure, so he said nothing.

"I took his amulet and then, while he was still alive, I fed him to his pythons. Two took his arms, two others his legs, another his head. When they all converged on his torso, well...better if I don't describe it further."

There was a beat of silence. He reached out, caressing Connors's cock. "Does that matter to you? That I murdered someone in so hideous a manner?"

Conners stared into those dazzling, incandescent eyes and knew, from the bottom of his heart, that Darius could have wiped out a class of preschoolers and he wouldn't give a fuck. His desire was beyond any morality, even beyond self-preservation.

"No," he heard himself say. "No, it doesn't."

"Good," said Darius, suppressed mirth curling the corners of his mouth as he fondled Conners's balls. "I knew you were the right choice."

"But..." Conners was at once sorry he'd spoken.

Darius looked up sharply. "What?"

"That stuff about—channeling demons—that's bullshit, right?"

"What if it weren't? Would it matter?"

There could be but one answer. "No."

"Good. Your lack of scruples makes you all the more fuckable. And you'll let me do anything I want with you, now won't you?"

Suddenly he kicked Conners's legs out from under him, sending him sprawling to the canvas on his hands and knees.

"Because you really don't have a choice."

There was no foreplay, no gradual opening up. The penetration was swift and cruel, and Conners had to bite back a scream. Darius grabbed a fistful of Conners's thick hair and yanked his head back, riding him brutally. Ramming and thrusting and gouging until the pain transformed itself into a terrible pressure. An ecstasy so intense it felt like dying.

When Darius came Conners collapsed flat onto the mat. He had just barely had time to recover his senses when Darius's huge arms closed around his rib cage, crushing the breath from him as he lifted him to his feet.

"That was just for starters," Darius said, climbing back into the sling. "Now it's just your turn to show me what you can do. Let's see how well you can fuck me."

Although his legs still quivered with weakness, Conners grabbed the sides of the sling and pulled Darius toward him. His cock penetrated the tight circle of muscle and entered the plush, dark warmth of Darius's interior. Moaning, he drove into Darius with all his weight, wishing his dick were long enough to penetrate past Darius's heart and pop out of his mouth like an enormous tongue.

"Stop!" ordered Darius.

Conners did so.

"Pull out."

He complied.

"How big is that cock of yours? Let me look at you again."

Conners moved around so that Darius could see his 7½ rigid inches.

Darius's silvery eyeballs peered from under slitted lids.

"It isn't big enough. Use your fist. Use your whole arm. *Fill* me."

The flesh underneath Darius's rib cage was deflating, expanding, deflating again. As if his whole body were gripped with the contractions of his enormous appetite.

Conners spit on his fingers and inserted two, then three, four into Darius's ass.

"More!"

His entire hand was engulfed now. Slowly Conners curled the fingers into a fist and began to thrust. The sling swayed and Darius's body shook from the pounding.

"It's not enough. I...need...more."

Conners pushed his wrist and forearm inside. He fucked until his biceps ached, ramming his whole arm in elbow-deep.

Darius began to shake and moan, as though his very skeletal system were unhinging.

Somewhere in Conners's mind, it occurred to him that he must be hurting the man, that he could be doing serious internal damage and that he should withdraw, but the realization only drove him to greater brutality. He worshiped Darius, but he wanted to hurt him too; hurting and having were one and the same. Faster and faster, his arm pistoned, fist-fucking his idol like a boxer battering a helpless, rope-bound opponent.

"More!"

The wrestler's rib cage heaved like staves about to burst. The flesh of his abdomen went concave, convex, concave again as though a bellows were working in his guts.

"More!"

Conners felt it then, the first mighty contraction inside Darius' rectum. It felt like his fist was snagged in undertow, like he was elbow-deep in quicksand.

Darius' sphincter muscle suddenly tightened on Conners' arm just underneath the elbow. Conners was getting ready to pull back for another ramming. He couldn't free his arm. His flesh was clamped as if in the maw of a shark.

Conners couldn't believe what was happening. Leaning back, he twisted to try to extricate his arm.

Nothing happened, or rather something did...something began to happen, but Conners was so stunned at first that it took a moment for him to recover his breath sufficiently to scream.

His arm was being drawn in. Inexorably, efficiently, in rhythmic powerful waves. Like a band saw pulling a cord of wood into the feeder.

"What is this? What's happening?"

"*More!*"

Conners's arm continued to disappear. Past the forearm, around the angle of the elbow. Darius's gut began to bloat and bulge beneath the pressure of the flesh it was stretching to accommodate.

"*No!*" screamed Conners. He was biceps-deep now in Darius's bowels, his arm throbbing as though constricted inside a giant blood-pressure cuff. He shrieked as bones began to give way, fingers and wrist being pulverized, his elbow shattering.

In a frenzy powered by agony, he fought to retract his arm, but Darius's asshole tightened and contracted with merciless force. His shoulder dislocated loudly. It stretched away from his body at an impossible angle and was swallowed up.

Conners felt the world tilting under him in hallucinogenic waves. He tried to stay on his feet, because to fall meant adding pressure to his dislocated arm, but he was growing giddy with agony.

"No, please! Don't do this!"

Darius looked up through eyes sheened as if with ice. "Oh, but I must. Like my predecessor with his pythons, I have to take my nourishment this way. After all, I am part python."

He gave a hellish grimace, like a woman in the last throes of a fatal labor. The hole between his buttocks distended, became a well impossibly deep and wide.

With a final scream Conners sank to his knees. Darius gave another huge contraction and sucked the rubbery meat of Conners's shoulder in up to his neck. Bones and tendons, ligaments, were being crushed, reduced. Conners's head was forced to one side at an impossible angle. Vertebrae unhinged. His bulging eyes wept blood. With the final snap of his spine, he became a quadriplegic.

And Darius opened himself up even wider until he could draw in Conners's lolling head.

Conners was still conscious as his face moved like a pallid slug into that moist and fetid dark. By now he was long past terror, and sanity was a remnant from another lifetime. The pain was gone, his ruined synapses incapable of transmission. A strange and languid peace, black and tropically warm as the bizarre new world which he was entering, enveloped him. He was becoming one with Darius. Soon his flesh and bone and marrow would be part of Darius; he would go into the ring with Darius, would eat and shit and fuck with Darius, would live and die with Darius. They would be forever as one.

It was like being born again, into the awful core of a dark and reeking universe and yet, as Conners's skull was slowly crushed, his dying brain put on a pyrotechnic dazzle brilliant enough to offset the other horrors. Gaudy lightning strobed behind his eyes. Tinsel and neon and fireworks.

It was as if he were showered in stardust.

Young Deputy: K-9 Cop
By Jack Fritscher

Jack Fritscher is one of the godfathers of leather fiction, creator of many an S/M icon. This lean, mean story of hairy, hard men bares its fangs and celebrates the beast within. Are you sure the cage is locked?

Dogmaster: You've seen him. Built like pit bull. Big. Squared-off heavy muscle. Vet. Professional trainer. Special Services Kennel for the county deputies' K-9 Patrol. Man in authority moving under thick pelt of full body fur. Nights, alone with Dane and Doberman, he clips his fast-growing body fur, naked, hard, in private quarters behind kennel—where young county deputy waits, stripped naked from uniform, caged, choke-chained, slow-stroking himself in the last hour before obedience training begins.

In Dogmaster's quarters, hum of grooming clippers in his big paw-hand, he shears his own fur to a mean, disciplined bristle. Low growl of his two big dogs dozing at his feet. Hungry for fresh meat. Dogmaster judges the sound of barking from kennel in the deep night. He grooms fur on the back of his strong hands, around square wrists.

He curries back pelt on powerful forearms that read by day like muscular hairy hams hanging from the khaki vet shirt he wears attending to big dogs brought by men proud of their studs. Broad mastiff shoulders hairy. Animal coat of fur on big barreled chest.

In the county: rumors of his Special Service Kennel. Knowing smiles. Then silence. Unbroken. In the county: Anything is possible.

Roll of abs defined in dark washboard cuts by fur, growth patterns not masking the pedigree of power but defining it. Men from the county bring their dogs to him for stud. Pecs and belly soft-bristled, outlined by the natural lay of his hair.

Dogdik: thick, long, mean, bulbous, red, ready.

Legs: squat, hard, powerful. For serious studwork.

Dane rolls over in doze, big balls rolling against inside of back haunch. Dogmaster turns at tight waist, looks down at dog who expectantly opens one eye. Dogmaster turns back to mirror. Butt: round, ripe, muscular; sweaty crack furred, dark, deep with promises he keeps. The animal spoor about him. The way he enlists a man to help mount stud over another man's bitch in heat. Together, intent on the perfect mounting. Dogmaster clips body hair the same careful length as his close-cropped beard. Thick growth rises high up cheeks, runs down muscular throat, meets rising curl of hair from chest.

A special grooming tonight.

Dogmaster's big arms raise up. Armpits run wet with sweat. One paw palms the length of hair on Dogmaster's head, low on his brow, bristling down the animal back of neck. Other hand running clippers an even length across his head.

Tonight's special weekend duty. Fucking Ultimate Obedience Training. New young deputy. Uniform strip. K-9 Patrol.

Dogmaster, erect, enormous, clippers in hand. Smoothing his body. Dogdik drooling. Rich head crowning uncut hairy shaft. His two stud dogs, eyeballing his moves, awaiting his command. Dane and Dobe, hungry, growling low, waiting, killer instincts set on edge by Master's hulking presence, held at bay by the cold eye of command presence.

Dobe's pink tongue flicks across black lips. White teeth bared. Hindquarters quivering. Dick spritzing. Dane growls in anticipation, starts up, anxious, nosing toward iron door to kennel, excited by the smell of fear a dog recognizes sweating out of a husky man's choke-chained body.

"Stay!" Dogmaster's voice resonates deep from big balls, echoes in the hard-tiled room. Two dogs freeze in total obedience. Big dogs are measure of the man. His own animal body: Marine-trained. Former DI. Respectfully nicknamed behind powerful back at Pendleton and LeJeune: DOG DIK. Disciplined trainer of mean and dogs for combat.

Trainer of USMC grunts forced by dare, high stakes, and his command, to fight naked with specially trained attack dogs, in the last days of Vietnam, in the backwash of the DMZ. Men placing hard bets on any good brawl for blood.

Now: best K-9 trainer in the county. Dane moves in close to Master: fur-to-fur, haunch-to-thigh. Dobe sniffs hungrily at kennel door.

In the county bars deputies laugh, wink, say, shit, they wish he'd work tighter with them. Independent. Animal loner. Sharp white teeth flashing easy grin through mat of beard rising to deep-squint of piercing eye. Deputies, quiet in silent fraternity, treat Special Services K-9 training as better left unspoken.

In dark fursweat kennel young deputy, naked, caged, heavy leather collar and choke-chain around neck, smelling dog piss ripe and fresh in territorial corners, delivered, handcuffed for stud, pulled from a prowl car, stripped from uniform—gun, gear, boots—by other tough deputies. Hosed down, readied for clipping shaving grooming, ordered to endure. Special services K-9 training. Waiting for the opening of the heavy metal door.

Around him, big dogs, caged separately, pad in expectant anticipation, streaming long wet piss-squirts, sniffing nose-to-butt hole, butt hole-to-nose. Quick lick of long tongue through cyclone mesh fence. Lick of dog tongue to low-swinging dog balls and fresh pucker hole. Natural animal instinct.

Hairy young deputy, recruited hunk, long-chained from collar to ring in kennel floor, awaits the first night of obedience training. Naked, warm in animal heat of the kennel. New to county. Fresh from the service. Twists nervously the gold ring on left hand. Special weekend duty never meant pissing in cage. Dick hard. Scared shit-less. Dogs howling. The hum, steady hum, of Dogmaster's clippers on other side of kennel door. Whine of Dobe. Low growls of Dane. He figures he better be ready. He figures maybe now his reality-run may be in for a shakedown he never expected.

He remembers deputies' talk. Overheard them. Until they noticed. Until they slammed locker doors loudly. Until they shut up. Now: clarity. Clarity coming. This is the county. In semidark he fig-ures how it might be: groomed, Dogmaster opening his kennel cage, come to shear his body, train him, force sniffing nose to command-ing butt hole, force licking of bulbous big red dick. Enormous. Powerful Dogman. Heavy paws hold him in position. Dogmaster's long spit into crack of ass. Wild barking. Dobe and Dane pacing, watching, eager. Dogmaster's snarl. Mount. Head sliding out of the heavy uncut skin. Insistent. Dogslickwet. Fucked in. Deep. Heavy fullness. Plowing. Holding. Pumping. Held firm by Dogmaster's big paws. Only commanding look from hairy Dogmaster's eye holding Dobe and Dane at bay. Only the whim of the Dogmaster not throw-ing open locks on separate cages of pack of huge male fighting dogs.

Only minutes now. Hum of the Dogmaster's clippers stopping. Whine on other side of the door. Sound of unlocking deadbolt. Deep-throated barks rising to full howl and salute, cage to cage, in dark kennel. Only moonlight breaking through high, barred, industrial windows. Sound of iron door opening. Blinding light from Dogmaster's bright, hard-tiled quarters. Dobe and Dane bounding into kennel around heavy legs of Dogmaster. Big, hairy body planted squarely in dark outline against light, shimmering in bristling halo, around the full measure, bulk and height and well-hung heft, of Dogmaster who waits one long moment in the Special Services Kennel door for night vision that is his alone, to carry him down the long growling corridor to young deputy's cage. Every move, driven by crossbred, massive Dogdik, unbeliev-ably beyond captive deputy's imagination, brings out latent beast in caged, choke-chained, naked, exultant manimal!

We conclude the book with this finely wrought story from England. Dave Chester examines the complex interplay between sex and the rest of our lives, taking us inside the head of a London leatherman as he tries to come to terms with both family and fucking.

Friday evening. I'm working out at the gym. Circuit training. Short of time. Too late at the office and due at his place in less than an hour. It's June and it's hot. A stinking hot summer day with diesel clouds pressing down on the city. Just at the end of the third circuit, 36 step-ups followed by 24 press-ups, I decide I won't shower. I go straight into the changing room and push the door so that it crashes against the wall. I dress, buttoning my creased cotton shirt, feeling my sweat soak into it. I pull on my trousers and, after getting my feet into damp socks, I step into my shoes, breaking the backs. I put on my jacket so roughly it almost rips and roll my tie into a knot and stuff it in my kit bag. It's funny how kit bags smell of men.

I feel hot and horny and stride down the street, pushing my way through groups of people ambling toward me. The traffic's at a standstill. I go straight to his flat. The 12th floor of a smart block by Regent's Park. We're due at some bar by 8 o'clock, but that's not what I have in mind.

When I open the door with the key he'd given me—the one that always makes me swear because it won't turn smoothly—he's naked except for white socks, the sort that have leaves of tissue paper between them when you buy them in department stores. He's changing from work clothes to casual stuff. He likes linen trousers and polo shirts.

I pin him against the bedroom doorjamb and begin working him over. The circuit's stirred my testosterone. I kick off my shoes, drop my trousers, and step out of them. I hear a rip, but what the fuck. I push down my CKs and force him onto my dick. I don't want any designer excuses and am faintly pleased when he doesn't try to make any. While he sucks and gobs on me (he remembers that I like it), I take off my jacket and shirt, dip into the pocket for a rubber, reach around the bathroom door for some grease, and raise him so that he can continue sucking me and I can grease him up at the same time.

He's a pushover. That's what turns me off with him, really. Too compliant. Too easy.

Anyway, back to business. I push him back off my dick. He's pleased to get a breather. I fit the rubber, lift him into a scrum position, make him lean into the bathroom, and fuck him till we both shoot. Me in the rubber, him on the bathroom floor. I thank God he shoots on the tiled floor, otherwise he'd have been into the cleaning cupboard and shampooed the carpet. I hate all that house-proud stuff. I can't see this lasting.

Saturday morning. When you don't have curtains and the summer light streams in, you tend to wake early. About 6:30. I have a flat on the top floor of a building with views across roofs, chimneys, fire escapes, and some pots of plants well dead. I have a headache. A thumper. I know I should have drunk a pint of water before crashing. Poppers always give me a headache if I don't dilute them. With sunshine and headache I can't go back to sleep, so grab a paper from the random pile on the floor. The money section from *The Sunday Times*. April, though. I must do something about this pit. Maybe change the sheets today. Headline: The Last Ever Personal Equity Plans. Well. I'd done all right. Piers—the

Wellington-educated, Ferrari-driving, Stubbs-collecting broker on my floor—and I had taken out four each in March. Before the budget. All lodged with different providers to take account of high maturing differences. Short-term investment. High returns. No initial fees and no need for withdrawal after five years. Laughing all the way to the bank. I glance over the article and feel self-satisfied. After all, it wasn't much to invest, but the returns are guaranteed. I smile, then laugh a bit. My head throbs. It wipes the smile off.

Piers, with his wife, Helena, and their sprogs, Jemima and Ajax, all tucked away in their Blackheath villa, will do all right too. They'll reinvest. I wanna blow it on some pink-pound indulgence. Maybe a new bike and some extraspecial leathers made from calf hide by those B-gay queens in Beverly Hills, Robin and Rick. I'll find some fatuous way of blowing the money.

I close my eyes. The paper falls over my face and feel myself fall off to sleep. Thank God. Maybe this headache will have evaporated by 11.

The phone rings. I reach for it and the whole lot bounces on the floor. I unravel the spiraled cord. It's Gretel.

"It's Mum."

"What's new?" I ask. Gretel swallows. I know this tactic. Her Japanese tension-control theory. I wait.

"I want you to come with me to see her. First of all…" she says slowly and rationally "…you haven't seen her since Christmas and secondly…" another pause "…I need your support!"

"Why don't they increase her medication?"

She's doesn't want to listen. "I'm up there every week. She has medication. This is different." Another breath. "Please…?"

I can't face Mum anymore. I feel like a shit. Not as far as Mum is concerned but for Gretel. She's never resolved it. I think she never will. Although it's Mum who should be the one who's sorry, Gretel spends too much time running, as soon as Mum has one of her fits. I don't think we'll ever sort this one out.

Gretel's said for years she wants me to go with her to a therapist, but as far as I'm concerned we don't need a therapist. We need to be firm and kind to Mum and that's that. I've sorted out all I need. I don't want to go over that cage stuff again. At the trial they said I was a normal boy. They should see me now. Maybe that's the cause. All that Freudian mumbo jumbo.

Anyway, it's me whose paying for Sunnydene. Gretel works in some soup kitchen–type place for street kids in Pimlico. She never has a penny. They seem kind enough to Mum at Sunnydene. They know all they need to know about Mum and the past. I'm certain: more or maybe different medication, the odd ride in a bath chair, and flowers at Christmas and birthday is enough. What more can the witch expect?

"This afternoon." Gretel concludes firmly.

"Ring me later, sis. I can't get my head round it."

I put the phone down and leave it on the floor. If it rings again at least I can't drop it.

When I open my eyes again the sun's moved so far west my room's cool and shady. I look at the electric clock. 15:34. I don't believe it and reach for my wristwatch. It reads 3:35. So it must be. As I tip myself out of bed I think, *What a waste of the day.*

I put the kettle on for tea, pull a dirty cup from the pile in the sink, and give it a rinse. There's something really crummy about tea in a cold, wet cup.

After tea I grab my Speedos and a towel and head for the pool. Twenty lengths and a sauna should see me right. Also eye up the talent maybe. Then head out for the night. Just as I'm going out I hear the phone ring and the machine click on.

On Sunday it's another clear sky. I wake again around 6. Eyes half open. God, this place is a tip. I can see most of my leather gear on the floor, and the wardrobe door is open, with an avalanche of sex toys draped out. What *have* I been doing?

Half-sleep. Yes, and I have a headache, and, yes, I can smell poppers. Open my eyes wider. The bottle's on the table. The cap's off. No wonder I can smell it. I roll over to try and ignore it. I'm certainly not getting out of bed to find the cap.

Christ! Who's this? I can't remember bringing anyone back. He's facing the other way. Cropped, with a great tattoo on his back. I wonder if I rogered him? I think to look on the floor for a used rubber but wouldn't be able to tell it from the others scattered about. I don't know if I should wake him. I've never done this before. Not *remembered*? Am I dreaming? I look out at the sky. No. Not dreaming.

The phone rings.

"Yeah? Gretel. It's just after 6. What are you doing?"

"You shit. Where were you yesterday? The machine was on and you said you'd come with me to see Mum. Well?" More Japanese technique. "She's much worse, they say. I went yesterday afternoon and she seemed quieter. But they rang me in the middle of the night. She's sleepwalking again"

"I told you it's a matter of drugs. Tell them to change what it is they're giving her."

"No, Hansel. It's not that. They think there's something deeply wrong."

"What a surprise!"

"Please. Be reasonable. She's our mother, for chrissake. Show some real compassion for once."

"I show compassion every month. Twelve hundred pounds worth of compassion."

I hear Gretel sigh. The Japanese technique wearing thin? "Will you come up this afternoon? If we get there just after lunch, we can have tea together on the way back at Bramble Heath? Yeah?"

Pause. I say nothing.

"OK, OK, I'll pick you up. Is that what you want?"

"About 11:30." I'm resigned to it ruining my day.

"OK. See you." I put phone clumsily on to the hook. Ugh. I want to break the phone.

He rolls over to look at me. Smiles. Inanely. "Hi! Good morning."

"Hi!" I sit up and light a fag. Matches. A book of matches from the Salmon and Compass. Where the fuck's that? "Smoke?"

"No thanks."

"I do. On Saturday and Sunday mornings. And sometimes in clubs. Makes me feel…" I run out of ideas.

"Yeah?"

"What?"

"Feel?"

"Fuck off."

His face drops.

I take a big drag. Exhale and use the breath to say, "Look. Sorry. You're in my bed, and I'm a fucking shit."

"Yeah." He gets out of bed and pulls on his leathers. He's a bit angry. I like that. I see his fat tits and rings and glimpse his big dick just as he tucks it in and zips up. Not at all bad.

"Stop!" I say, and jump out of bed. "Let's start again. I'm Hans." Shoot my right hand.

He reluctantly takes it. Looks coy. Christ, he plays all the cards at once.

"I know. Born in Bavaria. Came to London when 12. And fucks like a train."

I look at the floor and smirk. "You know about me, and I'm sorry to say I can't remember a thing about you. At least let me give you coffee. I've got some juice too, I think."

Coy-boy drops the anger bit and smiles. "OK."

I pull on some shorts and put my head through a T-shirt. I grab his tits and then sink my tongue down his throat. I thought so. Putty.

In the kitchen we establish that I'd gotten plastered in the Eagle and we'd come back. I just couldn't think why I'd never seen him before in the pubs. So good-looking and well hung. Cut too. I like that. A real mystery.

I make coffee. Kenyan beans from Annette Lancaster's shop in Covent Garden. I wish I'd invested when she asked me; we've missed the capital growth opportunity. She's off the map. Seattle's king coffee. AA peaberry ground by hand. The powder you want to lick up like sherbet. The Cona with the spirit lamp that people like and call an experiment. It makes great coffee, and finally hot milk through a strainer poured into big cobalt-colored bowls. Now I feel more myself. Not so aggressive.

"It was lucky I wasn't riding my bike last night," I say to make conversation.

"You were. I was pillion on the way back"

I laugh. "Well, you were daft as a brush!"

"It was good. You drove like the wind."

"I bet I bloody did. So boozed up I don't remember fuck."

"And you insisted you get out your dick and lay it on the petrol tank."

"Oh, fuck."

"We stopped at the lights at Tottenham Court Road and drove alongside a stretch limos packed with Essex girls and lads. The girls tried to grab it. One of the lads offered to suck you off."

"Oh, dear." Even I felt a bit ashamed. I hate leather exhibitionism like that.

"No. Never mind. The copper…"

"What?"

"The copper didn't even mind. He was laughing too, so, you know, I waggled my tongue at him…offering to give him a blow job? I think he might have dropped his trousers in different circumstances. You seemed cool. Have you always had bikes?"

"Since I was 18. I bought a Honda 250, and when I got my first full license I graduated to a 400/4."

"How long have you had the Triumph?"

So he knows a bit about bikes too. "About 18 months. I usually keep them for three years and then change. This is the second Triumph I've had. Got the first at the relaunch. Good acceleration..."

"Sure."

"...and sound. Like a real bike. Not a sewing machine." I light another fag. "You a biker?

"Sure. I've got a Fireblade, but it's in for repair. Wiring tree overheated. Fucking thing melted and I was stuck somewhere between Norwich and the coast. Some local guy helped me out. Put it in his barn until the transporters collected it..."

I drift off during the end of his story and think of him getting the Norfolk farm lad to suck on his big one. The fag burns my fingers and I throw it into the washing-up. I'm at the end of my coffee and want to make more. Maybe Coy-boy wants more too. The phone rings again. I grab it from the wall.

"They say there's a crisis. She won't speak in English anymore. We have to go. Now."

"Oh, Grets, I can't go now. Give me an hour."

"Now. Are you dressed?"

"No."

"Well, have a shower and put some clothes on. I'm on my way."

She hangs up.

I look weakly at Coy-boy. "Mother problems. My sis is coming to get me so we can go and visit. Nursing home in Aylesbury. The end maybe."

"I'm sorry."

"Don't be. It won't be a minute too soon. But it means that..." I stop and look at him "It means that...I could meet you tonight about 7." What am I saying? What if she does die?

"Why not? Nothing ventured..."

Oh, hell, he is much too coy for me! "Seven at the Eagle. No, come here. We've got to eat."

"If you're seeing your mother, I'll get something for us. Pasta, yeah?"

This is getting domestic.

"OK. Pasta."

"And some 1995 Merlot."

He knows his wine. Maybe not so coy after all. I'm on my way to shower. He catches my arm. We struggle. I put him against the wall with the notice board on it. Holding him against porno pinups. I smile. He's a fucking pinup.

"Then will you fuck me again like you did last night?" he says, sneering at me. I like that too.

"Maybe." Maybe he'll do for a couple of weeks.

When I come out of the shower toweling my hair, Coy-boy is putting on his socks ready to lace up his DMs.

"Like the DMs..." I say.

"Yeah...want me to lick yours clean?"

"Later."

I notice he has nice feet. Sun-tanned with long, straight toes. I could pinch myself. I've never been a foot fetishist. Then I notice his nipples through the shirt. The sight of those great rings and fat tits make me horny, so I move behind him and reach over his shoulders to pull on them really hard. He just smiles, lifts his head, and I kiss him upside down. I pull harder and he likes it. His tongue reaches far into my mouth and my hard-on gets harder. I work his tits hard and he moans a bit. I raise him, keeping hold, and get my dick in line with his rim.

I can tell Gretel's arrived by the sound of her clapped-out old car in the street below. Coy-boy and I are still naked after the quickie. He's covered with my dribbling spunk. I didn't want him to get the impression that I ride every fuck. Gretel's on her way up, and while she and I are both relaxed about my way of life, I urge Coy-boy to get into the shower while I wipe myself down with the dishcloth from the kitchen. After all, I showered ten minutes ago. As I pass the cloth under my chin, I can smell stale milk in it and make a mental note to soak it in bleach. Next week, maybe. The doorbell rings. First I grab some cologne and spray it on to cover the smell of the milk. Maybe I should have shaved. I undo the latch and let the door swing as I do up my jeans and button my shirt.

It's so strange how different Gretel and I are now. As children we were close. So close. We spent hours playing in a fantasy world of little dances and stories. It was a sort of protection. Life with Mum and Dad was odd. Now we don't hug or kiss.

"Hiya, sis!"

"Are you ready?"

"Sure. Five minutes."

Gretel looks pixilated. She always has. She never grew up. Today her straw-colored hair is woven into two rough plaits, and she's wearing a cotton print dress that she washed an hour or so ago. Even I think it needs ironing. Sandals and socks. She's jangling her car keys. That means she's in no mood to wait around.

"God, this place is a mess." Gretel picks up a cushion from the floor and throws it onto the sofa.

"Just give me a couple of minutes. I've lost my trainers." I go into the bedroom, and Coy-boy's coming out of the shower. "Go through and say hallo to my sis."

He wraps the towel round himself and tucks a corner in at his waist and goes into the sitting room. He's got one of those neat little belly buttons.

Gretel turns to him. "Hallo." She smiles. She's usually very civil to my friends.

"Hallo," I hear Coy-boy say warmly. I smile. "I'm Calvin," he says. I stifle a laugh. I think I'll stick with Coy-boy. I shove my trainers on and run my hands through my hair.

I get some spare keys from my chest of drawers and find Gretel and Coy-boy facing each other. "Here. Front door to the block is the silver one and door to the flat is the brass one and the pointed one. OK? See you about 7."

"All right."

"You ready, sis?"

"Yes." She tries to sound controlled. "You know this is serious; we'll need time."

"Yes. That's why he's got keys..." I try to sound grave, but it comes out patronizing. "We'll talk in the car." To Coy-boy, "OK? If there's a problem, I'll ring. Watch a video." I look at Gretel. "OK?"

"See you whenever," says Coy-boy.

Gretel has an old French car and drives it like a tank. It looks like an upturned jelly mold on wheels and sounds like a toy. There's a hole in the floor.

"How do you get this through the MOT?" I ask as we get in and slam the tin-plate doors.

"I have a little man in Chalk Farm."

"I should think he's living on another planet. You could get done for this."

There's hardly any traffic as we jerk and cough our way up toward Hampstead, jumping a couple of red lights on the way. I say a prayer. She crunches the gears as we climb the hill in Fitzjohn's Avenue.

"Sis..." I reconsider saying that there's an easier way to the A41.

"What?"

"Nothing."

I try to relax. Traveling with Gretel in this can is a sort of torment. I could have let her take the car and met her there on my bike. I look at the sky as rain begins to fall. She pulls an antiquated lever and a wand sweeps across the windscreen. The rubber is so worn it makes no difference. So Gretel squints and grabs the wheel like a blind man. Rain drips through the canvas roof. I'm dreading the rest of the journey.

Later—it seems like hours—Gretel swings the tin can into the gravel driveway of Sunnydene, a big Victorian house turned rest home. She turns off the popping engine, and it almost chokes itself to death by spluttering and jumping long after all electrical connections have been terminated. We sit. The engine cracks as it cools. I can smell burned oil. Neither of us really wants to begin this visit. The rain plops onto the car.

Sunnydene is a grotesque monument that should have won prizes for ugliness. It doesn't have the gothic mystique of St. Pancras Station or the self-confident glitz of the Rothschilds' Woddesdon Manor. It must have been built by a self-made merchant who designed it himself. It has several dumpy turrets and heavy stone balconies. It has large windows thick with dark stained glass. There are gargoyles and plaques that look like deathmasks and cast-iron barley-sugar drainpipes. The place is surrounded by overgrown laurels, yew hedges, and ubiquitous cypress trees. Any lawn has been overtaken by moss and the flowerbeds merge with the gravel path and driveway. Chickweed and convolvulus grow everywhere, even into the trees. To the side of the house is a greenhouse with broken panes, dock plants and bindweed growing so rampantly and smugly inside, it reminds me of a snake pit.

"God, this place is dismal, sis."

"I told you it wasn't worth the money anymore, but you wouldn't listen."

We get out of the car and crunch our way across the gravel to the front porch and push open the door. It's as silent as the grave. In the far, far distance a clock is ticking. Gretel rings a handbell on the hall table. There's a blue Chinese bowl with an arrangement of dried flowers and some back numbers of magazines lain in an overlapping row, like at the dentist's. *The Lady, House & Garden, Country Life*. I smile at Gretel, a sort of "it'll be all right" smile, and she looks down at the red-and-umber Turkish rug. Just then she looks like she did when she was ten. We hear footsteps, and Gretel moves next to me. She holds my hand. The stale smell of cooked cabbage floats on the air.

Mrs. Hextable is an ample woman. She owns Sunnydene with her husband. We negotiated with her when Mum came here as a resident. She wears a sneering grin matched by the tone of her voice. Her blue cotton frock is covered by a doctor's white coat, trying to mix the cosy with the professional.

"Mr. and Miss Smith. I am so pleased you could come up. Do sit with me in my room, please."

She sweeps away and we follow. Gretel squeezes my hand. I know this is going to be hard, and I resent it. I resent the time it's taking, the fact that Mum has the nerve to linger and not be taken by a hurricane of a heart attack.

Mrs. Hextable, or Matron as she likes to be called, has an office in a very tall, narrow room. The fireplace is boarded over, and in front of it stands an ancient gas fire. I see it has a nameplate: THE RADIANT GAS APPLIANCE. There are some prospectuses lying on the desk, advertisements for future residents. The photographs show Sunnydene as it would have appeared 20 years ago. We sit down on one side of the matron's desk. She sits on the other.

"The fact is that Mrs. Smith is very poorly." Matron puts her head to one side and removes her spectacles. "She falls in and out of consciousness and can no longer, it seems, understand English. I told you, Miss Smith, that last night she had been walking in her sleep, and we are anxious for her safety. If she speaks, which is rarely, she will only speak in German, and we have no one who understands German on the staff."

Mrs. Hextable leans forward, placing her bosom on the desk. "I am so sorry, but Mrs. Smith must go either into hospital or a fully equipped nursing home where she can be given 24-hour care. You'll recollect our license does not permit us to provide the medical support your mother now requires." Matron sounds resigned and smiles.

Gretel looks at me. I begin to imagine the bills and think of the thousands of pounds this place has cost over the years. Then I see Gretel is about to cry, so I ask quickly, "Can we see her?"

"Of course. She will be pleased, I think. Afterward, I would very much appreciate it if you could come to me here, in my office. I'll ask for some tea, and we'll talk about the best plan of action for Monday."

"Monday?" Gretel asks.

"Yes, Monday. That is when we'll undertake the transfer... I mean arrange for your mother's care. The local hospital is very good, or there is a nursing home we recommend..."

Upstairs we stand outside Mum's room. Gretel is breathing heavily. I am hardly breathing at all. We push open the door...

Light is filtered through colors: green, red, purple. Branches making patterns on the ground. The wood smell. Burning oak shards. Dead leaves. Brambles catching on clothes. Tear away from the brambles. Look at the faces in the half-light that are shadows only. In the distance, laughing. Hooting. The witches. They smell us. They sniff up and gargle with the spit. Gretel comes to me. The white clouds catch the moonlight and make patches on the ground. We are lost again.

Then, in a scything motion, a branch curls round us. Holds us tightly. Up in the tree, a face—not a shadow, one face—is looking down at us. Its crooked nose and pointed chin, its black hair, its fat tongue licking lips plastered with blood-red make-up. The branch-arm curls us to the figure. Her tongue lapping across our faces. We pull back. I try to break the arm—to snap the twig or break a finger. There is a shrill scream followed by laughter. The arm holds tighter. Tighter. It's suffocating, and when I can catch a breath, I take in ether or some kind of spirit, evaporated into the air. That makes me heady. I pull myself down. As I do, Gretel holds my arm and buries her face in my jacket. A voice sings out.

"My tongue's on heat to taste the treat of children's meat."

Gretel tries to pull me away, but I think we must look. Look up into her face. It's the last time. Maybe we'll finish it here and now. No more pretending to behave like mother and children. Just finish it once and for all time.

Another long branch folds round us. "My children, I'm coming. I cannot hold on..."

I look up and open my mouth, but she prevents any word, any sound. Just as she always does. Suffocating. Never allows us. Using stick to beat. Twine to bind. Teacloth to gag. Food to poison. And no one. No one sees, knows. No one to tell. No one.

"Guzzle, guzzle, stuff my muzzle."

The branches separate us. Gretel to one side, me to the other. The face above us lengthens and distorts. Laughs. Cries with laughter. The wind blows and blows. It blows away our words. Our cries.

"Grind the greasy gristle; these mites will whet my whistle."

The tongue slaps its lips, and as its sharp teeth show I draw in a huge breath even though it's really hard to do it. I breathe in a huge breath that makes my lungs feel like great balloons. I feel my breath go deep down to my stomach. I push harder to get the breath deeper. Deeper.

She will not. She will not make us guilty. Carry her guilt on. Let her take it away to another world. We will not be left with it. Gretel and I will not be left with those feelings.

I manage to scream out. "No!" The wind increases. It becomes a tornado, a whirlwind, and with my breath the whole room blows out of the windows and sucks the door open. Curtains flying, clouds evaporate up the chimney, the undulating carpet settles and on it the layers of dust. The medicine glass is broken on the floor.

Mrs. Hextable hurries in. Gretel has fallen down. I am standing by my mother. She is dead.

Saturday night back in the flat. I run my finger along a row of CDs on the shelf. I can smell something really good cooking in the kitchen and smile to myself as Coy-boy makes some noise with a saucepan lid. Goldberg Variations? The symmetry. The puzzle. Liza Minelli? No, not tonight. Pet Shop Boys? Mustn't give myself away. Mahler songs? *Kinder Toten Lieder*? In the circumstance, why not? It'll sound grave and it'll impress Coy-boy. Maybe I'll explain about the context and how Mahler fits into 20th-century music.

I touch the power switch and the CD drawer slides open. I fit the CD and press play. It always gives me pleasure the way the drawer slides out and in. I turn up the volume. Coy-boy comes in from the kitchen. He looks great in white shorts; I can see his limp cock hanging to one side. His singlet shows up his nipple rings and tits. I can't resist it, so I squeeze one. As he puts down two glasses of wine, he moves forward and we kiss. Then I pull back and look at him. He has a sweet face and such clear eyes...and he's smiling.

"Mahler? I'm surprised. I thought you'd be more of a Carl Orff man myself."

"Fucking cheek." I smile, grab him to me, and hold his arse, then sink my tongue down his throat.

We eat a fantastic meal. Not pasta but some fresh tuna in ginger and garlic, with a rocket and walnut salad. He's used some big white plates Gretel gave me last Christmas. The food sits on them as if on huge china islands. The wine's white. Sancerre. Later we eat some sort of berry tart with crème fraîche.

"What do you do? For a living?" I ask.

"I'm a cookery writer. But my degree's in music."

I'm gob-smacked. I knew he couldn't be a plumber but a nancy cookery writer... "Where do you write?"

"Wherever I'm asked. I have a column in GQ and do you know 'Fay Starch'?"

"*Pink Paper?*"

"Yes. That's me"

I choke on my wine. "You're joking!"

"I do it for a favor, really. The editor's a mate. Just now my serious work's on a book for Random House. Andalusian cookery. Publishing date next Easter. Do you know it?"

"The food or the country?"

Later Coy-boy asks, "Fancy a drink by the canal? That pub on Shepherdess Walk? If we go now, we'll catch last orders."

"I don't know about drinking. I feel...lethargic." I haven't told him about Mum. I don't seem to have much energy. Now that Mum's finally died, it's a huge relief. Even Gretel said so. I haven't got the energy to explain. When Gretel was driving me back to town, I was thinking of getting Coy-boy on the bike and have him piss in his jeans while we headed along the Westway breaking the speed limit. I've always liked leather that smelled of piss and bike oil. I thought we'd spend the night in some really heavy, noisy place, like the Blockhouse.

Now, home again, and heavy after a good meal, I take Coy-boy into my bed to sleep with him. Not the sort of scene I'm into at all—vanilla sex. He lets me snuggle up to him, put my head on his chest, and suck on his tits like a baby.

Tears wet my face, and he licks them up. It makes more tears come, then, later, laughter. When I kiss him I kiss him for love. It makes me feel tender—like I have never felt in my life. I hold him. He holds me and we are sort of...equal. I don't want to dominate him—not tonight, anyway. I don't want to ride his arse until he's so sore he can't speak. I don't want him to gobble my dick till he chucks up. Something has changed in me. I'm content, feel like I'm in another man's shoes.

Monday. I take the day off work. Bereavement in the family's about the only thing that counts in the stockbroker's world. So I get Piers to cover for me. Coy-boy and I go riding. Out to High Beeches in Epping Forest. There's a bikers' meeting place with a coffee stall run by an old man and his son. At weekends the place is packed with biker guys who go to look at each other's machines and, in some cases, dicks. This Monday's damp and cold, so we drink steaming coffee with far too much milk, cupping our hands 'round the warm mugs, smiling at each other like kids. We are both in our leathers and on the way back Coy-boy holds on tight and does piss in his jeans. I'm pleased and smile as the air rattles through my crash helmet. Some things never change.

Afterword

Do you feel safe?

If these writers, and Simon and I, have succeeded, then your answer might well be no. But we hope that if we ask, "Have we turned you on?" you'll have to answer yes.

In a time of disease and gay bashing—when young queer men die tangled in barbed wire, and a generation has been allowed to perish for no crime other than loving its own gender—it's easy to dream of a paradise where love is the only emotion, and the only conflict is deciding who'll pick up the dinner tab.

In these years of HIV and homophobia, there's a new proliferation of literate smut—recognizably human voices telling stories of desire, of lust. But even in this more-or-less acceptable venue, it's all too easy to turn away from the real nature of eros—to dress it up as polite "erotica." There are too many stories, novels, and movies that smile and sing about erections, about asshole fucking and blow jobs, without dealing with the fact that there is a dark side—and not just a black leather side.

Sex, especially the kind that deals with power, with force, isn't safe—and shouldn't be. Dynamite can move mountains, but it ain't a plaything for anyone who's not prepared to get a little, shall we say, burned. Sex that's as casual and empty as a polite handshake will have no other meaning, no other power. But when you understand that the proffered hand may also slap, may pinch, may punch, and not just stroke or hold or pat, then the excitement builds, breath comes in gasps, the beast gets hard.

Sex is an animal force, a contact with our primitive monkey selves. Sex isn't just about hard-ons, come, butt holes, rimming, and balls, it's about the deep stuff, the core things. Sex is about consumption, about being devoured. It's about being a *thing*, an object of someone's forceful will. It's about death, about passing beyond the thin veil of self and into Somewhere Else.

When you make sex utterly safe—and I'm not referring to matters of hygiene here—you diminish it, you mix it with lukewarm water, you put a smiley face on the raw power of the urge, the thunder of a cock, the deep tribal drums of a good fuck.

These stories are *rough*. They step over the edge. A hard-on isn't something refined and elegant. And even the best prose can't fully reproduce the gnarled, dark glories of lust. In a way, then, these stories have, inevitably, failed—but when you can't reach down and wrap a rough hand around a throbbing dick...well, these tales can then give you at least a *ghost* of the experience, a better illusion than some.

I've heard people decry this sort of smut—point quivering, frightened fingers at these writers, ashamed of them and their grand erection-making power. This stuff doesn't purvey the smiling queer poster-child images that they'd like Coors and Absolut to buy and repackage into happy one-Latino, one-black, one-Asian, one-woman, one-white queer-yet-straight marketing modules. In the rush to political visibility and social acceptance, these stories, and the flaming desire they represent, should be exiled, some say, to an asbestos closet. After all, when psychopathic bigots show their "deplorable" videos of queer celebrations, isn't it always the leathermen, their harnessed chests and tight chaps, who are singled out—the heights of the gay depths?

These stories tell some basic truth, take a wide-eyed look at the animal realities of cock, of sex and fucking; they attempt to wrap words around the baser drives inside us all. These tales celebrate and elevate the deeper channels of male lust. They rub our noses in our feelings, elucidate the growls and snarls of animal rut.

Judge these stories on the scale of your excitement, by the hardness of your own cock. Don't expect them to coddle you in the bathwater warmth of tenderness, kindness, and safety. There's love here but of a wilder sort.

As you close these pages we wish you well. May your sex be frightening and powerful, hard and animal...but only as safe as necessary to keep you here, and hard, for a long, long time.

—M. Christian
San Francisco, 1999

Contributor Biographies

B.J. Barrios, an edge-playing pig in the New York area, has previously published stories under his online persona/pen name, LTHR EDGE, including "Kidnapped" in *International Leatherman 17* and "Jack of All Trades" in *International Leatherman 20* and *21*. He also maintains an extensive personal home page at http://lthredge.com.

Bill Brent is the founder of *Black Books* and the editor of *Black Sheets*, a humorous sex 'zine that he started in 1993. His short stories and essays appear there and in various anthologies, including *Best American Erotica 1997*, *Eros Ex Machina*, the *Factsheet Five Zine Reader*, *Guilty Pleasures*, and all three of the *Noirotica* anthologies. He is writing *The Ultimate Guide to Anal Sex for Men* and working hard on his first novel. For a free catalog, write him at Box 31155 RS, San Francisco, CA 94131-0155. You can also E-mail RoughStuff@blackbooks.com.

Ken Butler is an arts administrator whose erotic fiction has been published in *Best Gay Erotica 1997* and *Daddy*, *MACH*, and *Chiron Rising* magazines. Although his degree is in music, he spends most of his time working in the theatre or in front of a computer keyboard.

Tom Caffrey is the author of the short story collections *Hitting Home & Other Stories* and *Tales From the Men's Room*. His work has appeared in numerous anthologies, including *Best American Erotica 1995*, *The Sportsmen*, *Ritual Sex*, *Flesh and the Word 3*, *Flashpoint*, *The Mammoth Book of Gay Erotica*, and *Wanderlust*.

Pat Califia takes pride in speaking at length about unspeakable topics. Pat lives in San Francisco with a boyfriend and several other pets. Previous work includes *Macho Sluts* and *Melting Point*. A new short story collection, *No Mercy*, is forthcoming from Alyson Books.

Dave Chester lives in London with his lover, Geoff. They share a motorbike, house, and cat. Summer weekends are spent in the garden; winter ones by the fire and at various leather venues. Dave directs opera and plays and writes articles and fiction. He likes playing Billie Holiday albums when he works.

M. Christian's work can be seen in *Best American Erotica 1994 & 1997,* The Mammoth Books (International, New Erotica, Historical Erotica, and Short Erotic Novels), *Leatherwomen III,* all the *Noiroticas, The Ghost of Carmen Miranda, Black Sheets, MACH,* and many others. He is also the editor of the anthologies *Eros Ex Machina: Eroticizing the Mechanical, Midsummer Nights Dreams: One Story, Many Tales,* and *Guilty Pleasures: True Tales of Erotic Indulgences.* He lives in San Francisco, where he endeavors to explore its nooks and, occasionally, its crannies.

Richard Cleaver was born in 1952, raised in Iowa, and enjoys opera, redheads, and torturing marines' feet. Since 1993 he has lived in Japan, where he is a columnist for the Japanese gay monthly *Barazoku.* He is also the author of *Know My Name: A Gay Liberation Theology.*

Samuel Cross has his own identity problem. Evenings he is Jen of the adult fetish site www.JenLynn.com. He has written for such magazines as *In Touch, Indulge, PowerPlay,* and *Firsthand.* His stories have also appeared in erotic and fantasy anthologies including Paula Guran's *New Blood.*

Jack Fritscher, winner of the BEA National Small Press Book Award 1998-1999, for *Rainbow County and 11 Other Stories*, is the founding San Francisco editor of *Drummer*. This diversely voiced author of 12 books, as well as stories and feature articles in more than 30 gay magazines, is noted for *Some Dance to Remember* and for his biographical memoir of his lover Robert Mapplethorpe, *Mapplethorpe: Assault With a Deadly Camera*. His Lammy-nominated novel, *The Geography of Women: A Romantic Comedy,* is an inclusive lesbigay story of extended family. His novella *Titanic* first appeared in magazines in 1988 and is the anchor fiction of his 12 tales in *Titanic: Forbidden Stories Hollywood Forgot*. His photographs appear in the coffee-table photobook *Jack Fritscher's American Men*. Reviews and gay literary history research at www.JackFritscher.com.

Kevin Killian has written two novels and a book of memoirs. He is also the author of *Little Men*, a collection of stories, and *Argento Series*, a book of poetry. With Lewis Ellingham he has written *Poet Be Like God: Jack Spicer and the San Francisco Renaissance*.

In the last six years Miodrag Kojadinovic´ has lived in Belgrade, Yugoslavia; Vancouver, British Columbia; Utrecht, the Netherlands; Amsterdam; a small town in Serbia; and Budapest. His erotica was published in Holland (pirated), the United States, Slovenia, Canada, and Serbia (in Hungarian only; Belgrade editors thought it too blunt). After becoming a Master Fag ("doctorandus") in the Netherlands, he is enrolled in yet another MA program.

Wendell Ricketts was born on Wake Island, an atoll in the middle of the Pacific Ocean, and raised in various small towns on Oahu, Hawaii. He now lives in Albuquerque, where he is the 1997-1998 Creative Writing Fellow at the University of New Mexico. His story "Blood Brothers" won the 1998

English Department graduate student fiction contest (and appeared in *Blue Mesa Review #10*), and his "Raspberry Pie" received honorable mention in the 1998 Heekin Group Foundation Fellowship Award competition. His work has also appeared (or is forthcoming) in *Tall House Review*; *James White Review*; *Blithe House Quarterly*; *Letters Magazine*; and the anthologies *Doing It For Daddy* and *For the Brother Who Would Be My Lover*. He recently completed a collection of short stories that he hopes will offend at least a few members of Congress.

Thomas S. Roche's short stories have appeared in the *Best American Erotica* series, *Best Gay Erotica 1996*, and *The Mammoth Book of Pulp Fiction*, among others. He also edited three volumes of the *Noirotica* series of erotic crime-noir stories. Some of his short stories are collected in his book *Dark Matter*. He can be found at www.thomasroche.com.

D. Travers Scott is the author of a novel, *Execution, Texas: 1987,* and editor of an anthology, *Strategic Sex: Why They Won't Keep It in the Bedroom*. He lives in Seattle, where he is editing *Best Gay Erotica 2000* and writing a new novel as well as a nonfiction book about male heroism.

Simon Sheppard's fiction, poetry, and essays have appeared in dozens of anthologies, notably *Best American Erotica 2000* and *1997;* the 2000, 1999, 1997, and 1996 volumes of *Best Gay Erotica; Friction, Volume 3*; and a whole bunch more. Sex Talk, his weekly column, appears on the Web and in queer papers nationwide. His short-story collection *Hotter Than Hell and Other Stories* is forthcoming from Alyson Books. *Rough Stuff* is his first editing gig. He lives in San Francisco with his lover, enjoys tying up and spanking bottom boys, and worries entirely too much.

Wickie Stamps work appears in numerous anthologies, including *Flashpoint, Close Calls, Brothers and Sisters, Doing It for Daddy, Leatherfolk, Queer View Mirror, Switch Hitters, Once Upon a Time, Sons of Darkness*, and the forthcoming *Strategic Sex*. Wickie is a prior editor of *Drummer*.

horehound stillpoint's work can be found in *Poetry Nation, Queer View Mirror II, Best Gay Erotica* (1997 and 1998 editions), and *Sex Spoken Here*. In 1996 and 1997 he helped represent San Francisco at the National Poetry Slam and survived. He recently finished his first play: *The Queerest Thing on Earth*.

Lucy Taylor's work includes the collections *Close to the Bone, Unnatural Acts and Other Stories, Painted in Blood,* and the Stoker-award winning novel *The Safety of Unknown Cities*. She has recently published two novellas, *Spree*, and *Sub-Human* and a novel, *Dancing with Demons*. She and her boyfriend share a home in Mean, Colo., a boat named *Venom,* and seven wonderful cats.

Karl von Uhl gratefully lives in rural central Iowa, where no one can hear your scream. For 3½ years he wrote the column Vox Clamavis for *Bear* magazine. His fiction has appeared in *Bear* and *Powerplay* magazines under the pseudonym Cord Odebolt. He thanks John Chambers for his tireless research in the writing of this story. He may be contacted at leathernk@hotmail.com.

alyson
books

BOY IN THE SAND, *by Roger Edmonson.* Cal Culver, better known as gay porn star Casey Donovan, was a fascinating, tragic figure. This examination of his life places him in the context of his times—from Stonewall to the mid 80s—and shows his effect on the more hedonistic aspects of gay culture. From his beginnings as a stage actor to his forays into the world of gay porn, he always maintained the aura of being the golden boy.

FRICTION, *edited by Gerry Kroll.* **FRICTION, VOLUME 2,** *edited by John Erich and Jesse Grant.* This series of gay erotica presents the sexiest stories by the top erotic writers from the country's most popular gay erotic magazines. Variety is, after all, the spice of life in all things—including sex—so *Friction* has a lot of everything for everyone!

HEAT: GAY MEN TELL THEIR REAL-LIFE SEX STORIES, *edited by Jack Hart.* Sexy, true stories in this unbridled gay erotic collection range from steamy seductions to military maneuvers

MY BIGGEST O, *edited by Jack Hart.* What was the best sex you ever had? Jack Hart asked that question of hundreds of gay men, and got some fascinating answers. Here are summaries of the most intriguing of them. Together, they provide an engaging picture of the sexual tastes of gay men.

MY FIRST TIME and **MY FIRST TIME, VOLUME 2,** *edited by Jack Hart.* You never forget the first time! And Hart is the expert in getting gay men to tell it like it is. Evoking the trembling, heart pounding, sweaty-palmed excitement that fuels the first trip down the road of carnal knowledge, these first-person accounts provide some of the hottest reading of the season.

STRAIGHT? *edited by Jack Hart.* Hart has compiled a new anthology in which gay men describe in their own words the couplings they've had with men who did not seem on first appearance to be open to having gay sex. Truth indeed can be stranger—and hotter—than fiction.

WONDER BREAD AND ECSTASY: THE LIFE AND DEATH OF JOEY STEFANO, *by Charles Isherwood.* Drugs, sex, and unbridled ambition were the main ingredients in the lethal cocktail that killed gay porn's brightest star, Joey Stefano. He was a child from the country's heartland, but Joey's rise and tragic fall in Los Angeles's dark and dangerous world of gay porn paints a grim portrait of American life gone berserk.

These books and other Alyson titles are available at your local bookstore.
If you can't find a book listed above or would like more information,
please visit our home page on the World Wide Web at **www.alyson.com.**